'How dare you?' Miranda snapped.

'You. . .you. . .abominable creature! How dare you suggest that I—?'

'I suggested no such thing,' retorted Adam, all innocence. 'I merely remarked—'

'I know what you said! You have no need to repeat your insulting remark! I could do many things—I could become a nanny, or a companion, or. . .or. . .'

'Has your invention run out?' enquired Adam kindly. 'You could, I suppose, find work in a laundry, or a shop, or even in a tavern. . . Have you ever done a day's work in your life, Miss Dawson?'

GW00691736

Sarah Westleigh has enjoyed a varied life. Working as a local government officer in London, she qualified as a chartered quantity surveyor. She assisted her husband in his chartered accountancy practice, at the same time managing an employment agency. Moving to Devon, she finally found time to write, publishing short stories and articles, before discovering historical novels.

Recent titles by the same author:

SEAFIRE

Sarah Westleigh

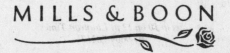

MILLS & BOON

DID YOU PURCHASE THIS BOOK WITHOUT A COVER?
If you did, you should be aware it is stolen property as it was reported
unsold and destroyed by a retailer. Neither the Author nor the publisher
has received any payment for this book.

*All the characters in this book have no existence outside the
imagination of the author, and have no relation whatsoever to anyone
bearing the same name or names. They are not even distantly inspired
by any individual known or unknown to the author, and all the
incidents are pure invention.*

*All rights reserved including the right of reproduction in whole or in
part in any form. This edition is published by arrangement with
Harlequin Enterprises II B.V. The text of this publication or any part
thereof may not be reproduced or transmitted in any form or by any
means, electronic or mechanical, including photocopying, recording,
storage in an information retrieval system, or otherwise, without the
written permission of the publisher.*

*This book is sold subject to the condition that it shall not, by way of
trade or otherwise, be lent, resold, hired out or otherwise circulated
without the prior consent of the publisher in any form of binding or
cover other than that in which it is published and without a similar
condition including this condition being imposed on the subsequent
purchaser.*

*MILLS & BOON, the Rose Device and
LEGACY OF LOVE are trademarks of the publisher.
Harlequin Mills & Boon Limited,
Eton House, 18–24 Paradise Road, Richmond, Surrey TW9 1SR*

© Sarah Westleigh 1996

ISBN 0 263 79761 9

*Set in 10 on 12 pt Linotron Times
04-9609-78217*

*Typeset in Great Britain by CentraCet, Cambridge
Printed in Great Britain by
BPC Paperbacks Ltd*

CHAPTER ONE

MIRANDA gazed dolefully after His Majesty's ship *Othello* as she heeled with the wind, ploughing her way across a heaving Atlantic lit by the red glow of the setting sun and diminishing in size with every moment that passed. Soon, despite her age, the damage she'd suffered and the long tendrils of weed growing on her bottom to slow her down, only her depleted pyramid of sails would be visible as she rose on the crest of a wave. Then they, too, would sink completely out of sight, taking with them her last link with home, family and everything familiar.

The raised voice of the second lieutenant brought her attention back to the great cabin of the American frigate *Seafire*, where the surviving officers of the *Othello* were, like herself, confined.

'Stop snivelling, Mr Welland!' snapped Mr Piper. 'You are in no worse case than the rest of us! The Americans probably treat their prisoners of war better than the French!'

Miranda rose from the cushions covering the locker beneath the ship's stern lights and moved over to the youngest of the *Othello*'s midshipmen, a skinny lad of only twelve, making his first voyage. His eyes were fixed on the streaks of blood drying on his white duck trousers and she felt sympathy rise up in her on a tide of indignation.

'He is only a child!' she protested to the grim-visaged officer who had spoken.

'As a young gentleman he is training to be a King's officer! He must learn never to show fear! He should take his example from Mr Keeper,' retorted the lieutenant, indicating the other midshipman present, at fourteen an insensitive boy and a bit of a bully, who smirked.

Miranda put her hand on Will's shoulder. 'The worst is over now,' she consoled him softly, ignoring the lieutenant's exasperated grunt of 'Women!' 'We have been fed. The captain will not ill-treat us, I think.'

He had a hard face, the captain of the *Seafire*, cold, slate-grey eyes and a square, uncompromising chin. Despite the lines of experience etched on his weathered face he looked young to be in command of a frigate.

He had ignored them since sending them across in a ship's boat under marine guard. Apart from his servant, a tall, broad-shouldered black man who had brought them their food, crouching to avoid the low beams overhead, the scarlet-coated marine sentries at the door were the only persons they had seen since being thrust into the cabin.

'But Tom Bright was killed,' gulped Will, trying to stifle his sobs. 'I was standing right by him when he fell.' He sniffed before adding in a barely audible voice, 'Captain Blackmore and Mr Stannard are gone, too.'

Will had been carrying a message up from the lower gun deck to the quarterdeck. Otherwise he would have been below when disaster had struck, when the heavy balls of the frigate's broadside had smashed their way, one after another, through the back of the *Othello* and along its length, to cause chaos on the two gun decks and to wreck the quarterdeck.

Their own guns had scarcely been fired; only the two aimed astern had caught the agile enemy in their sights. Mr Piper, the second lieutenant, the most senior officer left alive and therefore in command, had surrendered almost immediately.

The American, she thought angrily, was an inferior warship. The *Othello*, with her two decks of guns, should have been able to defeat a mere frigate. But for that unlucky shot which had killed Captain Blackmore, the arrogant Captain York—for that was the *Seafire*'s captain's name—might now have been the one to be confined, aboard the *Othello*.

The thoughts raced through her mind as she squeezed Will's shoulder. 'I know they are,' she told him sadly, setting the frightening memories firmly aside. 'So are a number of the seamen, and many others were injured. But we are at war, Will. We must grow used to the idea of death.'

Who am I to talk? she thought, stifling her own grief. For Captain Blackmore had been more than just the captain of the ship taking her out to join her family in the West Indies, he had been her father's particular friend, almost an uncle to her. That was why it had been arranged for her to sail with him in the supposed safety of a seventy-four-gun warship.

And his first lieutenant had been killed too. Her breath choked in her throat as she remembered Peter. He had become the first object of her heart the moment she had seen his handsome face beneath his bicorn hat and noted the splendid figure he cut in his uniform. A sigh escaped her as she thought of what might have been, for she had never admired any man so much. During the days at sea as they had sailed down towards the Canary Isles, where they had intended to pick up the trade winds before crossing the Atlantic, her admiration had grown. He had sought her out whenever she appeared on deck while he was there, had been attentive and charming when invited to dine at the captain's table. She had dreamed dreams— But what good to remember now, when the man with whom she had fallen in love was dead?

It was the waiting getting on their nerves. She shifted impatiently and spoke sharply out of grief, anger and a lurking fear of the future.

'You surrendered too soon, Mr Piper,' she accused. 'You lowered our colours before we had once fired our own broadside!'

'Only the guns at the stern could be brought to bear! What did you want me to do?' demanded the lieutenant grimly. 'He was racing down wind to rake us from behind again with another broadside. Should I have fought on until the entire crew was dead? You too Miss Dawson, make no mistake!'

'Of course not, but Captain Blackmore—'

'Had failed to turn the ship in time to meet the first broadside and had been killed! What can you know about it, Miss Dawson? A mast and all its sails and rigging were strewn over the deck and trailing over the side in a tangled mess. The men couldn't cut away the wreckage in time for me to turn the ship before the next broadside did for us.' A plaintive, defensive note had entered his voice. 'What else could I have done?'

'We could have –' began the third lieutenant diffidently. Despite his weedy appearance the fire of frustrated enterprise blazed in Mr Gander's brown eyes. He would have fought on.

The sailing master, the warrant officer responsible for navigating the ship under the captain's orders, a solid trunk of a man with many years of experience behind him, smiled in sympathy with the young lieutenant's bitterness. 'We could have done many things,' he interrupted in his rich, throaty voice, 'but in the end it'd still have been strike our colours or be sunk with all hands.' He made a rueful face. 'Captain York is a fine seaman and an inspired tactician,' he said, showing reluctant admiration for an enemy.

Miranda sighed. 'I suppose you are right, Mr Haskett. Down below it seemed an age while we waited in vain for our guns to fire back.'

'Our stern chasers did!' snapped Mr Piper, still defensive. 'We had been trying to escape him during the night watches, and failed. With the captain fallen and the ship disabled, I had no choice.'

He might be right, thought Miranda reluctantly. In a way he *was* right – she did not know much about the sailing of a ship and less about fighting one; her knowledge was all hearsay. He was only troubling to argue with her at all because of who her father was. But all the same, after the stories Papa and her brothers had told her, the surrender had seemed precipitate.

She remembered the moment a youthful midshipman had almost fallen down the ladder to inform the surgeon that the action was over. Hearing him report, she had climbed the ladders to the ruined quarterdeck, glad to escape the foetid atmosphere below. The American captain was already aboard taking possession of the ship, having introduced himself as Captain Adam York of the US Navy's frigate *Seafire*. Shortly after this they had been rowed across to his warship. For the rest of the day they had sat about, wondering what was happening aboard the vessel they had so recently been forced to surrender. Now they were unlikely ever to know, for the *Othello* had quite disappeared from sight.

Despite her best efforts she could not banish memories of the morning. They were too close, too devastating to be easily thrust aside. The dull boom of a gun, the splash of a ball landing a couple of hundred yards astern had confirmed an enemy presence beyond doubt. The squeal of the bosun's pipes, the rat-tat-tat of the marine drummer's tattoo, the stampeding feet had already warned Miranda of the imminence of action. A Rear Admiral's daughter, she knew the ropes. Everything, including herself, had to go below, allowing the whole deck to be opened up so that all the great guns could be fired.

She eyed the monsters which intruded even in this smaller captain's cabin. This, too, had no doubt been taken apart earlier and put back together again to accommodate the officer prisoners while the captain oversaw the urgent repair of both vessels. Despite being covered with sailcloth the cannons still emitted a strong smell of gunpowder, an unwelcome reminder of the devastation they had wrought aboard the *Othello*.

She lifted her head to listen as, through the open skylight, she heard the lookout's hail.

'Deck, there! *Othello* has hoisted a signal!'

Her heart thumped. So she was still visible from the masthead. Not quite gone yet.

'Mr Stirling, take a glass aloft and see what she says! Bear a hand there!'

Captain York's voice, resonant and clear, came from the quarterdeck above their heads.

'Aye, aye, sir! Telescope it is, sir!'

Soon the piping voice of the midshipman came floating down, his words indistinguishable in the cabin.

'Return to deck, Mr Stirling.' Then, as a thump proved the speed with which the midshipman had obeyed the order, 'Acknowledge and make the signal, "Goodbye and good luck."'

With Will looking a little more determined and swallowing the last of his tears, Miranda resumed her seat beneath the windows. Dusk was falling now; darkness would be upon them in no time at all. What did Captain York intend to do with them?

Most of the crew of the captured ship, including the surgeon and the wounded, had been left aboard, under the guard of a detachment of American marines. Like the officers here, they would all end up as prisoners of war in the United States of America.

A series of shouted orders on deck, the screech of the ropes through pulleys, the heeling of the ship as the wind filled her sails told Miranda that the part of the *Seafire*'s rigging brought down by the one shot from the *Othello* which had found its mark had now been repaired.

Once under way, her companions concluded that the *Seafire* was sailing almost due south.

'Heading for the Canaries?' wondered Mr Gander.

'They're Spanish,' observed Mr Piper. 'Spain is Britain's ally now. He wouldn't dare put in there.'

'But the Americans are not at war with Spain,' pointed out his junior lieutenant.

Mr Piper shrugged. Apart from taking out his frustrations on poor Will Welland, he had little constructive to say.

The captain's servant, whose name, he had informed them with dignity, was Daniel, came in to light the candles in the lanterns hanging from the beams, putting a stop to speculation. Immediately, the view through the windows disappeared, lost in reflections. Daniel pulled heavy wine-coloured velvet hangings across and the cabin became a strangely shaped, cosy room, all shadowy beams and curves.

The snapping to attention of the four marines guarding the door heralded the long-awaited arrival of the captain himself.

He strode in, his bent head bare, his cocked hat tucked under his arm, and Miranda strongly suspected that he had just shrugged into his watch coat with its tarnished epaulettes and gold lace, for one of the buttons remained unfastened. But none of this, not the crouch he was forced to assume, the streak of dirt marring his cheek nor the filthy state of his hands, detracted from the aura of confident authority with which he greeted his captives. Or prevented the alarming frisson of awareness his close proximity sent streaking through Miranda's unawakened body. Mortifying colour rose in her cheeks. She swallowed.

The *Othello*'s officers rose. Mr Gander, jumping up unwarily, knocked his head on a beam and gave a yelp of pain before joining the others in standing up as straight as the low headroom allowed and saluting. York returned the salute and flung his hat across to land near Miranda, who still sat, obstinately determined not to allow this man to frighten or dominate her despite the curious, breathtaking effect his presence seemed to have on her. She owed him no deference apart from that due to any gentleman she met. She inclined her head. He did no more than glance at her and nod back.

'Please be seated, gentlemen,' he invited—or commanded, it made little difference—as he crossed to the big chair behind his desk. A lantern, hanging above, threw light down to burnish his black hair and throw a shadow from his clubbed queue—a pigtail looped up and tied with a piece of black cloth.

As he sat he placed a pierced and weighted strongbox on the mahogany surface in front of him. The key evident in the lock, doubtless found on the dead captain's body, left little doubt that the box had been opened and the contents scrutinised. Miranda, glancing at Mr Piper, saw his pallor and the way he chewed at his bottom lip. It looked as though he had failed to throw the weighted box overboard and thus destroy the ship's papers before they could be taken by the enemy.

'So, Lieutenant. You were headed for Barbados, I see, to join the squadron stationed there. Your captain was to report to the admiral commanding His Majesty's ships and vessels upon the Windward Islands Station.'

The lieutenant nodded.

'I shall wish to question you more later—'

'I know no more than what the orders say, Captain,' interjected Mr Piper earnestly.

Captain York acknowledged the interruption with a nod. 'That I understand. And now you would doubtless like to know that the *Othello* is headed for Annapolis. She has been made seaworthy and your crew will be well treated so long as they do not conspire to retake the ship. As for yourselves, gentlemen, I require your word, as honourable officers and gentlemen, that you will not attempt to cause trouble aboard the *Seafire*. My crew is depleted but is still quite adequate to fight this ship or to defend it should it become necessary. Do I have your word?'

He looked along the rank of officers, one a mere child, another almost old enough to be his grandfather, and one by one they gave their word.

'Capital. Your swords will be returned to you. You will have the freedom of the quarterdeck, of course, unless requested to remain below. No doubt, like myself, you would now like to retire to your quarters and perhaps—' with a glance at Midshipman Welland's trousers '—change your attire. Since my first and fourth lieutenants have left the ship their berths are vacant. Your chest, Lieutenant, and that of Mr Gander, has been brought across and placed there. The carpenters have erected another cabin for your sailing master. My officers will entertain you in the gunroom, gentlemen, where you may recover your weapons.'

A murmur of assent greeted these arrangements. Captain York turned to the two midshipmen. 'I am putting your young gentlemen in with mine, in the midshipmen's berth. I have nowhere else to accommodate them.'

As the boys shuffled their feet and Mr Piper nodded,

Captain York, for the first time, looked directly at Miranda. 'As for you, young lady—'

'My name is Miranda Dawson. Miss Dawson. My father—'

'Is an admiral; I am fully aware of that fact, Miss Dawson, since Captain Blackmore was to place himself under his orders.' He shot her a distinctly unfriendly look. 'You are, miss, a confounded nuisance. I do not like any female aboard my ship, let alone a green girl scarcely out of the schoolroom.'

Miranda scowled; she could not help herself. She was almost eighteen and, despite her delicate looks, as strong as a horse. If only she had been born a boy! Then, instead of cowering in the bowels of the ship, she could have been on the quarterdeck with the officers, helping to fight this arrogant creature, fear forgotten in the exhilaration of danger faced! How she envied her brothers!

And how she wished her hair had not degenerated into a salty mop of straw-coloured tangles, that the hem of her elderly gown had not become sodden in the water sloshing about in the bottom of the boat which had brought them across, and dried in streaks and creases. And that she had not caught it with her heel while climbing the side and torn a great rent in the material. Men had nothing so stupid as skirts and petticoats to hamper them while they clambered about a ship!

Her fulminating blue gaze met and caught that of the captain. The cold grey eyes under the heavy dark brows narrowed, the impatience in them changed to amusement and a smile curved his shapely mouth. He was not handsome, like Peter, Miranda decided, noting the bony, flattened bridge of his nose and suppressing the stupid tremor that shot through her again.

'However,' he went on more amiably, 'I could not leave you aboard the *Othello*; my first lieutenant will have quite enough on his hands without coping with your presence aboard. The *Seafire* is not a large ship but Daniel has agreed to sling his hammock in a corner of my storeroom so that you may use his sleeping place. You will find the chest you were using aboard the *Othello* in there. Your other boxes have been brought across and stowed below with my other stores. Daniel will, of course, allow you access to them if necessary. Luckily,' he enlarged, 'we are homeward bound and he managed to find room for them.'

'You are most kind,' said Miranda, the irony in her voice not lost on the object of it.

His face suddenly creased into a real grin. All the lines which had been showing up white against his sun-baked skin disappeared into the furrows. 'Wait until you see your accommodation! It is scarcely luxurious. You will, of course, be my guest.' He waved an expansive arm. 'My cabin is at your disposal, except for those times when I need to be private for my own purposes. You will oblige me by allowing the sentry to announce you before you enter. My supper will be served in half an hour. He gave a slight bow. 'I shall be honoured if you will join me.'

That captivating grin meant nothing. He did not mean he would be honoured at all. He was treating her like a naughty schoolgirl! Miranda composed her emotions, her mind and her features as she rose to her feet.

'Perhaps Daniel will be kind enough to show me where my quarters are. I regret—although no doubt it saves you a deal of trouble—that I have no maid with me. A girl was hired in Portsmouth but failed to turn up before we sailed.'

'As you say, another female would have been an added embarrassment. However, her absence leaves you without a chaperon, Miss Dawson. I must ask you to be circumspect in your behaviour. My men are excellent seamen and normally well disciplined, but they are not saints.'

'I can assure you, I know how to comport myself, sir,' retorted Miranda with frigid dignity.

'Daniel will show you all where to go,' said the captain, springing to his feet with sudden decision, impatient to be rid of his unwelcome guests. 'Gentlemen, I wish you joy of your quarters. Supper is, I believe, about to be served in the gunroom.'

By the light of a swinging lantern, Miranda saw the shallow wooden box of a cot standing on its side along the wall of the tiny space, some eight feet by five, in which the captain's servant normally slept. The cabin was squeezed in beyond the store, which housed a huge gun besides sundry chests and boxes containing the captain's more immediate needs which would be humped below out of the way during an action. The cot, supported in a netting, would be slung later, she supposed, from the strong hooks screwed into the beam above. In addition to her sea chest, the compartment contained a stand supporting a canvas basin, a small butt of water and a folding stool. A mirror had been

hung on one of the battens framing the thin partitions, a
thoughtful touch for which she would like to thank
someone. Daniel, probably, since it had been his cabin.

Although air could circulate from the companion
hatchway just outside her door through vents in the
partitions, the cabin was stuffy. During the day a little
light would reach her from the hatch, provided she left
the door open. Otherwise the candle in the lantern must
suffice.

She had soap in her baggage and there was enough
water in the butt to wash her hair, as well as herself.
Miranda set to. Half an hour was not long but her hair
was short and would soon dry. Better damp than filthy,
she decided as she dug some soap from her chest and
extracted some clean garments to wear.

The basin swayed with the easy motion of the ship
and so did she. She dried her hair as best she could and
disposed of the dirty water in a wooden bucket provided
for her convenience. Daniel would know what to do
about her soiled linen.

A midshipman came to inform her that the captain's
supper was about to be served. With a last glance in the
mirror and tweak of her shining golden curls, still
slightly damp, Miranda doused the candle in the lantern
and emerged into the gangway by the companion
ladders, which went up to the quarterdeck and down to
the officers' quarters in the gunroom. Facing her was
the door to the captain's servant's pantry, where Daniel
could brew drinks for his master, produce limited
snacks, wash a few dishes and keep the silver clean.
Between ranged two doors giving access to the captain's
quarters, one to the store, the other to his sleeping

place. Entry to the great cabin was through one or other of these. A solitary marine sat on guard between them.

At sight of her he jumped up, snapped to attention, head canted because of the low headroom, and called, 'Miss Dawson!' loud enough to be heard inside the great cabin, and pointed her towards the door to the store.

A voice called for her to come in but it was not the captain's. He was still washing and changing, she guessed. She squashed down a feeling somewhere between relief and disappointment as she passed through the storeroom. Entering the cabin, she nodded at Daniel, who greeted her with a wide smile and continued fussing about the table, arranging the glasses and the wine decanter to his satisfaction and putting a final shine on a creditable display of silver. A wooden trough of hard ship's biscuits, which passed for bread, stood in the centre of the table.

'Thank you for leaving me your mirror, Daniel,' Miranda said, unable to keep a certain condescension from her tone. She had never had dealings with a black servant before, let alone one who was presumably a slave.

A huge smile split the dark face. 'It's not mine, it's the cap'n's, missie,' he replied. 'You'll need to thank him.'

'Really?' Miranda could scarcely conceal her astonishment. 'I will.' Dismissing the question of the mirror, she sought to satisfy her curiosity about the servant himself. It did not occur to her that it might be rude to ask, so she came straight out with her question. 'Are you a slave, Daniel?'

He shook his head, his smile still wide and white. She was to discover that it took a great deal to wipe that smile from Daniel's face. 'Ah was given to Masser Adam when he was five, Miz Dawson. Ah must'a bin some ten years older. Ah belonged to him. When he ran away to sea Ah went with him and, so's Ah couldn't be dragged back to the plantation in chains, he granted me my freedom. We always managed to serve in the same ship and when he was given a brig of his own he took me for his servant again. No, missie, Ah'm no slave,' he said proudly, his face now grave. 'Ah serve the cap'n'cause Ah love him.'

'He ran away?' Now her curiosity spun off in another direction. 'How old was he then?'

'Twelve, missie. Too young to go off alone by my reckoning. He needed me to look after him.'

'And that is what you've been doing ever since, I collect,' said Miranda with growing respect. Apart from a certain drawl, the man spoke almost as well as his master, certainly better than most of the seamen. She was beginning to realise that the last thing he deserved was her condescension. 'Thank you for answering me, Daniel. Pray tell me, are you able to arrange for my laundry to be done?'

'Ah'll put it with the cap'n's, missie. Done on a Monday. But—' he looked a little embarrassed and his eyes rolled '—you'll understand we can't have your.. er...petticoats hanging about the rigging to dry.'

'Perhaps,' said Miranda helpfully, 'someone could rig me a line in the cabin?'

'Ah'll ask the bosun to see to it, missie.'

'Supper ready, then, Daniel?' demanded Captain

York, emerging from his sleeping place looking scrubbed, shaven and much more tidy than he had earlier. He had donned a clean frilled shirt, pristine white against his dark blue uniform trousers, but had not bothered to put on his jacket or even his waistcoat. She did not blame him; it was hot and stuffy in the cabin. His stock looked as though it might choke him and his only adornment was the grey silk bow on his queue.

'Ah, there you are, Zack.' He greeted a newcomer as the marine sentry snapped to attention and cried, 'Lieutenant West, sir!'

'Cook's getting impatient, Cap'n,' murmured Daniel. 'He says the meat'll be ruined if you don't hurry.'

'It'll be tough anyway,' grimaced Adam York. 'That last sheep he killed was stringy and old as the hills. Never mind; those we brought aboard at Casablanca look younger. Tell him he can send it up straight away.'

As Daniel sent word to the cook, the captain turned to Miranda. Having so far ignored her, he now made up for his neglect. With the utmost courtesy, he bowed over her hand.

Stifling her surprise at this belated show of manners, Miranda dropped him a small curtsy. 'Thank you for thinking to provide me with a mirror, Captain.'

'My sisters declare they cannot manage without at least six,' he observed, appraising her slowly from head to toe, taking in the low neckline and high waist of her graceful blue gown. 'You seem to have managed extraordinarily well with one small one,' he decided, his examination over. 'You find your quarters adequate?'

Small flags of embarrassed annoyance appeared on

Miranda's cheeks as his gaze travelled over her. She had considered the gown most becoming when it had been made for her, part of her school-leaving outfit. and his scrutiny confirmed her in her opinion, but how ill-mannered of him to examine her in such a way! He must have noticed how much the material needed the attention of an iron, but beggars could not be choosers and it was all his fault anyway.

'Barely, sir,' she answered him, 'but they will suffice. I cannot expect to enjoy luxury aboard an enemy man-of-war.'

'I am glad you appreciate the fact. Allow me to introduce my acting first lieutenant, Mr Zachary West. Mr West is taking supper with us.' He indicated their dress. 'You will appreciate that I am not treating this as a formal occasion.'

'Cap'n Adam needed moral support,' grinned Zack, in his turn bowing over her hand.

Shorter than his captain and stockily built, Zachary West none the less had need to mind the beams of the deck above. His round face reminded her of a pug dog's, though it was not so squashed. In fact it was a good-humoured, audacious face which rather appealed to Miranda.

He was clearly on excellent terms with his captain. He had called him Adam, though for form's sake he had prefixed his rank.

'You will pay for that,' murmured Adam with a sour smile. 'I ask you, how often do I dine alone? One or two of my officers always join me; today is no exception You, my friend, are in danger of never being invited to eat at this table again!'

'Do not say so! What a desperate punishment! To have to exist on the gunroom fare entirely! And all because I dared to speak the truth! He is afraid of women,' he whispered in a loud aside to Miranda.

She blinked. Surely he had gone too far!

He had. 'But not of little girls! Enough, Zack; I can take a joke with the best, but you abuse my tolerance.'

The reproof was the more effective because Adam's tone, although holding irritation and a measure of embarrassment, had become coolly distant where before it had been warm. This was how he maintained discipline, then. Mr West could be in no doubt as to who ruled aboard this warship.

'My apologies,' said Zack stiffly.

'Here comes the mutton!' Adam's tone was back to normal and he sounded glad of the interruption as an excuse to restore a more relaxed atmosphere. 'We do not normally eat so well at supper,' he explained to Miranda as he seated her at the table, a slight flush showing under his brown skin, 'but dinner scarcely amounted to a meal at all today. And being so lately out of Casablanca we are well supplied with fresh victuals.'

Miranda concentrated all her attention on the pot-roasted mutton being put on the plate before her with helpings of various vegetables, afraid that if she did not she would dissolve into shaming tears. Because now the tension had subsided she realised that he had referred to her as a little girl! How dared he belittle her so, when she had been forced to endure a long, extra year at the Academy waiting for suitable transport to take her out to Barbados? Most girls were wed and probably the mother of a child at her age. It served him right if the lieutenant's gibe had embarrassed him! But if there were only a fragment of truth in the accusation—she eyed him balefully from beneath her golden lashes—she would delight in showing him how much of a woman she was!

As they ate, the men talked easily together, their difference forgotten. They covered a variety of subjects but never once touched upon the events of the morning or the business of running the ship. Miranda listened, afraid to offer a remark in case she made a fool of herself and the captain heaped more scorn upon her head. The men discussed the fish and birds and other creatures they had seen, the islands they had visited and mentioned their families with wistful affection.

Adam, it seemed, went home sometimes between commissions, but his father's attitude had softened very little since he had cast Adam off for running away.

'He does deign to speak to me now,' he said with a wry grimace, 'but at heart he still regards me as a disobedient child. The atmosphere between us is not easy. I visit for my mother's sake, and I like to see my brother and sisters and their families.'

Mr West, she discovered, had a wife and a baby girl in Philadelphia.

'He hasn't seen little Catherine yet,' Adam said, addressing her directly for the first time. 'The mail caught up with us and he discovered he was a father when we were in Casablanca disposing of our prizes.' He grinned, a buccaneering grin which caused Miranda's stomach to lurch. She blushed and quickly looked away as he went on, 'Every member of the *Seafire*'s crew will be rich when we reach Annapolis.'

'If that agent can be relied upon to transfer the money,' remarked Zack.

'I've dealt with him before,' said Adam confidently. 'He is an honest man. At least, more honest than most. You'll be able to set your family up in fine style, Zack.'

'You must be rolling in wealth by now,' observed Zack with a wry grin. 'That's why all we Seafires follow you so eagerly, of course—we know we can rely on you to take more prizes than any other captain! What will you do with your share? Invest it?'

'That is what I usually do, yes.'

'My father invests in our Funds,' ventured Miranda, emboldened by being so directly addressed. 'When he retires he intends to purchase a small estate.'

'Of course, he takes a percentage of all the prize money won by the captains under his command. Barbados used to be a rich station, did it not? But now the Spanish are your allies. . .' Adam shrugged. 'But I wonder he is happy in a shore commission.'

Miranda bridled anew at the censure she detected in his tone. 'He served as a sea-officer for many years,' she said tautly. 'He was knighted for his valour during the battle of Trafalgar but unfortunately he lost a leg in a minor action later.'

'A brave man! How he must dislike being posted ashore!'

Miranda smiled gratefully at Lieutenant West. She might secretly criticise some aspects of the admiral's treatment of his family but she was fond of her father and proud of him. 'He would rather be at sea, but he has an important job to do at Carlisle Bay and he does have a flagship anchored there, so he is not absolutely tied to the beach. Mama likes it in the West Indies despite the heat and the risk of fever. I was looking forward to joining them.'

'I fear,' said Captain York repressively, 'that it may be some time before you achieve your object. I cannot see an early end to this war between our two countries.'

'We do not talk politics at table,' Zack reminded him with a wry glance.

'You have the right of it, Zack,' agreed Adam readily, 'but the occasion is somewhat peculiar and I had forgot. Will you take a glass of wine with me, Miss Dawson?'

The ugly moment passed. He had made a gesture of peace. She did not wish to drink wine with him but it would have been churlish as well as bad manners to refuse. They had to rub along together for an indefinite period. It normally took a month to cross the Atlantic, although it had been done faster in ideal conditions. So after Daniel had refilled both their glasses she lifted hers in silent response to his similar salute and drank of the quite splendid Rioja.

Miranda wanted to discuss the war. Obviously the table was not the place to do so. She would have to seek a more suitable opportunity. He must be made to see how much she resented America's declaration of war on her country when it was locked in mortal combat with that fiend Napoleon. It had been a real stab in the back from a former colony.

She could almost forget that Mr West was an enemy, but the captain had made it impossible for her to regard him as anything else. Which was just as well since his proximity had such a peculiar effect upon her nerves. . .

CHAPTER TWO

ONCE the cloth had been drawn Miranda rose from the table as she had been taught, leaving the two men to enjoy their port and to talk without her inhibiting presence.

She had nowhere to go but to her tiny cabin unless she went on deck. She glanced uncertainly at the companion ladder. She had not been introduced to any of the *Seafire*'s other officers and she was doubtful of her reception were she to venture up to the quarterdeck alone.

So she turned into her sleeping place, only to find that her cot had been slung in her absence, leaving no room for her to do much else but slide in and lie down. Whoever had done it had lit the lantern and left a spare candle, with tinder and flint in case of need. On deck there would be stars to see and perhaps a glimpse of the new moon. Was it only last evening she had stood at the rail of the *Othello* with Peter Stannard to watch it rise?

Tears pricked her lids and she brushed at them angrily. She must not repine over the past but make the most of the present and plan for the day when she was free again.

She prodded the well-stuffed mattress in the cot experimentally. The bed felt as though it would be comfortable enough, swinging with the motion of the ship, and was provided with more than enough covers

27

considering the warmth of the night. The wooden sides would hold her in should the ship pitch and roll in a storm and, like the one she had been using in the *Othello*, its main drawback would be the difficulty of getting in and out. Her chest would have to double as a footstool.

But she did not feel tired; rather, she felt disturbed, restless. She had been shut up below all day and needed to breathe fresh air before she could hope to sleep.

With sudden determination, she opened her chest and took out her cloak. It was of a dark colour and intended to keep her warm in less balmy climes, but she could scarcely go up on the deck of a warship without covering a gown intended for an evening function in some genteel drawing-room!

She flung the cloak about her shoulders, left her cabin and began to climb the companion ladder. Daniel was occupied in his pantry and the marine sentry, roused from a doze, ignored her once he had seen she was not bound for the great cabin. Her soft, flat-heeled slippers made no noise and offered no hindrance to her progress. With her dress and cloak bunched up in one hand she ran up the ladder almost as nimbly as a midshipman might. It was, after all, little different from climbing into the hayloft of the empty stables at home and, unlike this one, that ladder did not have a rope handrail to cling to.

Silent as her approach had been, the officer on watch spotted her the instant her fair head appeared above the hatchway. He walked across to assist her to the deck.

'Good evening, Miss Dawson,' he murmured, saluting. 'Lieutenant Windsor, at your service. Is there something I can do for you?'

So he knew who she was. She supposed everyone aboard did by now. His shadowy form in the darkness seemed only slightly taller than her own five feet three. He must be one of the few men aboard who could walk across the great cabin without ducking—even her hair brushed the beams.

The sliver of moon was behind a high cloud at that moment and she could see little of Mr Windsor's face in the starlight, just a rather long white blur punctuated by darker shadows emerging from under his cocked hat. His voice sounded young, full of self-confidence. She smiled, hoping that his eyes, adjusted to the dark, would be able to detect her amiable response.

'With your permission, Lieutenant, I should like to walk for a while. I feel in need of exercise and fresh air before I can sleep.'

'Of course, Miss Dawson.' He made a gesture with his hand. 'If you would care to pace the starboard—that is,' he added hastily, 'the right-hand side of the deck—you will not be in the captain's way should he come up.'

'Very well,' murmured Miranda.

The bottom sails had been furled for the night. Those left to catch the brisk wind and drive the ship forward were far above her head, two on each of the three masts, leaving the entire length of the decks open to her view: the gangways along each side leading to the foredeck, the dark hole in the middle where part of the main gun deck below was open to the sky. Vague shapes in the shadows at the lower level she knew to be the ship's boats, hoisted aboard and lashed down until they were needed again. Few of the crew were to be seen, apart from the men at the wheel and the lookouts—six shadows posted along the sides constantly scanning the darkness for any hazard. The men of the watch would be huddled in dark corners trying to catch some sleep. A cry from a lookout or a shift in the wind and they would appear from nowhere to swarm over the decks and up the masts to do whatever was necessary, as she knew from her time aboard the *Othello*.

But for the moment everything was quiet. She walked the length of the quarterdeck, from the forward rail, just behind the main mast, to the stern, to and fro, passing a lookout each time, his shadowy figure barely discernible as he scanned the horizon—that almost invisible line which divided a midnight-blue sky studded with stars from the slate-grey sea. She wondered what he was thinking as he stood there, whistling softly to keep himself alert. Of home? Or of the captain who held his life, and the life of every man—and woman—on board, in his hands? Who could jump on the lookout for making an unseemly noise but, she knew instinctively, would not. Or the lieutenant would long ago have ordered the man to keep quiet.

Enjoying the breeze, the starlit night, the slender arc of the moon, now fully visible, the creak and groan of timbers and rigging, the chuckle of water under the hull, Miranda found it difficult to believe the events of the day.

To think that she had ended it as a prisoner of war! But. . .was she? Captain York had implied as much, but surely America did not make war on women? No, once they reached the United States she would be free to make her way to join her family in Barbados.

With this comforting thought in mind, Miranda leant on the aftermost rail—the taffrail, wasn't it called?—to watch the wake creaming away behind, with green phosphorescence causing it to shine in the dark, making it look almost as though the sea was alight. No wonder sailors called it seafire, it was a spectacular sight and this frigate had been named after the phenomenon.

He was an intriguing man, Captain York. Was he truly afraid of women? Mr West must have been teasing him but the captain had not been slow to register his displeasure. No, he could not be. Not a man as self-assured as the captain! Why, you had only to look at him to know that if he gave an order the men would race to carry it out—and because they wanted to please him, not because they were afraid of being punished. The ship had a happy air about it, borne out by Zack West's easy relationship with his captain until he over-stepped an invisible mark and became over-familiar, something which no commander could tolerate. Yet there was no sign of lack of discipline—discipline could not be slack or the *Seafire* could never have achieved the victory of the morning. He had that necessary quality of true leadership—the knack of keeping his men on a loose rein which could be tightened when necessary.

The sound of muted voices behind made her turn. Even after so slight an acquaintance, she knew that the tall shadow conferring with the short lieutenant could be none other than Captain York. Miranda's senses sharpened. Why had he come on deck? Did he know she was here? Was he about to chide her for leaving her cabin?

The captain's final words were spoken more loudly as he turned away. 'Very well. Carry on, Mr Windsor,' he said, very formally. The lieutenant said something else, rather quickly. Captain York, halted in his stride, looked her way and then said, 'Thanks, Abe,' before changing direction and heading towards her.

Miranda straightened, nerves taut. Was he about to deliver a verbal broadside? A strange excitement overtook her as he approached. She would welcome an exchange of fire with the captain! A fitting end to an eventful day!

However, he merely inclined his head before saying, 'You desired to take the air, I believe, Miss Dawson. Will you join me on the larboard side of the deck?'

The windward side, his exclusive territory. A captain was entitled to privacy—the only man aboard who was. No one, except an officer on duty with a need, would dare to intrude on the windward side without invitation when the captain was there.

Miranda did not know whether to feel flattered or not, but she was not about to argue. It would be more comfortable to walk on the high, dry side of the frigate.

'Thank you, Captain,' she murmured, accompanying him past one of the two guns pointing astern. There were guns at intervals along each side of the deck too, all tightly lashed down and covered to keep the salt spray off them. There was little chance of forgetting that this was a warship.

Or that Captain York commanded an enemy naval vessel.

'I normally try to walk at least two miles every day,' Adam explained as they began to pace the deck together, 'which means about seventy-six lengths of the deck twice a day. And this is one of the times when I most enjoy doing it.'

'I'm sorry to have intruded, Captain.'

'Not at all, Miss Dawson. I gather you feared being unable to sleep?'

'I felt the need for some fresh air.' And, she added silently, time to think, to sort out my emotions.

As they passed the lookout on that side of the quarterdeck the captain paused. 'All well, Roper?'

'Aye, sir,' said the man, knuckling his forehead. 'Not a glimpse of a sail, friend or foe, sir.'

'Perhaps it's just as well, eh? We've had enough excitement for one day!'

'Aye, sir,' returned the man with a grin. 'But she were a fine prize, sir!'

'And you'll get your share of the prize money. Keep your eyes open.'

It was smooth, assured, the popular captain at ease with his crew while maintaining a necessary distance. But Miranda had questions to ask which should ruffle him and the answers would either make it easier or harder for her to sleep.

'Must I consider myself a prisoner of war?' she demanded abruptly.

He hesitated a moment before replying. Perhaps she had managed to surprise him.

'Your position is unusual, Miss Dawson,' he finally pronounced. 'You were taken from an enemy man-of-war and so, technically, yes, you are my prisoner. But on the other hand you are a female and I have never heard of females being held as prisoners of war. So your position is also ambiguous. I shall leave it to my admiral to decide once we reach America.'

'I am certain *he* will not wish to detain me! I shall be able to take immediate passage to Barbados.'

'In what kind of ship, Miss Dawson? None sail from America to British-held territory.'

'Then I must travel via a neutral country. Really, Captain, you are presenting quite unnecessary problems!'

'Do you have enough money with you to cover the cost of the fare?'

Even in the shadows of the quarterdeck he saw her face drop. Why was he being so obstructive? wondered Adam to himself. It would be easy enough to reassure the child that if all else failed he would pay her passage to Barbados. But he did not want to; he wanted her to believe that she would have to remain in America... where he could see her whenever he was ashore?

Damn it all, she was English, England was the enemy he was commissioned to fight, and he had only met her today! A chit out of the schoolroom! Of what possible interest could she be to him? Yet how different she was from his sisters, from all the other simpering, insipid misses he met when he spent any time at home—or anywhere else on land for that matter—apart from the whores, who exhibited quite opposite traits. She looked no different, appeared so fragile, yet had shown no trace of fear, had challenged his intentions towards her, had put up a spirited defence of her father...

An admiral, he reminded himself grimly. No wonder

she was sure of herself! An enemy admiral's daughter had little to fear from his naval authorities, although they might attempt to use her as a bargaining counter. He would have to treat her like precious porcelain, for if anything happened to her he would be held liable. His masters might consider her a valuable hostage rather than a prisoner of war. Safe delivery of Miss Miranda Dawson might secure his own future in the service—

He cut his thoughts off sharply. He needed to use no child to help further his career! Had he not already become a full captain, in command of one of the USA's latest frigates? Some officers remained lieutenants all their lives! Had he not had enormous luck in capturing enemy prizes, making him a rich man in his own right, and no longer dependent upon his father for succour should he be forced to leave the service?

He watched Miranda's chin come up, saw the blaze of defiance in her blue eyes. Yes, he could see the expression, though the colour came from memory, for although they happened to be walking within the glow cast by a candle illuminating the compass, and the sliver of moon had long ago emerged from behind the bank of cloud, the light was not strong enough for him to determine the hue.

'Then I shall work to earn the money!' Miranda declared.

Adam could not help the chuckle which rose from him at her defiant words. What a spirited creature she was! They turned to retrace their steps and he could feel the anger emanating from her, the way she almost stamped her feet as she walked. He allowed the silence to stretch. At last, 'How do you propose to do that?' he enquired mildly. 'I can think of only one easy way. . .'

They were almost at the taffrail and she came to a sudden, incredulous halt. 'How dare you?' she snapped. 'You. . .you abominable creature! How dare you suggest that I—'

'I suggested no such thing,' retorted Adam, all innocence. 'I merely remarked—'

'I know what you said! You have no need to repeat your insulting remark! I could do many things—I could become a nanny, or a companion, or. . .or. . .'

'Has your invention run out?' enquired Adam kindly. 'You could, I suppose, find work in a laundry, or a shop, or even in a tavern. . . Have you ever done a day's work in your life, Miss Dawson?'

Miranda sought the support of the rail. She found she was trembling. With anger, not with fear or. . .or anything else. Her hand shook as she brushed a tendril of hair from her face. Short as it was, it could still reach an eye if the wind whipped it forward and sideways. And as she straightened up again she bounced off the rail and stamped her foot to let the odious creature know that she had lost her temper with him.

'I have just come from an academy where I was sent to learn the manners of a young lady, Captain. You are tempting me to forget all I have learned and to treat you with the contempt you deserve! If my brothers annoy me I slap their faces and pull their hair!'

'How very interesting,' murmured Adam. 'Would you like to try it with me, Miss Dawson?'

Miranda was tempted, but prudence forced her to reject the invitation. She imagined she would end up in some undignified position—possibly across the captain's knees being spanked, since he was determined to treat her as a child.

'No,' she returned with dignity. 'I have no wish to waste the money my father paid for my education. We have not always been rich, Captain, and, yes, I have often worked hard, though not for money. I helped my mother in the house and garden in the days before we could afford enough servants. A captain's pay is not generous and my father had no private source of income.'

'No prize money?' wondered Adam, one dark brow raised.

Miranda took the enquiry as a criticism. 'Any luxuries we enjoyed, including our house and extensive gardens, came from prize money, but he was never stationed where prizes abounded. Blockade duty is both tedious and unrewarding. But the battle of Trafalgar changed his fortunes. And now, posted to the Windward Station, his frigates are taking plenty of prizes. Both French *and* American,' she added with a touch of malice.

'Huzzah for him. So you can do housework and tend a garden. You will not find either employment lucrative, Miss Dawson.'

'My dear Captain,' she said with as much condescension in her tone as she could muster, 'do not allow my predicament to concern you. I shall find work and save for my passage, even if it takes me years. But long before that I trust this unnecessary war between our countries will end. My father will be able to remit my fare and I shall be able to sail direct to Barbados.'

'If he is still there,' murmured Adam, some powerful force impelling him to keep up his baiting of her. From self-defence he was determined to continue to treat her as an infant, but he could no longer delude himself. She was not. She had hidden her womanly charms beneath that cloak, but he could not forget they were there. He had been all too conscious of them during supper.

He was not afraid of women, as Zack had accused—he had been in love once long ago and had had several liaisons since—but he had learned to be cautious in his dealings with the female sex. Generally speaking, he avoided young ladies like the plague, and must have given Zack and others the wrong impression. But if he dallied with one of the few marriageable females who did not bore him to tears he might so easily find himself leg-shackled. A naval officer had, in his opinion, no business to marry, leaving wife and children, if any, to manage on their own while he was away, perhaps for years on end. Look at Zack! A father who had not only missed the period of his wife's pregnancy but also those first, magical months of his daughter's life. At least, he had always imagined that they must be magical. He was certain they would be for him.

He hadn't thought about marriage for years. And now, because an unusual chit of a girl possessed of both beauty and spirit had been foisted upon him, he found himself brooding on the only aspect of naval service which could possibly bother him. He had long ago considered himself wed to the navy. The sea was a harsh mistress but one he loved above all others. Damnation take Miss Miranda Dawson! He'd been without a woman for too long! What quirk of fate had made him decide to take the *Othello*, against the odds? Not fate, he admitted grimly, but sheer arrogance. To prove himself able.

'I shall join my family, wherever it is!' declared Miranda, bringing his thoughts back to her with a jolt.

Adam relented. 'I admire your spirit, Miss Dawson, and have no doubt you will succeed,' he admitted.

'Are you sailing for the Canary Isles?' demanded Miranda, since an idea had suddenly occurred to her.

The black brows descended in a frown. 'I do not think I can confide that information.'

Miranda's voice held scathing contempt. 'Why? Whom could I possibly inform?'

'There could be circumstances. . .but what would it matter? Yes, I am headed for the Canaries, where I hope to replenish my water and wood before embarking on the Atlantic crossing.'

Miranda stopped. 'But they are Spanish!'

He halted beside her. 'So they are.'

'And Spain is now an ally of England!'

'But not a very willing one. Their common enemy is Napoleon. America is not at war with Spain. There are plenty of places where an American ship may still put in to find the supplies it needs. I had hoped to put into Madeira—'

'That is Portuguese!'

'True, but the natives are not averse to selling their delicious wine to an American! Chasing the *Othello* took me too far south. I shall have to content myself with a further supply of Spanish wine. But I prefer Madeira to sherry.'

'Well,' said Miranda, quashing any irrelevant discussion on the merits of wine, 'you could put me ashore on one of the islands. I'm sure I could find a King's ship or a merchantman willing to take me on from there.'

'A merchantman? Er. . .the fare?' murmured Adam.

'The navy would arrange it,' declared Miranda with more confidence than she felt.

'So they might,' admitted Adam, if doubtfully. 'But I am afraid I could not risk abandoning you on one of the Canary Isles, even if I thought it within my remit. I have to answer to my admiral. In any case, we shall be calling at one of the smaller, more remote islands where you might experience some difficulty in contacting any naval personnel, and I shall feel happier about your safety if you remain aboard the *Seafire*.'

'Of course it is within your remit!' snapped Miranda, latching onto the circumstance which made her fume. She felt quite capable of looking after herself and making her way either to the West Indies or England from there, but the power of decision Captain York now exercised over her life was another matter altogether. She hated it. And him because he possessed it.

The last sliver of the new moon had disappeared as it set, leaving the deck in velvety, starlit darkness. Miranda looked up into Captain York's face, trying to assess his response to her fierce declaration. He appeared to be eyeing her with amusement.

'Of course it is!' she repeated angrily. 'Why, you can even put prisoners of war ashore on enemy territory—'

'But only with the written agreement of an enemy officer that they shall not take part in the war again until an equal number of American prisoners have been exchanged. And I think we are agreed that your exact status is not at all clear, Miss Dawson. I must, I fear, err on the side of caution. I am not an entirely free agent, you must realise.'

'Your admiral!' sneered Miranda.

Adam sighed, tired of trying to explain to a child who refused to understand. 'My admiral,' he agreed. 'He has the power to have me brought before a court martial and dismissed from the service. I am not willing to risk such an eventuality.'

Miranda seethed. 'I perceive that you are not afraid to take your ship into action, sir, to risk your own life, that of every man aboard, as well as the ship itself! Yet you will not risk—'

'A different matter altogether, miss! I am paid to take the first risks you mentioned and could be called to account if I failed in my duty to do so! But I am not paid to pander to the whims of adolescent females who can think of nothing but themselves and their own desires!'

Miranda's hand lifted without any other thought than to wipe the sneer off the face hanging above her in the darkness. But it had risen no further than her shoulder before her wrist was grasped by what felt like an iron band.

'Oh, no, you don't, you little termagant,' muttered Adam wrathfully and, still holding her wrist, pulled her towards him.

Miranda saw the kiss coming and compressed her lips into a tight line. His were hard, punishing, bruising the tender flesh that had never felt the touch of a strange man's mouth before. Yet his closeness had a curious effect upon her, making her short of breath so that when he released her she stood before him, chest heaving, fighting to regain control.

'Your first kiss?' enquired Adam, his anger abating and being replaced by a wry regret that he had so far forgotten himself as to treat the chit so. But at least it should prove to her that Zack's opinion was wrong— that he did not fear women. Her lips, despite being pressed together against his marauding mouth, had tasted sweet. He could wish he had taken them under different circumstances.

But he had no business taking them at all! He considered himself a gentleman and gentlemen did not make free with their kisses when in the company of respectable young ladies. And, whatever else she was or was not, Miss Miranda Dawson was a respectable young lady. He should apologise.

'How dare you, sir?' cried Miranda, forestalling any apology he might have offered. Had it been so obvious to him that she had never been kissed before? 'You forget yourself.' she stormed on, rubbing her wrist, certain that by morning it would show a bruise, ignoring a slight, placatory gesture he began to make. 'I am in your charge; you warned me against your men, but it seems to me I had best beware of their captain!'

Adam revoked his resolve to apologise. She had spirit, this child: most of the young ladies of his acquaintance, admittedly not numerous, would have swooned at being kissed in the way he had kissed Miranda.

'Perhaps you should, Miss Dawson. Beware of provoking me. I mean. I can scarcely order you to be flogged at the gratings. What better punishment can I devise for you?'

'You mean—'

'I mean I shall delight in kissing you every time you cross me, Miss Dawson. So be warned. The more you dislike it, the better I shall be pleased. I suggest you go below while I complete my evening mile. I shall expect to see you at breakfast, which will be served at one bell in the forenoon watch. That is, at half past eight.'

'Thank you,' said Miranda tightly. 'I do not need to listen for bells. I have a watch with me.'

'Capital. Until the morning, then, Miss Dawson.'

He bowed, turned, dismissing her, and resumed his pacing of the deck. Miranda stood for just a moment watching the upright figure stride away. Then, with an inarticulate choke, she turned and made for the hatch.

'Give you a good night, Miss Dawson,' offered Lieutenant Windsor, saluting as she passed.

'And you a trouble-free watch, Lieutenant,' retorted Miranda, hoping he would not detect the tremble in her voice.

Not until she reached her cabin below did she give way to the storm of tears she had been holding back ever since that dreadful creature had threatened his punishment for any disobedience.

How could she bear to be kissed by him in such a way again?

But somehow, in her dreams, he kissed her quite differently. And she actually enjoyed it.

CHAPTER THREE

MIRANDA woke at dawn, disturbed by the sound of knocking and scraping as the deck above her head received its daily rubbing with holystones. It seemed that the American Navy was as devoted to maintaining its ships in scrubbed and polished condition as the British, she thought resignedly, abandoning further thought of sleep. At least, Captain York was.

Captain York! She tossed restlessly in her cot, her face burning with embarrassment, thoroughly disgusted with herself as memory returned. How could she have dreamed of the creature and imagined herself enjoying being held in his arms and kissed? She was nothing to Captain York but a nuisance he wished to punish and he meant no more to her than a hated enemy with whom she was forced to consort; but her unconscious mind had taken no account of these hard facts. For some reason it had turned her impotent submission to his assault into a ridiculous desire to sample more of his kisses!

Oh, Peter! she wailed to herself, turning her burning face into her pillow. Why did you have to die? You would never have treated me so! You never shamed me by seeking to kiss me! And I loved you so much!

She tried to recall the features of the man her romantic heart had found so attractive. He had been handsome—even-featured with a noble brow—and had looked so manly in his naval uniform. The white breeches and silk stockings—so much more elegant than the trousers worn by Captain York!—beneath the uniform frock coat, with the recently introduced epaulette on his right shoulder, had become his excellent figure, and wearing his cocked hat he had looked every inch an admiral in the making. She had felt so proud that he had even noticed her! How well he had executed his duties under Captain Blackmore. But, she had to admit, without possessing that extra something so apparent in Captain York.

Captain York never needed to raise his voice in anger; his men vied with each other to obey his slightest command. He exuded confidence, his authority was instinctive, as was his seamanship—that inherent knowledge and use of wind, tide and current to get the best performance out of his ship—which had been immediately recognised by the *Othello*'s master, that elderly and experienced man of the sea.

She lay there for a while coming to terms with the fact that Peter Stannard was dead. He had been charming, attentive, and so much more agreeable than Captain York. How she hated the American for killing her dreams. She had nothing to sustain her now, except the distant prospect of joining her family in the West Indies.

With the noise of the ship coming alive all about her, and fully awake, she knew it was no use lying in bed feeling sorry for herself. She could cope. She must. She must look upon the actual crossing of the ocean aboard the frigate as an adventure. She had never done anything half as exciting in her life before, and here she had no quasi-paternal figure like Captain Blackmore to criticise her every action. She had no intention of misbehaving, of course—the social etiquette instilled in her at the hated Academy had been well learned if resented—and she would most certainly keep her promise to Captain York. But, at home, she had been wont to borrow a pair of her brother's breeches and pull long socks up to her knees in order to jump ditches and climb fences and trees. She could do with them now: clambering about the ship would be so much easier. She became very thoughtful.

Determined to make the most of whatever lay ahead, she sat up, stilling the swing of the cot by putting a hand on the partition, and gingerly extricated herself from its clutches, deciding as she did so to fill in the time before breakfast by taking another turn about the deck. She had always enjoyed fresh air and exercise. And if Captain York was there she would keep strictly to the lee side of the ship and ignore him.

So she rose, relit her lantern, washed in cold water and put on a fresh day dress of patterned muslin in shades of brown, cream and green. It was of a darker hue than she usually wore, but would not show the dirt should she brush against any of the tarred ropes or other hazards littering the deck. And it did become her, she decided as she peered into the mirror in the flickering light. Not that there was anyone aboard the *Seafire* that she wished to impress. Far from wishing to entice Captain York with her feminine charms, she was now desperate to avoid another kiss.

Soon after she emerged on deck the sunrise came in spectacular fashion, lighting the eastern horizon with golden splendour, while to the west the sky was still black. Gradually the light spread to encompass the entire heaving ocean, or at least that part of it she could see. The lookouts were already aloft rather than posted about the sides and so able to see for miles in every direction, but so far they had not reported any kind of sighting. The *Seafire* seemed to have the ocean to herself.

There was no sign of Captain York, for which Miranda gave sincere thanks. The longer she could put off facing him again, the better she would be able to cope, because the acute memory of that disastrous kiss must fade. Zack West was on watch and had greeted her in friendly fashion as she had appeared from below. Now he came forward to join her at the forward rail of the quarterdeck, where she stood drinking in the sight of the sky and the sea, watching the men going about their work, cleaning, polishing and mending, eyeing the bright paint of the boats stacked on the main deck below and the row of guns on each side lashed down behind closed ports. These things would constitute the boundaries of her vision for many days to come.

'A splendid sunrise,' Zack remarked with a smile.

'I had never realised how beautiful it could be until I came to sea,' admitted Miranda. 'Before embarking on the *Othello* I had seldom been up in time to see one at all, let alone one as wonderful as this!'

Zack chuckled. 'Being at sea has turned you into an early riser?'

'There seems little choice!' Miranda grimaced ruefully. 'The men make such a noise holystoning the decks! And they start before first light!'

Zack leaned companionably on the rail beside her, his grin teasing.

'When you've been at sea a while you'll learn to sleep through it,' he asserted. 'We have to, or we'd never get any rest between watches. The normal sounds of a working ship become a soothing lullaby, an assurance that all is well. Silence would wake the captain or me in an instant!'

'I can forget the chuckle of the water- ' she waved a hand upwards '—the slatting of the sails, the creaks and groans of the timber; they seem natural. It is the men clumping and scraping about overhead I cannot, as yet, ignore!'

'There should be no slatting!' Zack, brought to realise a fault in the trim of the sails, snapped an order and men rushed to haul on various ropes until all shivering in the canvas had been eliminated and the sails were taut as drums, drawing strongly again. 'A slight shift in the wind,' he explained once his attention returned to her.

'Yes,' agreed Miranda, whose thoughts, while this had been going on, had turned to her fate in America. If only she could be certain that she would not be held as a prisoner, or used as a bargaining counter to secure the release of some important enemy.

'Do you think I shall be treated as a prisoner of war once we reach America?' she asked Zack.

He eyed her quizzically. 'What does the captain say?'

'He doesn't seem to know. Says it depends upon his admiral.'

'And so it does, I suppose. But you'd be given parole. You could go and stay with my wife,' Zack added on sudden impulse. 'She would welcome your company, I'm sure.'

Miranda turned to him, her face glowing. 'Could I? Really? How kind you are, Mr West!'

'Mr West is supposed to be on watch,' came an acerbic voice from behind. 'What kind of watch are you keeping, Mr West, when your captain can come on deck without your noticing? And your tardy sail-trimming did not go unremarked. As for you, Miss Dawson, I will thank you not to distract my officers from their duties.'

Miranda could feel Zack stiffen beside her and glimpsed the frown between his eyes as he shot his captain a startled glance. He was not used to being spoken to thus. Nothing he had done deserved such a set-down and she suspected that, normally, a mild reproof would have been all he would have received for that momentary lapse of concentration. But for some reason Captain York was in a foul mood and had put her in a cleft stick. If she defended herself, said she had not sought the lieutenant's company, things would look worse for him. And he had been friendly—more, kind, offering her the hospitality of his home while she must remain in America. She would have to take the blame, although rousing Captain York's further wrath did not appeal. If provoked he would punish her. An obscure frisson of almost pleasurable anticipation ran through her at the thought, which she immediately denied.

'I am sorry, Captain,' she said stiffly. 'I came on deck to watch the sunrise. Mr West was kind enough to be civil to me. I will now take my morning exercise.'

Saying which, she moved as far away from *his* side of the deck as possible with all the dignity she could muster. She walked to the stern and stood at the taffrail, gazing abstractedly at their wake, taking deep breaths to calm her nerves. Then she turned and, taking care not to trip over any of the numerous obstructions littering her path, began a steady pacing of the sloping deck. How many lengths had he said? Seventy-six to the mile, she remembered. How did he count them? Perhaps he knew how long it took him. She, she decided, would walk until the watch changed, half an hour before breakfast, for which she was already ravenous. Then she would go below, freshen her face and wait in the great cabin for the meal to be served. After all, he had said she could use his cabin.

Captain York stalked his side of the deck while she paced hers. The daylight grew stronger, the sun began to radiate its heat. Lost in her thoughts, Miranda was startled to hear eight bells strike from the belfry—the signal for another bout of wild activity and much twittering of bosun's pipes as the watch changed. It seemed to be the cue for the *Othello*'s officers to emerge on deck to take the air too. But the bells had reminded her that in half an hour she would be able to satisfy her hunger so, having greeted them, she made for the companion ladder, passing Zack, still engaged in handing over the watch to another officer. With her foot on the top step she was halted by Captain York's voice hailing her.

'Miss Dawson!'

She stopped and turned, her stomach clenching. What had she done now?

He approached with long, easy strides. He did not smile, but she was relieved to discover that his voice held no anger or censure as he said, 'My hens are laying well at present. If you would care for eggs for breakfast, please inform Daniel. He will see them cooked to your liking.'

Astonished at his change of front, Miranda nodded. 'Thank you, Captain. I should enjoy a boiled egg above anything.'

At least, she thought as she descended the ladder, the meal would not be eaten in hostile silence. He would never apologise for his ill-humour, of course, but she felt cheered that it seemed to have passed. Perhaps she would continue to escape punishment for aggravating him and not be called upon to endure another of his lowering, mortifying kisses.

Mortifying, unwelcome, yet strangely disturbing! She really could not understand why a hard, angry kiss from that man—an enemy—should cause her a moment's disquiet other than the sort occasioned had he slapped her face. Then she would have been furious, resentful, suffering from hurt pride. She was angry, of course, for how dared he treat her with such disrespect? But, like the crossing of the Atlantic, that kiss had taken on the aspect of a challenge, an experience she could savour in retrospect. She did not, she declared vehemently to herself, like Adam York, but it had been her first kiss and had made her realise that, should she meet a man she could truly love and respect, she would enjoy his advances. Something she had not been too sure of before. She had longed, against all the lessons she had had dinned into her, for Peter to ignore convention and kiss her, but of course, unlike Captain York, he had been too much of a gentleman to do more than touch her fingers with his mouth. Which had had no more effect upon her than her brothers' occasional gestures of affection. Yet even Captain York's courteous salute before supper the previous evening had set her nerves quivering. She could not understand why the touch of a man she loathed could affect her in such a way when that of the man she had loved had left her unaffected. It must, she decided, be because she was in York's power and she hated him for it.

Yet when he entered the great cabin later, smiled at her and greeted the two young midshipmen invited to join him in his repast with formal yet warm hospitality, putting the anxious youngsters at ease with a few well-chosen words, she could not find it in her to dislike him entirely. The young gentlemen, clearly in awe of the occasion, relaxed perceptibly as, having been helped to fried salt pork and beans and told to help themselves to bread—in the form of ship's biscuits— he began to chat easily with the lads, asking them questions about their progress with seamanship and navigation, encouraging them to express themselves freely but warning them that he would be inspecting their diaries—supposed to contain a record of everything that happened aboard the ship—later in the day.

He could not be all bad, she recognised. From what her brothers had told her, such understanding from a captain was rare. The inquisitions they had been subjected to by their captains had left them stammering and unsure.

She had no need to speak as the meal progressed, for the captain's questions and the youngsters' answers kept the conversation flowing. As soon as they had

finished eating the midshipmen rose to leave, bowing
formally to her as they did so.

'I trust you were not bored, Miss Dawson,' said
Captain York after they had disappeared. 'I invite the
midshipmen to take breakfast with me in turn; it is my
duty to see that they learn their lessons well and to
prepare them to take the lieutenant's examination in
due course. I find eating relaxes them, makes them
more ready to talk freely.'

'I was not in the least bored, Captain; in fact I found
the conversation most interesting. They certainly
seemed well informed, even if they did need correcting
from time to time. You are to be congratulated.'

'As are you, Miss Dawson. You have settled into
your enforced sojourn with us with the minimum of
fuss.'

Miranda flushed. She had not expected any word of
appreciation or praise from him. But even as he finished
speaking the smile faded from his lips and he turned
away, as though impatient to relieve himself of her
company. Nevertheless, she decided to go ahead and
say something she had been rehearsing ever since she
had come below.

'I am sorry if my speaking with Mr West was wrong,
sir. I did not think a few words could do harm, since we
had met socially over supper last evening.'

He swung back to face her, the expression on his face
difficult to read. He might almost have been feeling
guilty, but that impression was fleeting. He was, in fact,
annoyed, though whether at her apology or her actions
she could not tell.

Then, as he spoke again, the reason became all too plain.

'For many reasons I have always disliked the idea of having a woman, any woman, aboard any ship I command, Miss Dawson. Firstly, a warship is not a comfortable place for a lady to find herself, as you have discovered, and my hospitality must necessarily be lacking. But, more importantly to me, any female is a disturbing influence among the men, who lack feminine society for long months together while at sea. The officers are easily distracted from their duty—even Mr West, as I had occasion to observe. Such a distraction could cause disaster if a sudden change in the wind went unnoticed or the ship drifted off course. The officer of the watch needs to be constantly on the alert. Any slackness on his part could prove lethal.'

Miranda swallowed. 'I know that, Captain. I just did not think. It will not happen again.'

He relaxed, and suddenly a rather mischievous grin lit his countenance. His grey eyes lightened with humour.

'I shall rely upon that, Miss Dawson. I do not wish to have to punish you again for provoking me.'

Miranda's face flamed. So much for her apology! He thought that kiss a joke, did he? Just as she was beginning to like the man a little, he had to remind her of it and the threat that had come after. And why didn't he want to have to kiss her again? Hadn't he enjoyed it?

Too confused and mortified to make a coherent answer, Miranda contented herself with an unladylike snort as she flounced out of the cabin.

* * *

She was alone with Adam York for no more than a moment or two as the frigate sailed slowly south. She began to wonder whether he was avoiding such an eventuality. Officers joined him for each meal, his clerk spent most of the day working at the desk in the great cabin, completing the mass of records they were obliged to keep, and Daniel was constantly on hand. He had to be in and around the cabin in order to keep it and Adam's clothes spotless and be ready to carry out his master's smallest wish. So there was always someone else present. The arrangement meant that she became acquainted with members of the gunroom, including Captain York's master, Tom Crocker, a much younger but experienced navigator with whom Mr Haskett of the *Othello* soon became friendly.

'York will not go far wrong with Crocker aboard,' Mr Haskett confided to Miranda as they paced the deck together one afternoon. 'And Tom says the captain is no mean navigator himself.'

'So we should fetch the Canaries and then cross the Atlantic without going too far astray. Some consolation, I suppose,' muttered Miranda rebelliously. Hard as she tried, she could not help resenting her position, and because of it she was not enjoying the warm weather and excellent sailing conditions as much as she might.

'Are you afeared, child?' murmured Mr Haskett. 'You've no need to be as long as I'm around.'

'I am not fearful, just annoyed,' declared Miranda. 'I had not expected to be confined aboard an enemy warship!'

Most of the time she felt as out of place aboard the frigate as she must have looked in her long skirts. They made her an obvious target for the seamen's curiosity and added to Captain York's impatience at having a woman not only aboard his man-of-war but invading his personal privacy. All her original intention of showing him just how much of a woman she was had died a violent death when he had kissed her. So she decided she might as well follow up on the idea she had conceived earlier.

Some of the officers from the *Othello* were promenading on the deck with her. Young Will Welland seemed to have made friends with the *Seafire*'s good-natured midshipmen and was busy talking, laughing and helping a couple of them in their duties on the foredeck.

'I'm learning a lot,' he'd confided to her. 'They're treating me with great goodwill. If only the fellows and officers aboard the *Othello* had been like those here! I like it on this ship.'

Miranda had been pleased for him. He had needed the friendship of his shipmates and understanding of his superiors to give him confidence. He seemed to have found it on the *Seafire*. That he was helping to sail an enemy ship did not seem to trouble him and, truth to tell, under the present circumstances it did not trouble her, either. She was glad to see the boy happy.

A subdued Tony Keeper, on the other hand, seemed determined to seek the protection of his senior officers on the quarterdeck. He was sporting a badly damaged eye.

'How did you get that?' Miranda asked him sympathetically as an opening. She did not normally indulge in conversation with a young gentleman whose nature she found rather unpleasant, but she wanted an excuse to talk to him.

Mr Keeper coloured up—the first time Miranda had ever seen such a sign of embarrassment from him. At the same time his lips pouted truculently. 'I fell over and hit my eye on a belaying pin,' he muttered.

'Oh, how unfortunate,' murmured Miranda, who did not believe him. Word was that, caught victimising Will, he had been taught a lesson by the American midshipmen. 'Could you help me, do you think? Being aboard a ship, I should like to dress in an appropriate manner, and you are not far above my size. Could you let me borrow a spare uniform? Trousers would be so much more convenient for climbing up pitching and rolling ladders and threading my way amongst all the gear littering the decks.'

The midshipman gaped at her as though she were mad. 'Dress as a boy, you mean?' he asked, aghast.

'Yes. At home I was used to wearing my brothers' clothes sometimes when I wanted to be free of my skirts. Mama did not object,' she added hurriedly, seeing the disbelief written on the boy's face. She did not add that this had been before her parents had decided that their tomboy daughter should be turned into a young lady.

'I could not possibly do such a thing!' declared Mr Keeper virtuously. 'You would be ruined, Miss Dawson. And I should be blamed!'

'No, you would not. And as for my being ruined, who is to know, once I am on land again and among strangers? Please, Tony.' She gave him her most bewitching smile. He was younger than she and so she felt at liberty to address him in this familiar way. 'You would be doing me the greatest service.'

He wavered. A calculating look entered his good eye. The other was black and half-closed. 'I could not lend my clothes to you, Miss Dawson. But if I had some I had grown out of and decided to sell—'

'And I bought them!' cried Miranda. 'You could scarcely deny me that right!'

A smug expression of satisfaction settled on Mr Keeper's heavy features. He was quite a big lad for fifteen, two or three inches taller than Miranda, having grown apace during the last six months. 'I'd be right glad to receive payment for them,' he admitted. 'I owe a bit of money.'

Miranda raised her brows. 'Gambling?'

He nodded. 'One has to join in, you know. And I've had a run of bad luck.'

'What with damaging your eye and all, I collect that you have.'

Keeper shrugged, assuming indifference. 'My luck will change. I shall come about. But the money for my things will be useful.' He inspected her figure boldly. 'The trousers should be about right and the jacket ought to fit, though the buttons might be a bit tight across the chest,' he observed, grinning, eyeing her well-developed figure with adolescent relish.

'I can easily alter them,' said Miranda quickly, wanting to set the impudent lad down but unable to do so under the circumstances. 'I shall need a couple of shirts and a hat and some stockings, too. I don't know about shoes, though,' she mused, eyeing his large feet.

'You could buy a pair of shoes from the purser,' he

suggested. 'He'd be sure to have some your size, he fits the boys out.'

Miranda did not relish having to approach the purser, though he had the unusual reputation of being honest. 'How much do you want for the clothes?' she enquired, mentally reviewing her scanty stock of money.

He named a sum which made her wince. 'I cannot possibly afford so much!' she protested. 'I could buy new for that, and yours are second-hand!'

'But you're not in a position to buy new, are you?' said Keeper with a barely concealed sneer.

'If I can buy shoes from the purser, I could buy other things.'

'But not a British midshipman's uniform,' he pointed out.

'I could make do with trousers and a shirt if necessary! But—' she moderated her sharp tone '—I'd rather wear a full British uniform. The clothes available from the purser would be American navy issue. She simply could not appear dressed in the style adopted by an enemy country. She thought quickly and offered a sum which was less than she could afford and thought reasonable and a long way below Keeper's demand. A short haggle ensued. In the end they came to an agreement which suited them both. Miranda would have very little ready money left, but she could always sell the clothes again when she had done with them.

'I'll go and fetch them now if you like,' offered Keeper.

'Bring them to my cabin. You know where it is. And I'll have the money ready.'

He nodded and made for the hatch leading to the

midshipmen's berth, obviously eager to secure the cash to ease his penurious plight.

Knowing he would be called to his dinner in a few moments, Miranda waited anxiously for him to appear. The captain ate at a later hour so she would have time to change and surprise him. But while she waited she decided not to do so. She would try the things on after dinner, make any necessary alterations and appear dressed in her young gentleman's clothes on the morrow.

Her nerves quivered as she imagined Captain York's reaction. She hoped he would not think her improper dress worthy of severe reprimand.

But he would never kiss her while she was garbed as a boy. Would he?

His astonished expression as she walked in to breakfast the following morning instantly gave way to one of distinct disapproval. He did not even greet her other than to demand, 'What on earth has possessed you to dress as a midshipman, Miss Dawson?'

With some difficulty, Miranda maintained her outward calm. She had known he would not approve and had therefore not risked meeting him on deck earlier but had spent the time down on the lower deck rummaging in her largest trunk to find the pair of nankeen half-boots stowed in the bottom. A pair of new shoes from the purser would probably be uncomfortable but she could wear her boots all day and all night too, if necessary.

She had expected his challenge and was braced to meet it, yet her stomach did an additional flip as she retorted, 'To avoid disturbing the sensibilities of your-self and your crew, Captain. And also,' she added defiantly, 'to make moving about this warship easier. How would you like to have to climb ladders trailing a skirt?'

Adam ignored her question for the moment. 'And exactly how, Miss Dawson, do you hope a change of costume will assist in rendering the presence of a female aboard the *Seafire* less disturbing?'

'Why,' said Miranda with exaggerated innocence, 'you are so used to seeing young lads caper about the decks displaying lively high spirits that if I look like one of them no one will notice me.'

Adam treated her to a disparaging scrutiny. 'You truly think no one will notice the difference?' he enquired harshly. 'I do not believe either of the young gentlemen due to share the table with us this morning will be bursting out of their jackets in quite the same manner as you are. They may have grown in other ways, but they will not have developed. . .er. . .' Even in his anger he retained enough delicacy to avoid mention of her breasts, so he sought another phrase to cover the matter. 'In the same places,' he substituted stiffly.

Miranda coloured in confusion. The uniform fitted her well enough elsewhere, except, perhaps, for a certain tightness round her bottom, but even shifting the buttons on the jacket had not prevented the strain they were under from showing. Being generally so slender, she had always been glad of her well-endowed figure until this moment. Not that her breasts were huge by any means—she would have been embarrassed if they were—but at least they were there, unlike those of some of the more unfortunate girls at the Academy.

To add to her discomfort, she found the coat far too warm and could not prevent herself from running a finger round her neck to ease the choking effect of her stock. But even the captain was wearing his jacket in anticipation of the arrival of two of the young gentlemen, so she could not discard hers.

'I am aware, Captain,' she managed at last, 'that my figure is a different shape from that of Mr Keeper's, but I think it ungentlemanly of you to mention the fact.'

'Indeed, Miss Dawson, I am distressed to hear your opinion,' he said with pointed sarcasm. 'But you force me to inform you that I find your behaviour unladylike.'

'In that case, neither of us should be troubled by the other!' snapped Miranda, but as the two visiting midshipmen arrived at that moment she was compelled to assume a more equable stance and to greet them with a show of composure.

Neither could hide their grins at her appearance. 'You look better in that garb than that oaf Tony Keeper,' chuckled the elder of the two.

'You will oblige me by minding your manners, Mr Lightfoot,' rasped the captain, and the lad subsided, his face scarlet.

But the boys' reaction forced Miranda to realise that far from becoming inconspicuous she was likely to suffer enhanced interest from both officers and hands. This served to make her even more determined not to abandon the freedom of movement her new outfit afforded her. The diversion caused by her new appearance was likely to be of short duration—they would soon become used to seeing her thus garbed and forget to stare. Then she would indeed blend into the background. She would change into a dress for dinner, but that was as far as she would go to placate Captain York.

The meal progressed in a stilted manner, none of them being quite at ease and the captain remaining unusually silent.

Once the young men had left, he discarded his coat and eased his neckcloth.

'I could order you to change back into women's clothes, Miss Dawson,' he observed, 'but I will not. I can understand your desire for freedom of movement. But please remember that some members of my crew may find your attire provocative. You will do well to remain as inconspicuous as possible, at least until the men grow used to the sight of you so dressed.'

'I am willing to promise you that, Captain.' How she wished she had the courage to remove her coat, but the shirt beneath would reveal even more of her womanly contours, damp as it undoubtedly was. 'I have no wish to attract unwelcome attention.'

This was said in a barbed tone which informed the captain that *his* attention would be as unwelcome as anyone else's. His grey eyes sparked with sudden amusement at her defiant stance but before he could answer her a hail from the lookout, heard clearly through the open skylight, made him cock his head to listen.

'Deck, there! Sail on the larboard bow!'

As Daniel cleared away the last of the breakfast dishes Adam, his eyes bright, subsided in his chair in an attitude of languid boredom which would not have been out of place in a London drawing-room.

Miranda was puzzled as to how he could remain so calm. 'I wonder what kind of a ship it is?' she ventured, curiosity overcoming her reluctance to make any friendly overture. 'If you will excuse me, I shall go up on deck and find out.'

'Stay here,' murmured Adam, a warning note in his voice. 'Someone will come to inform me within a few moments. Then I shall go up to see for myself and you are welcome to accompany me. But I must not show impatience and they probably do not know as yet.'

This last assertion was borne out by the continuing dialogue on deck. Apparently only the very top of the sails was visible, making identification of the strange vessel difficult.

Before long the marine sentry announced the arrival of a midshipman.

'Mr West's compliments, sir, and the lookout has seen a sail on the larboard bow,' panted the boy.

'My compliments to Mr West. I will join him at once.'

As the midshipman disappeared Adam rose to his feet and reached for his jacket. Unless circumstances were unusual he never appeared on deck without it, or his hat, which Daniel handed to him as he ducked towards the door. Miranda put her cap on, glad she wore her hair short, though she would have to see about getting it cut soon, and followed Captain York up the companion ladder. Without the encumbrance of a skirt she really was able to run up it like a midshipman.

All the same, before she had properly reached the deck Adam had grabbed a telescope and was swarming up the main mast to join the lookout, perched as high as he could go.

After a tense five minutes Adam came down.

'Set full sail, Mr West,' he ordered. 'We need to overtake before I can be certain, but I think it might be a British frigate. If it is, we shall give chase.'

Zack's face creased into a wide smile. 'Another prize?'

Adam's answering grin held all the anticipation and daring of the adventurer he was. 'With luck, Zack,' he agreed.

A buzz went round the deck, then passed through the frigate. Every eye brightened, the seamen executed their tasks with renewed enthusiasm.

Only Miranda and the small group of Othellos taking the air on deck were not so enlivened by the prospect of a chase.

'Although,' said Mr Piper, brightening, 'the tables may be turned. If it is a British ship and it prevails—'

'We shall be freed,' completed Mr Gander eagerly.

Mr Haskett, eyeing the purposeful activity on deck, the *Seafire*'s sailing master conferring with his superior officers, failed to look as hopeful as the others at these comforting words.

'In a one-to-one encounter,' he observed morosely, 'the more heavily gunned American frigate is usually victorious.'

'But the *Shannon* captured the *Chesapeake*,' protested Mr Gander.

'That's true enough, sir,' agreed the master, 'and that victory has done something to raise British morale, but the navy is still reeling under that unexpected series of reverses. We're used to winning battles, not losing 'em. I wish I knew who was captaining that frigate.'

'Wait until we know her name,' said Mr Piper. 'I can remember a great part of the Navy List.'

While the officers discussed the prospects, Miranda wondered why she had such mixed feelings over what Mr Piper and Mr Gander still considered the likelihood of imminent rescue, even though the British frigate was undoubtedly attempting to outrun the American.

CHAPTER FOUR

A CHASE! Another chase, to be exact, although, having been aboard the hare on the previous occasion, Miranda had been only dimly aware of what was going on. Now she was on the hunter's quarterdeck and Adam York's nose was twitching every bit as eagerly as that of a hound.

A scurry of activity soon had every possible sail hoisted. The extra pressure of wind canted the deck to an uncomfortable angle beneath her feet. The wash chuckled beneath the *Seafire*'s hull, she seemed almost to skim the water despite the pitch and roll, held in suspension above it by the enormous pyramid of canvas, itself held aloft by creaking spars and taut, singing ropes.

It was exhilarating sailing under that cloud of sails but that of itself could not account for the predatory excitement which had seized every member of the crew. They scented action, a prize to be taken and before long they were confirmed in their expectation. Adam went aloft again to perch perilously high up that wildly swinging mast and confirmed the lookout's opinion. The other vessel was definitely a British frigate. And thus far in this war, as the Othellos had just been lamenting, the Americans had so often emerged the victors.

Miranda could not imagine Adam York losing the

battle if he could catch his prey. His record was too formidable. He had spent the last months successfully harrying the supply ships taking much needed equipment and ammunition to the British army in the Peninsula, and had crowned his achievements by joining battle with the *Othello* and overcoming her.

The British frigate was still far ahead but the captain and the master kept taking sightings. As the hours sped by their expressions became positively exultant. Even Miranda, without the aid of an instrument, could see that they were overhauling the other vessel, and fast.

'Pass the word to the cooks to put the fires out immediately dinner is done,' Adam told Abe Windsor. 'Call me if anything changes.'

Mr Windsor repeated the order to a midshipman, who slid down the sloping deck to reach a ladder and disappeared, scrambling to deliver the captain's message.

Miranda had kept well out of the way until then but nothing much seemed to be happening, in fact Adam was preparing to go below. She waylaid him by the mizzen mast.

'Excuse me, Captain, but are you expecting to go into action?' she asked.

'I hope so! If we can overhaul that fellow before nightfall, I shall certainly bring him to action. If we do not, he will escape, for he has now laid a course for Tenerife and will find shelter among the Canaries long before daybreak.'

'Oh. We are that near the islands?'

'We made good progress yesterday, considering the poor wind. I had planned to lay off Herro tomorrow to take on supplies, and weigh anchor again before night-fall. But if we capture this fellow I shall have to change my plans.' He suddenly lifted a dark eyebrow. 'Are you enjoying the chase?'

Miranda frowned and looked down at her incon-gruous yellow half-boots. 'The sailing, yes,' she admit-ted, her fingers gripped hard around a stay. 'But you cannot expect me to welcome the thought of another battle, especially one in which one of my own country's ships will be engaged. I wish you would not attack it.'

'You need know nothing of the fighting, my dear.'

That, thought Miranda, looking up into his eyes with anger in hers, was no term of endearment but one of condescension.

'No?' she enquired sarcastically. 'Shall I become suddenly deaf to gunfire, to the death and destruction, the cries of the wounded? They bring them down screaming, you know. But that is not what worries me. Being a sailor's daughter, I am not squeamish; I know what service in the navy entails. What concerns me is the knowledge that you are about to attack a British vessel and there is nothing I can do to prevent it.'

'Indeed there is not, Miss Dawson.' He had climbed on his high ropes and looked down his nose at her as they stood swaying by the mast, he with his arms crossed, she still hanging on. 'I am glad you appreciate the fact. I must confine the prisoners of war once we go to quarters. By the time we go into action they must be locked up in their cabins. You—'

Miranda gripped her stay with both hands as the ship ploughed into a trough and rose like a corkscrew to the following crest. Adam snapped an order to Tom

Crocker, his master, to have the helmsmen mind their business.

'Please do not confine me below!' Miranda hated pleading with him, especially when he peered at her over that flat bridged nose of his. 'I cannot bear the idea of being shut up below again, not knowing what is going on, imagining the worst.' To her mind that was far more threatening than the actual sight of battle. 'If you will allow me to remain here,' she went on, 'I give you my word I will do nothing to hinder you. But you cannot imagine what torture it is, not being able to see what is happening.'

Adam shook his head, but his expression had softened. 'I can, you know. But you would be safer below. And I doubt you would have the stomach for what you might be called upon to witness.'

'I repeat, I am an admiral's daughter, no squeamish miss who faints at the sight of blood! My greatest regret is that I was not born a boy!'

She thought his lips twitched. 'You are making a fair imitation of a young gentleman at the moment, if I may say so. But you are not a boy, Miss Dawson, and even boys can be frightened by their first sight of battle. Young William Welland, for example. He will make a fine officer one day, given the chance to overcome his natural distress at the sight of his best friend being cut down at his side.'

'And if he is not bullied and scared out of his wits!'

'Precisely. Why else do you think I had that pair brought aboard? It took little understanding on my part to see that he needed encouragement and Keeper needed some sharp discipline. I believe both are receiving what they need aboard my ship.'

Miranda simply looked at him, her blue eyes wide. 'How could you tell. . .?'

Adam shrugged. 'It was fairly staring me in the face. They would both have been ruined had nothing been done.'

'You would do that much for enemy midshipmen?'

'For young gentlemen who are also human beings, like the rest of us, Miss Dawson.'

Miranda swallowed. This Captain York was a different creature from the one who treated her so severely—yet not all the time, she had to admit. He had often shown her a surprising degree of understanding. 'Will does seem much happier,' she whispered. 'I tried—'

He smiled. 'I know you did. And now, if you will excuse me. . .'

With his foot on the top rung he made a sketchy bow. Miranda disengaged one hand and touched his blue-clad arm, detaining him a moment longer.

'Will must not assist your officers when you go into action. He should not help them at all, really; he could be charged with traitorous behaviour, brought before a court martial, even hung! But it gives him great pleasure to be appreciated, and does no real harm. Just so long as Mr Piper and the others do not report his behaviour.'

'I asked his lieutenant's permission. Mr Piper was glad to be rid of the unhappy lad. He gave limited consent for him to go and amuse himself.'

'I see. But in action—'

'I am fully aware of that, Miss Dawson.' His tone was warm. 'If you wish to remain on deck you may,' Adam went on, 'as long as you keep well out of the way. Welland and Keeper will be confined with the other officers, but separated.'

'Put Will with Mr Haskett,' suggested Miranda. 'He needs the reassurance of an older man.'

'Very well—an excellent idea.'

Miranda smiled her thanks and watched him clatter down the ladder with a strange yearning in her heart. Adam York was a fine man, but an enemy. Not that most soldiers or sailors actually hated those on the other side they were ordered to kill. That was one of the ironies of war. In peacetime they would all probably be friends. In the same way, she thought that she and the captain might have been friends had they met under different circumstances and not been on opposing sides.

The chase was nearing its culmination when it came time for the captain to sit down to his dinner. Miranda abandoned her intention to change into a gown. The seamen, having eaten earlier, had already been beaten to quarters. With the men stationed for action and the deck largely cleared, she followed Adam below. They consumed a hurried meal under Daniel's watchful eye and conversation was minimal. Before he had swallowed his last mouthful Adam was on his feet.

'Finish the meal at your leisure,' he told Miranda as he shrugged into his coat, buckled on the sword Daniel handed him and made for the door. Miranda did not linger for more than the moment it took to finish her wine and then followed him to the deck, hearing the sounds of partitions being raised and the guns being uncovered as she did so.

Miranda tucked herself in amongst the rigging and

watched Adam as he stood, taut as a bowstring, every sense concentrated on the task in hand, issuing orders in clear tones, changing the course slightly, trimming the sails to gain maximum advantage from the vagaries of the wind.

'Discharge half our water,' he suddenly snapped.

Water, precious drinking water, spewed out of the scuttles as men worked the pumps. It was a legitimate ploy to enable the frigate to move faster, but what a risk! thought Miranda, her mouth parched with anxiety. Supposing he could not fill those barrels again?

But the *Seafire* began to pick up speed.

A smile lifted the corners of Adam's mouth. In the prevailing light airs their speed was good. 'That captain knows how to sail his ship but he'll not escape us now. Another half-hour and he'll be within range of our bow chasers. Then we'll see if we can take some of the wind from his sails!'

The two great guns, one on each side of the bow, were run out and ready to be fired, their crews crouched down beside them waiting for the order, while behind them a ship's boy, known as a powder monkey when the ship was in action, squatted in the middle of the deck by piles of balls, waiting to be sent scurrying down to the powder room for more charges. It had been one of those guns, remembered Miranda, which had woken her from her sleep aboard the *Othello*.

The British frigate was still far ahead when it opened fire on its pursuer. The *Seafire*'s seamen were all crouched about their guns, the marines at their stations. The entire crew watched the splash of the shots hitting the water half a mile ahead and gave a jeering cheer.

'Practising his aim and range,' commented Mr West with a grin. 'Shall we respond?'

'Not yet.' A frown formed between Adam's intent eyes. 'I wonder. They are approaching Lanzarote. They may hope that the sound of gunfire will bring a friend to their aid.' He raised his voice to reach the men perched high in the rigging. 'Lookouts, there! Keep a sharp watch for other sails!'

The whole scene was etched on Adam's inner vision as he assessed the possibilities, his mind almost unconsciously computing the set of the sea, the wind, the course and a dozen other factors which must govern his actions. So many lives depended on his getting it right. In another half-hour, if he could not come up with the enemy and bring him to action, he would be forced to give up the chase, wear away and chart a course for Herro. Having discharged half his water, he now had no choice but to put in to replenish it.

By the time they brought the enemy within range of their long guns the splendid red ball of the sun was dipping below the horizon, its reflection turning the blue of sky and sea into shades of crimson and gold and adding warm tones to the pyramid of sails billowing above them. Adam gave the order to fire. He would not abandon the chase without aiming a few shots at the enemy. A lucky shot might cripple her.

A shout came from a lookout, a thin sound penetrating the comparative silence between the roar and thunder of the two bow guns.

'Deck, there! She's going about, sir! Coming straight back at us!'

Adam already knew. His glass had been glued to his

eye for most of the past hours. He assessed the other's course once it was settled and then ordered a slight adjustment to his own. He could not allow the enemy to cross his bows. But excitement rose in him, that enhanced awareness and exhilaration which came in the face of danger. Quite clearly, while he had hoped for reinforcements which had not come, the British captain did not want to be accused of cowardice—a hanging matter in any navy—and so was preparing to engage.

Adam had no wish to disengage. The trusting anticipation on his men's faces told him that they expected him to fight and to win.

The lower sails must be taken in, leaving the frigate in fighting trim. As he turned from watching his topmen swarm down the rigging after carrying out his order, he became aware of the slender figure of a midshipman standing silently behind him. A midshipman in British uniform. Miranda! He swore silently to himself as his body reacted automatically to the sight of her. He had forgotten the girl's presence in his absorption with the chase. She had not, of course, being Miranda Dawson, gone below with the enemy officers. He, in a soft moment, had told her she could remain on deck. But with action imminent he knew he would have to send her down. It would be far too dangerous for her on the exposed quarterdeck.

He spoke to her quietly. 'Miss Dawson, I think it is time for you to leave the deck.'

'But you promised—'

'I know, but I cannot take the risk of your being injured, even killed, during the action. The gap between us and the enemy is narrowing fast.' A ball hissed overhead, punching a hole through one of the topsails. 'As you can see, his shots are already damaging our rigging. Before long we shall be exchanging broadsides. This is no place for you.'

'But I do not wish to go below!'

Adam made his voice stern. 'Nevertheless, Miss Dawson, you will obey my order! Mr Stirling,' he addressed one of his midshipmen, 'be so good as to escort Miss Dawson down to the gunroom. I will not condemn you to the lowest deck but you really must go below,' he added, firmly but kindly.

Miranda opened her mouth to argue and then closed it again. Adam had turned away, had already forgotten her in the press of more urgent duties.

'This way, Miss Dawson,' piped James Stirling nervously. He was about the same age as Will and, like the British midshipman, with whom he had become friendly, his voice had not yet broken. To him she must be a strange, incongruous figure in her borrowed uniform, she thought wryly.

She followed obediently, taking a last glance along the length of the frigate. With the great lower sails furled she could see all the men at their stations, the marines in the tops ready to fire down on the enemy officers, even glimpse the British frigate approaching over the bow. She descended to the gunroom without further protest. A marine stood on guard at the door, a swivel gun set up to cover the room. It could scatter small shot at a great rate, a much more effective deterrent than a single musket. Adam was taking no chances.

In the narrow, ill-lit, ill-ventilated space between the

tiny cubicles lining either side stood a long table, leaving just enough room for crouching movement on either side. The headroom here was even lower than in the great cabin and the bottom of the mizzen-mast passed like a column through the end nearest her. She settled into a chair and propped her chin in her hands.

'Thank you, Mr Stirling. I shall be quite safe here, I'm sure.'

'I'll get back on deck, then. The captain might want me again,' said Mr Stirling, and scampered off, eager to be near his idol.

'Miss Dawson!' The call came from behind the locked door of Mr Piper's cabin. 'Miss Dawson, are you there?'

Miranda sighed. She did not wish to enter into conversation with Piper or any other of the officers. Not at the moment. Her emotions were far too mixed. 'What is it, Mr Piper?'

'What is going on? Is there to be an engagement?'

'So it seems. That is why I have been sent down to safety.' She did not want the marine to imagine he had to keep her under guard too.

'Do you know the name of the British frigate?'

Adam had read the name through his glass. There could be no harm in passing on the information. 'The *Osprey*.'

'Ah!' There was a moment's silence while Piper thought. 'Captain Godfrey, I believe.'

'Do you know him, sir?' asked Mr Gander. The partitions were canvas and conversation between the prisoners was quite possible.

'Not personally. But you served under him once, didn't you, Master?'

'Aye, sir. A fine officer. He'll give a good account of himself.'

'So we have a chance!'

'I would hope so, Mr Piper.'

Their conversation had been punctuated by the boom of the chasing guns and now a crashing sound above brought Miranda's head up and raised a faint but penetrating squealing and bleating from the pigs in their sty and the sheep in their pen under the foredeck. The commotion propelled her to her feet. 'I refuse to remain down here where I cannot see what is happening. I'm going up again.'

She smiled at the marine, who frowned uneasily but came smartly to the salute as she passed. She had gambled that he would not stop her. The marines knew she enjoyed a privileged position aboard the warship.

Passing through the main deck, she saw that Abe Windsor was there, with a couple of midshipmen, ready to supervise the firing of the broadsides. The crash she had heard appeared to have been caused by one of the cannons coming off its truck. Sweating, heaving men were struggling to get it back into position while the officers and gun captain cursed them for carelessness.

'The captain requires a full broadside, you lubbers!' roared Mr Windsor in a voice Miranda had never heard him use before.

Leaving them to it, she climbed the next ladder and poked her head out of the hatch. All the officers were fully occupied. No one, except the nearest powder monkey, noticed her as she crept across the deck and crouched by his side. She put a finger to her lips and the child, who could not have been more than seven, grinned. Miranda felt the urge to take him in her arms and protect him. It seemed almost criminal to her that such young boys should be taken on board a warship at all, let alone made to carry the dangerous charges up from the powder room and wait about on the exposed deck. But, like the drummer boys in the army, the officers thought nothing of placing children in grave danger. Even Adam. It had always been so. Men took it for granted.

She squatted with the boys, her eyes fixed on Adam as he stood fighting his ship, directing its course, ordering his guns to fire as the vessel turned and they could be brought to bear. Broadside answered broadside; fountains of water rose into the air as the balls fell short or landed ahead or behind. An occasional thud below or crack overhead told her that not all the British balls had missed their mark. Cheers went up when a gun crew saw their shot hit the enemy. The thunder rang in her ears, making her deaf.

As the ships drew nearer to each other the short-range guns on the quarterdeck opened fire. The powder monkeys ran down for more charges and staggered back again carrying the pipes containing the bags of gunpowder carefully, so as not to drop them.

Soon musket fire rained down on the deck from British marines lodged in their tops. Adam stood like a rock, unconcerned by the balls whining past his head as he fought his ship. Zack gave a cry and clapped a hand over his upper arm. She saw Adam urge him to leave the deck, but Zack shook his head as a seaman tightened a bandage about the wound to staunch the flow of blood.

Miranda flinched as she felt the heat of a musket ball rush past her face to bury itself in the deck behind. As her friend the powder monkey trotted across to his gun, an enemy cannonball passed over her head to career across the deck, missing everyone until it killed a marine and ruined the hammocks beyond him. The child crumpled. Miranda leapt up and rushed to his side.

'Pass me the charges,' roared the gun captain, and such was his urgency that Miranda picked up the wooden pipe containing the charges and finished the journey the boy had begun. When she returned to him she found him quite unconscious.

The shot had not hit him but a large splinter—well, a ragged chunk of wood, really—torn from some timber it had damaged lay beside him. A bruise and gash on his temple indicated where it had struck.

Miranda bit her bottom lip at the sight of the carnage. Adam had been right—this was no place for a woman. Already several seamen lay about the quarterdeck either dead or nursing a wound. There would be more casualties on the main deck. And yet. . .and yet she would not have missed the experience, would not have been anywhere else. She still wished she were a boy; she would surely have been less squeamish if she were, and the excitement of the battle had fired her up, made her want to be part of it.

But on whose side? she asked herself guiltily as she gathered the child into her arms and staggered towards the hatch. Something strange was happening to her loyalties.

'Someone assist with that boy,' yelled Adam, and

then gave a smothered curse as Miranda turned her face towards him. 'Take him below to the surgeon and stay there!' he grated before the exigencies of the battle made him forget her again.

A seaman obligingly helped her down the ladders, perhaps glad to escape the heat of battle on the deck. She descended to the main deck, where more chaos reigned, although the guns were being loaded, run out and fired with undiminished efficiency, and went on past the gunroom to arrive at the head of the ladder leading down to the lowest deck, where the doctor was busy attending to those wounded who had already been brought below. She gagged on the stink coming up from below and turned back to the gunroom, dismissing the seaman, who immediately returned to his duties.

Miranda, with the boy in her arms, passed the sentry at the door of the gunroom and laid the child on the table. He needed something beneath his head so she removed her jacket and folded it as a pillow.

She found a bottle of brandy in a rack and brought it out just as a crash made her jump and the ship lurched. She clasped the bottle to her bosom while she tore off her stock, looking at the marine enquiringly.

'One of the masts gone, miss,' he opined calmly.

'I told you Captain Godfrey would give a good account of himself!' called Gander jubilantly.

Miranda quickly dampened the linen and dabbed at the contusion on the boy's forehead. Then she poured a little of the spirit on a clean patch and pressed it to his lips. He sighed and his tongue sought the moisture. He swallowed, but did not open his eyes. At least he was not dead.

'See he comes to no harm,' she said to the marine. 'I want to go up on deck again.'

'You'd best stay here, miss.'

She shook her head. 'I may be able to help some of the other wounded.'

She simply could not remain below not knowing what had happened, if Adam was dead, wounded or still alive and well. Her concern took her by surprise. As did the realisation that she could not bear for him to lose this fight.

Where was her patriotism? Her father would surely be thoroughly ashamed of her! Adam York was fighting on the side of the enemy. How could she possibly want him to win?

Guiltily, she told herself that she didn't, really; it was just that she wanted him to come through unscathed.

She poked her head out of the hatch into the dusky light and her eyes sought the tall figure of the frigate's commander, standing close to the huge double wheel, not far from the hatch. His hat had gone. Stray strands of black hair had escaped his queue and one side of his face was covered in blood. Her heart began to pound with anxiety. But he was still on his feet and his voice came firm and decisive as he ordered men forward to deal with the tangled mass of rigging brought down with part of the foremast.

She shivered, aware that although she missed the warmth of her jacket, feeling cold was not the cause of it but rather the shambles that met her eyes on the quarterdeck. And then a cry went up from those who could see.

'The *Osprey* is disengaging, sir,' came Zack West's voice, which sounded horribly weak and hoarse.

'Her captain does not relish the thought of a night action, I collect. Very well. We are in better case than he. We will give chase. Mr Crocker, make what sail you can; we will attempt to overhaul him, but we must do so quickly. It is not yet completely dark, we should be able to keep him in sight. Mr Stirling, pass the word to Mr Windsor to have the guns reloaded and primed and ask him to repair to the quarterdeck. The men may stand down for the moment, but they must rest by their guns if not required to assist in clearing and repairing the damage. You remain to supervise them. Mr Merrick—' to his senior midshipman '—be so good as to organise the removal of the dead and wounded. And now you must use the lull to go below and have your arm attended to, Mr West. Mr Windsor will take your place here.'

Zack, who looked deathly pale in what little light was left, nodded. He had the hand of his injured arm tucked between the buttons of his coat. 'Very well. I must confess it is confoundedly painful.'

'You should have seen the surgeon before!'

'Not while the ship was in danger, sir!' protested Zack. 'But now. . .'

He turned for the companion ladder and Miranda quickly stepped out on the deck to make way for him. He gave her a tired, uncomprehending nod as he passed. I don't believe he recognised me, she thought, feeling a stab of anxiety, for she had grown fond of Zachary West in the short time she had known him. But although unsteady on his feet he passed one-handedly down the ladder without help, seemingly in control of himself.

The other officers went about their duties, and as, in response to the master's orders, the huge lower sails on main and mizzen masts billowed out in the wind, Miranda padded to Adam's side.

'Did neither side win?'

'You here?' demanded Adam in exasperation. Damnation! He did not need the distraction of her presence just now. But he answered her question. 'No, the *Osprey* has not struck yet, but we gave your compatriots a pounding. The next engagement should decide the issue.'

'When?'

'As soon as we can overtake her. Excuse me, but I must go forward and supervise the cutting away of the wreck of the foremast. Its drag is hindering us.'

'Let me attend to your wound first.'

He brushed her aside. 'It is nothing—a mere scratch. The people will sleep by their guns tonight, but we will use this respite to serve supper; it is some time since anyone has eaten. It will be cold, for I cannot allow the galley fires to be relit. Your cabin will be reinstated within minutes; you may wish to use its facilities. After you have eaten I suggest you retire there and get what sleep you can.'

She could not hide her anxiety. 'Are you certain you are all right, Captain?'

He gazed at her down his nose again, denying the pleasure her concern gave him. 'Stop fussing, woman. And for God's sake do as you are bid for once.'

'Aye, aye, sir,' riposted Miranda, giving him a smart salute.

Adam's face relaxed into a reluctant grin. 'Get along with you, you little baggage. I have much to do before I may rest.'

CHAPTER FIVE

MIRANDA clambered down to the gunroom, where she
found that the boy, Billy Crow, had recovered consciousness and been carried to his hammock by a kindly
seaman. The prisoners of war had been released by the
marine guard and Piper demanded to know the out-
come of the action. Miranda gave a brief account and
then left the more senior officers to chew it over
amongst themselves while the stewards prepared a meal
for them. While Tony Keeper made for the midshipmen's berth, Will left with her to go in search of his
friend James Stirling.

'Was he hurt?' he asked her apprehensively.

'No,' she reassured him. 'He escaped unscathed. But
he's on the gun deck busy supervising the clearing up of
the damage there, Will.'

'I can help,' said Will cheerfully, and darted off up
the ladder.

After an action or a drill it took the men only minutes
to replace the partitions, which were hinged up and
bolted to the beams, and by the time she sought her
own cabin her cot had already been slung, though her
possessions were still stowed below, for the ship
remained largely cleared for action. Daniel, who had
been captaining one of the gun crews, had already set
the table in the stripped down great cabin and was busy
in his pantry. Miranda wondered at the speed and

efficiency of the limited restoration operation. But practice made perfect and many hands made light work, as she had always been taught, and despite depleted numbers, there remained some two hundred tired but experienced hands to set the captain's quarters at least partially to rights so that he could use it while the lull lasted.

She washed her face and hands, brushed the dirt from her recovered coat, combed her unruly hair and replaced the midshipman's cap to hide the mess it was in. When Daniel came to tell her that a meal had been served, she was calm and tidy.

She walked into the great cabin to find Adam already there.

He had changed his shirt and was without his watch coat, which, Miranda had noticed on deck, was liberally stained with blood. His own and others, she suspected. But, seeing him rise courteously to greet her, she was comforted that he appeared quite oblivious to his wound.

Someone—Daniel, no doubt—had attended to his injury, for a band of linen held a wad in place to stop the bleeding. From what she had seen earlier, he would be left with a scar running into his hairline. The relief she felt at seeing him greet her with a cheerful smile must have shown in her response.

'As you can see,' he said, sweeping her a bow, 'I am still in one piece. So, essentially, is Zack, although he stopped a musket ball.'

'Is it bad? Where is he?' asked Miranda anxiously as Adam moved to seat her at the table.

'Bad enough. Being so stubborn cost him a quantity

of blood and he is still down in the sick bay. The ball had lodged in his upper arm. Thank God it was spent. Once the doctor has dug it out I will have him returned to his cabin. Unless the wound mortifies he should make a good recovery.'

'I pray so. How happy his wife will be when he returns home!' Miranda shuddered delicately, unaware of how the contrast of her ladylike reaction with her boy's uniform affected her companion. 'I could not weather a visit to the sick bay, Adam, but will you mind if I visit him once he is back in his cabin?'

Adam regarded her with a touch of censure, she thought, not knowing how difficult he was finding it to retain his composure in the face of a sudden stab of illogical jealousy. His confused emotions only served to fuel his anger. 'Of course not,' he answered her question, though not with the enthusiasm she might have expected. Then he went on, his voice brusque, 'Having carried the boy down, most females would have remained in the sick bay in order to assist. You, I collect, preferred to face the dangers of the quarterdeck.'

'Most women?' queried Miranda bridling at his tone. 'I think not, Captain. Most women would faint. Some would no doubt go down to that hell-hole to do what they could for the injured, but I am not made of such intrepid stuff. I may not faint at the sight of blood, but would most certainly succumb to the vapours were I forced to breathe that foul air. The stench is overwhelming. How the sick and injured can be expected to recover under such conditions I fail to comprehend.'

'It is,' said Adam, grimly defensive, 'the best we can

do under the circumstances. Yet,' he went on, pursuing his theme, 'I wonder at your fortitude on deck. And the atmosphere was thick with gunfire smoke.'

'It was different,' said Miranda simply, quite unable to explain exactly how.

But Adam's smile flashed out. 'I know how different it is. I myself see that place as a hell-hole and view the surgeon's knife with horror. Above everything, I fear being subjected to his ministrations. By the way, how is Billy Crow?'

'Recovering well, as far as I am aware. He is another I must visit soon.'

Adam nodded. 'I'm glad to hear he was not badly hurt. Have some wine.'

'Thank you.' Her heart warmed again. Adam knew the child's name and showed concern for even the smallest of his ship's boys.

'And do eat your supper. The sooner you are in bed the better. We are overhauling the enemy fast and I expect to resume the action soon. She is making for the Canaries again, so we must attack quickly or not at all. The moon will give light enough for the gunners to fix her in their sights.'

'And us in hers.'

'Unfortunately, that is so,' agreed Adam drily. Miranda's stomach clenched at the prospect of another action and yet, as she eyed the cold pork on her plate, she discovered that despite everything she was hungry. As she cut into it she remarked, 'The pigs on board are a great blessing, but I'm sure the berth deck would be a more pleasant place for the seamen and marines without their being quartered so near!'

Adam shrugged. 'They grow used to the farmyard aroma!'

'You are fortunate here, but otherwise the entire ship's crew must get used to it—even the officers—for the odour wafts throughout the vessel! And so does the noise! The squealing of the pigs, the bleating of the sheep and the clucking of hens in their coops! Not to mention the goat!'

'Would you have me and my officers live entirely on salted beef and pork except for any fish we can catch as we sail? The goat gives milk for your tea and coffee and takes up less room than a cow, you'll allow!'

Miranda found she could laugh. 'Papa says some captains carry cows too, on the larger ships of the line!'

Adam answered her laugh with a smile. 'I do not doubt it. Every ship, naval or merchant, must carry livestock if the officers and passengers are to eat fresh meat.'

'The ordinary seamen have to make do, do they not?'

'The livestock is paid for out of the officers' own pockets. The men do not have the means, and even if they did there would not be room enough to ship enough animals to feed them all. They do have fresh meat and vegetables whenever we touch land and the purser can purchase them ashore.'

Miranda nodded. He had not said that most of the fresh food for the seamen was paid for out of his own pocket, but she knew it was so. 'Papa used to buy vegetables and fruit for his men, but could not afford meat,' she observed.

'He sounds like a captain who cared for the welfare

of his men,' said Adam, though his glance was a little sceptical.

'He did his best,' Miranda defended him. Her only quarrel with her father concerned his long absences from home, and he couldn't help them.

'Did he flog?'

Miranda frowned, made uncomfortable by the question. He had always spoken so casually about the punishments he meted out, as though flogging a man were of little moment. Yet she could not blame her father for obeying King's Regulations. 'Not unnecessarily,' she said reluctantly. 'Only when discipline demanded it.'

'Naturally.' Adam read her reaction to his question as an admission that she did not fully agree with her father's interpretation of discipline. He drank some more wine while he studied her flushed face. 'What is he like? Has he been a good father?'

Miranda pushed a piece of fat pork around her plate. 'How could he be,' she demanded at last, 'since he was so seldom at home? Every now and again an exciting stranger came to visit us—at least, that's how it seemed to us children. Even the boys. After Trafalgar he became a hero. My brothers both followed him into the navy and so would I have done had I been a boy.'

'Did you really want to?' Adam sounded surprised.

Miranda nodded vigorously. 'It didn't seem fair that I couldn't! How I longed to be a boy!'

Adam's wickedly challenging smile made her blush anew.

'And now?'

'Now I'm not so sure,' she admitted.

His smile broadened. 'What changed your mind?'

Miranda met the challenge in his eyes as she told a half-truth. 'Falling in love with Lieutenant Peter Stannard of the *Othello*. He was killed at Captain Blackmore's side.'

Truth to tell it had been Adam's kiss which had finally woken her feminine instincts, but her admiration for the young lieutenant and Peter's attentions had begun the process.

Adam's eyes narrowed. He had not expected that answer. 'I'm sorry, but your grief will pass. You're young. You'll find someone else.'

'Thank you, I'm glad you think so,' muttered Miranda ungraciously. She took a gulp of her wine, realising that she hadn't thought about Peter Stannard for quite a while.

Adam decided not to pursue that subject. He hadn't realised she was recovering from the death of someone special. So she'd been in love, had she? What had Stannard been like? Tamping down something suspiciously like a stab of jealousy, he reverted to what he thought a safer subject but one in which he was particularly interested. 'You said once that life was not easy at home with your father away so much. Were you terribly unhappy?'

'Oh, no, not at all. Mama missed him, of course, and had to shoulder all the day-to-day worries of making ends meet. Neither of them had a private income, you see. But I was happy enough. I had lots of freedom.'

'You ran wild, you mean,' he teased.

Miranda grinned. 'I did rather. That was why I was sent to the Academy.'

'A wise move on your parents' part, no doubt. But, you know, you have just confirmed me in my belief that it is wrong for a sea-officer to wed. He is bound to have to leave his family to fend for itself for much of the time.'

Miranda's eyes widened. 'Is that why you have never wed?'

'Partly.'

He paused while Daniel cleared the table, drew the cloth and placed the decanter in front of him. He offered her a glass of port. She refused, saying she preferred to finish the wine she had so far only sipped.

As Adam filled his glass Miranda twirled hers on the oak tabletop, considering the clarity and colour of the claret before raising the glass to her lips. Adam York could not be allowed to evade her question like that. The moment Daniel had left the cabin she challenged him.

'What do you mean, "partly"?' she demanded.

Adam pushed his chair back to the limit of its tethering ropes and stretched his long legs. He raised his glass and tasted the tawny liquid. 'I've only ever met one female I wanted to marry. She promised to wait for me but while I was away at sea she ran off with a rich landlubber. I've never considered marriage a possibility since.'

The words sounded bald; his despair at the time now seemed ridiculous. He'd thought he'd never recover from the disappointment. He had, but the experience had taught him a hard lesson he would never forget.

'Then she didn't love you,' said Miranda calmly. 'You were better off without her.'

He stared at her from beneath drawn brows. 'More wine?'

Miranda shook her head. Adam had withdrawn; he hadn't liked her remark any more than she'd appreciated his words of supposed comfort. They sat in silence for a while, both lost in their own thoughts. Yet the silence was not strained.

'Did you lose many men? Is the ship much damaged?' Miranda asked eventually, reverting to matters of the moment.

Adam stirred. 'Seven dead, including a midshipman; three more are likely to join them, and some dozen or so received less severe wounds. That number includes Zack.'

Miranda winced and replaced her glass on the table. She did not want Adam to see her hand shaking. 'So many?'

Adam leant forward to place his glass on the table. 'Fewer than I feared,' he told her. 'As for the ship, she is damaged, but can easily be repaired. She is sailing well enough, though not as fast as I might like. I suspect the enemy is badly holed below the waterline and may not be able to reach the safety of Lanzarote before having to abandon ship.'

'So the Ospreys are likely to have suffered more casualties than the Seafires?'

'It would appear likely.'

'And yet, as soon as you can, you will finish off a foundering ship.'

Miranda could not prevent her tone implying censure. Adam gazed at her, his eyes wide, amazed that she should blame him.

'The captain can still defend himself—he has his guns. And he has the option to strike, when the rescue of his crew would be assured. I wish he would. Regrettably, a prize is of no value if it sinks.'

Oh, dear, thought Miranda, hearing the stiff offence in his voice, we are at odds again. But how can it be otherwise when we belong to warring nations? How can I help but feel for the men aboard the *Osprey*, when one of them might be my brother?

She had no idea in which ship either of her brothers was serving at the present, both had been transferred while in foreign waters and communications were notoriously slow. The last news from Barbados had told her that Dick, still a midshipman, was cruising somewhere in the China Seas aboard a ship of the line but no name had been mentioned. Probably for strategic reasons.

Seeing that Miranda was not about to respond, Adam drank more port, eyeing her over his glass with a frown. 'Being from a naval family, you should know that there can be no sentiment in battle. One fights to win.'

'But always honourably, for a noble purpose!'

Adam's chair scraped on the deck as he leapt to his feet. 'Do you impugn my honour, ma'am? Question my purpose?'

'You seem extremely interested in prize money,' retorted Miranda with spirit, regretting the hurtful words which had escaped her lips but not about to retract them. 'I have never heard my father put the acquisition of wealth above the need for humanity and honour!'

'And neither, madam, do I! Do you think me a pirate,

a man who preys on any ship of any nation as long as it brings him profit? No, Miss Dawson. I fight for my country. as does your father for his. The *Osprey* is an enemy vessel. If I have to sink her, I will. But I am certain that her officers and men would prefer that I did not!'

'Oh, why did your country declare war on mine in the first place?' wailed Miranda, deeply sorry to have caused a new flare of antagonism between them. 'First you collude with France, then stab us in the back! You gained your independence—'

'For which we had to fight, I would remind you! We have no reason to love our British cousins! Especially as they do not consider anyone born before the Declaration of Independence in 1776 to be an American citizen. Any American sailor with more than eight and thirty years behind him fears being pressed from our merchant and naval vessels to serve in your Royal Navy. He is still considered by your government to be a British citizen! Who gave you the right to stop and search every vessel on the high seas, of whatever nation, in order to impress members of its crew?'

'But our ships are searching for deserters! They must be recovered.'

'True deserters and mutineers, maybe. But even so it is an unwarrantable liberty to stop and search the ships of nations with which you are not at war.'

'And you had designs on Canada,' said Miranda, abandoning that argument for a grievance of her own. 'You are tying up part of our army when every man is needed to fight Napoleon in the Peninsula!'

'Many people in America see France as an ally, a

fellow republic, a land free of the whims of debauched royalty—'

'But suffering first under the tyranny of the Terror and now under the ambitions of a man who has declared himself Emperor and aims to conquer the world!'

'And in addition,' said Adam forcefully, brushing aside her interjection, 'your country imposed a blockade against all trade with Europe! Our manufacturers and merchants resented that. You were ruining them, and the country too. It was they who pressed the government to declare war!'

'Our trade is suffering as well,' admitted Miranda, remembering rumblings of trouble—high income tax, rising prices and shortages—at home. 'But do you not see we have nothing against the French people, any more than we have against the Americans? It is Napoleon and his ambitions we must oppose if we wish to remain free. And your intervention has made conquering his armies so much more difficult.' She drew a breath and then came out with an argument she had often heard voiced in England and aboard the *Othello*. 'It suited Napoleon for your country to declare war on us. He waited until you did to invade Russia! I'll wager his diplomats and spies had a hand in shaping your policy!'

Adam grinned, a wolfish grin which angered Miranda. 'It has stretched your navy, has it not? You can scarcely raise a squadron to blockade our ports!'

Miranda jumped to her feet. 'The French fleet is the one we must keep in port! Your fleet is almost non-existent apart from small vessels!'

'We do have a few successful frigates,' Adam

reminded her drily. His initial temper had cooled. The chit could raise a convincing, stimulating argument when provoked.

'And both your nations issue numerous licences—letters of marque—to privateer captains which allow them to attack our shipping. They do your dirty work for you, capturing our merchant ships and their cargoes, not to mention attacking our whalers and stealing the blubber and whalebone and all the other valuable parts of the fish the men worked so hard to obtain!'

'Oh, I had a go at the whalers,' admitted Adam smugly. 'Filthy, smelly things. The merchant ships supplying your army in the Iberian Peninsula made far more agreeable targets.'

'Some of the supply vessels are American, trading under licence!' snapped back Miranda. 'Your government bends the rules easily enough when there is profit in it! Did you attack those?'

'No. So some supplies must be getting through to your precious army in Spain! And the Russians—or perhaps, rather, the Russian winter—have defeated Napoleon's grand army, which he cheerfully abandoned, as he did the one in Egypt. I don't know what you are complaining about.'

'Oh!' cried Miranda, reduced once more to stamping her foot. 'It is no use talking to you! You are an abominable creature!'

With which, she retreated to the privacy of her cabin, where tears of frustration and anger could be allowed to fall.

She removed her jacket but otherwise remained fully dressed as she climbed miserably into her cot. She no longer enjoyed quarrelling with Adam York, although perhaps it was best that they did not become too amiable together. She would never sleep, she thought, stifling her inclination to sob into her pillow. Yet the next thing she knew was the feel of a hand shaking her shoulder.

'You must get up, missie. The cap'n has ordered the deck cleared again,' came Daniel's soft Southern voice.

Reluctantly, Miranda left the cot and as she did so the memory of the battle returned.

'What time is it?' she asked.

'Four bells—' He caught himself up. 'Two o'clock in the morning, missie.'

Miranda groaned. 'The call would have to come in the middle of the graveyard watch,' she grumbled. No one on board seemed to realise that she knew a great deal of nautical language and did not need to have things explained to her. But Daniel, like everyone else, was only trying to be helpful. 'Have we caught up already?'

'Almost, missie.' He already had her cot unslung; another sailor took it away and Daniel reached up to bolt the bottom of the partition to the beams overhead, revealing the gun of which he was captain, with its crew already preparing to run it out. 'But that isn't all. It's not a dark night and we can distinguish a couple of strange sail approaching from the north-east.'

Miranda's stomach began to churn. She wished she had not eaten so much pork. Were they more English enemies, or French warships coming to the American's assistance? There was only one way to find out. Ask.

'Whose are they?' she enquired apprehensively.

Daniel turned from his gun as she hovered anxiously at the foot of the companion ladder. 'British. They hoisted recognition signal lanterns and the frigate replied.'

'So we are outnumbered. What will happen?'

'Normally the cap'n would manoeuvre and use his speed to escape, but with the foremast badly damaged. . .I don't know, missie.'

Of course he didn't; it had been a stupid question. Only Adam knew what he would do. He was nowhere to be seen. He must have been roused long before her. She wished they hadn't parted so at odds. They might never have the chance to talk again.

The intermittent thunder of guns from the bows had already told her the ship was firing on the damaged *Osprey*. She began to climb the ladder to the quarterdeck.

He was preparing to fight the others; that was obvious. The strange sail were still some distance away, vague, pale shadows in the darkness, but bearing down fast from windward, not directly behind but off to the left on a converging course. The frigate they were chasing was ahead and slightly to the right. Even if he gave up that chase he would never outrun the other two. If he did not, the *Seafire* would swiftly be caught between all three British ships. As he had already pointed out, the *Osprey* still had most of her guns and to prove the point was firing behind her as she ran.

Wherever the two new warships had come from, they left no doubt as to their hostile intentions. A ball splashed into the sea astern, followed by a distant boom. Soon the booms wove into a continuous thunder and shots fell all round the *Seafire*, but so far not one had found its target.

Adam stood by the mizzen-mast, a nightglass to his eye. Miranda had looked through one once. The image was upside down and it took practice to work out what it was showing.

'Their gun crews are not well exercised,' he remarked to no one in particular as he turned towards the master. 'Mr Crocker, prepare to change course when I give the word.' There followed a string of instructions which Miranda only dimly understood, but some of the men left their guns and ran to their sail stations, ready to haul on various ropes.

The two large warships had caught up to within half a mile and a couple of shots had found their mark on the *Seafire*'s hull.

Their own stern guns had begun to reply when Adam cried, 'Now!'

The great wheel spun, the sails bellied as the yards were hauled round to a different angle to the wind and to her astonishment the frigate heeled, turned, and headed for the gap between her two chasing enemies. 'Mr Windsor, the stern chasers to target the *Osprey* if you please, and a broadside from both larboard and starboard batteries on the others as they bear!'

Midshipmen ran to pass the order to the deck below. So he would fire at both ships but they would batter him from both sides. Miranda did not want to contemplate the result. She crouched down quite near to where he was standing, wedging herself in among the rigging of the mast. He exuded an air of confidence which was infused into all his men. She caught the infection and waited quietly for what the next few moments would bring.

They brought chaos. He must have been expecting it, for he began issuing orders to change course before the last ball had found its mark.

The helmsmen shouted as they spun the wheel.

'What is it?' demanded Adam.

'The ship is no longer under command, sir, the helm won't answer!' cried the master, himself desperately lending a hand to test the lack of response to the wheel.

'Mr Windsor, the rudder!'

The lieutenant hurried to the stern to peer over the taffrail.

'No wonder,' he roared above all the noise and confusion. 'The rudder is smashed!'

Without a rudder the wind was blowing them round, back towards their enemies. Adam shouted an order and the sails began to shiver and flap. The frigate lost speed. Soon they would be wallowing helplessly in the sea. 'Can it be repaired?' he demanded.

'Certainly not quickly, sir.' Abe Windsor had come back to report. 'What is left of it is swinging uselessly with the movement of the sea, so the linkage is broken, too. We may need to ship a new one.'

'Which we do not carry,' observed Tom Crocker unhappily.

Abe eyed the movements of the other ships warily. 'Their guns will be brought to bear again in a moment, sir.'

'I am aware, Mr Windsor.'

Adam's grim visage shook Miranda to the core. Their situation must be desperate. Every man aboard relied upon the captain to extricate them from this mess. So did she. But, for the first time, her confidence in Adam's ability to overcome all odds wavered. The British must win. She would be rescued.

He shook his head in an uncharacteristically helpless gesture. 'Given time. . .but we have no time. Well, we've landed some lucky shots in the past. We cannot always expect to escape being on the receiving end,' he observed grimly. He straightened his back, standing with feet planted apart as he swayed with the movement of the deck. 'We have a choice, gentlemen: to be pounded to a pulp, boarded by the crews of two large ships of the line who will outnumber us at least four to one, or to strike. I cannot bring myself to condemn every man aboard to injury or death. Strike our colours if you please, Mr Stirling.'

No one protested. All knew that their situation was hopeless. Already a new, rolling broadside was dealing death and destruction on the helpless frigate. The men watched in silence as the stars and stripes descended to the deck to become a heap of red, white and blue bunting, followed by the battle lantern, which had been hoisted to illuminate the flag because it was dark. Firing from the other ships ceased immediately.

Adam walked to the quarterdeck rail and addressed the faces peering up at him from the darkness of the deck below, a darkness relieved only by the dim glow emitted by a few horn-enclosed lanterns.

'You have conducted yourselves splendidly, my lads. We've had a lot of luck on this commission, but it has run out. I had no choice but to strike. Better to be prisoners of war and live to enjoy the prize money due to us when we are freed than dead, eh?'

A murmuring greeted his words until a voice shouted, 'Three cheers for Mr York! Hip, hip, huzzah!' As the cheer echoed up from below it was taken up by the men on the foredeck and quarterdeck.

Adam made a dismissive gesture, unused to being cheered in defeat, but as he turned towards her Miranda could sense that he was moved by his men's reaction.

What must she be feeling? Adam wondered as he eyed the small, crouched figure jammed in amongst the rigging. No doubt she would rejoice at the defeat of her country's enemy and at her release from his custody. Be happy at the prospect of her imminent return to the bosom of her countrymen, if not yet her family. As for himself, he scarcely felt any emotion at all. This was his first experience of defeat and, despite the people's cheers, it tasted bitter. He had always known it was possible, even probable, as was his death in action. But somehow he found it hard to believe that it had actually happened.

'A boat is putting off from the nearest ship, sir,' reported Abe Windsor, who had the nightglass to his eye.

Pride made Adam square his shoulders and issue the necessary orders in a firm voice. 'Prepare to receive the boarding party.' He looked round. Normal, glass-enclosed lanterns had been lit and seamen were already tending their wounded comrades. 'Carry on with clearing the decks. We do not want them to find a complete shambles.'

He stepped nearer to Miranda.

'Well, Miss Dawson, you have no more need to fear what may befall you in the United States.'

Miranda straightened stiffly, shivering despite the comparative warmth of the night. Her small face looked haggard rather than joyous.

'I am sorry, Captain,' she whispered. 'I would not have had you forced to surrender.'

'But it must please you to see your countrymen victorious.'

She shook her head. 'Not under these circumstances. You stood no chance against such overwhelming odds. Oh, Adam!' she exclaimed violently, 'How I wish you had not sighted the *Osprey*! Chasing her has resulted in this!'

She wanted to fling herself into his arms, to comfort and be comforted. It was nonsense, of course, as was her overwhelming fear of never seeing Adam York again.

'Without urgent dispatches to deliver I could scarcely have chosen to ignore her presence,' Adam pointed out. 'It was both my duty and my pleasure to chase an enemy man-of-war. My people expected it. They know the risks as well as I do, but have confidence in me to bring them through to victory. On this occasion I failed them.'

She tried to answer the prickly pride in his voice. 'No, luck failed you.' After a pause she asked, 'Where did those other ships come from?'

He shrugged. 'We shall no doubt discover.' He went on more gently, 'You must go below and change into a gown, Miranda. You will not wish to lose your reputation.'

'I do not care if it is in shreds!' declared Miranda mutinously. 'Besides, my gown is in my chest, which was taken below.'

'Daniel will see that it is returned to you and ensure some privacy while you change. You really must, my dear. The English are coming to take possession. What will the captain and his officers think if they find you dressed in boy's clothes? It would create a great scandal which would spread throughout your navy. The officers would dine out on the story for years. And I could be condemned for allowing it.'

'Very well,' she agreed reluctantly, then asked, 'Adam—shall we be parted?'

He smiled. Against his will he had grown fond of her. It seemed that she returned the compliment. She had been the first to shed formality and use his given name. From the start he had been drawn to her, been filled with desire, enemy or not. Her removal from his custody would at least bring an end to temptation. They had been brought together by a war which was far from over yet and he had no time for dalliance. 'I fear so, my dear. But, after the war, I shall enquire after your safe return to the bosom of your family.'

Miranda caught her breath. 'Thank you. I shall be glad to know that you are safe and well.'

Adam almost gave in to his instinct to take her in his arms when he heard the wistful note in her voice. Instead, he made his own brusque. 'And now, Miss Dawson, please go below and change while I dispose of my ships's papers. And hurry. The boat will be alongside within five minutes.'

* * *

The following half hour passed in something of a daze for Miranda. She watched, hiding her private distress, as the officers from His Majesty's ship *Victorious*—the very name rubbing salt into the Seafires' wounds—were received on board and Adam handed over his sword. As well as throwing his box of papers over the side he had found a moment to don his dress uniform and, to her, looked more like the victor than the vanquished. Her heart bled for him.

The *Othello*'s officers had been brought up on deck, cheerful and bubbling over with high spirits. She stood with them, the only one not smiling.

The lieutenant from the *Victorious* was, naturally, surprised to find a woman aboard the American frigate. But explanations, he declared, could come later. Meanwhile she would be taken across to his ship with the *Othello*'s officers.

On her way to the entry port, where seamen were waiting to hand her down into the boat, she paused beside Adam.

'Thank you, Captain, for your chivalrous treatment of me while I have been aboard your vessel.' She held out her hand.

Adam took it and bowed over it as though they were in a drawing-room rather than on a pitching deck. 'It has been a pleasure, Miss Dawson.'

Such commonplace words they both used, words which nowhere near expressed the stormy relationship which had been the reality of her time aboard his ship. Yet, insidiously, against both their wills, they had come to respect, even to like each other.

CHAPTER SIX

MIRANDA woke from a light doze and straightened up on Captain Ferris's settee. Dawn was already breaking as the *Victorious*'s captain, short, thick-set and balding, ushered in Adam and his officers, wearing their swords, the midshipmen their dirks, so they must have given their parole. Zack was on his feet, looking wan. Daniel hovered at Adam's shoulder. So Captain York had been allowed to keep his servant with him.

Apart from the furnishings, this cabin was identical to that of the *Othello* since both ships were of the same class. The headroom being much higher, only Adam and Daniel were forced to mind the beams. The occasion reminded Miranda of that aboard the *Seafire* when Adam had interviewed his prisoners.

This time he and his shipmates were the prisoners of war. The thought gave her no pleasure.

'You will not be with me long, gentlemen,' began Captain Ferris cheerfully. 'I shall make arrangements for your disposal at Las Palmas, which we should fetch before sunset, even towing your damaged frigate, Captain.'

'You would leave us incarcerated on a Spanish island?'

'If I have no other choice. It is no secret that both *Victorious* and *Argus* are bound for the Cape and beyond. I cannot transport American prisoners of war

108

halfway round the world and back. The *Argus* is taking off the crew of the *Osprey*, which is sinking, so you achieved your victory there, Captain. Those men who are not required to make up my full complement will be appointed to the other British men-of-war I expect to find at anchor off Las Palmas or Santa Cruz de Tenerife. No doubt all the captains will be glad to sign on seamen to help remedy their chronic shortage of people. And a prize crew must be put into the *Seafire*. Once the foremast has been repaired, a new rudder fitted and she is seaworthy, Captain Godfrey will doubtless be glad to take her back to Portsmouth to claim the prize money in which he will share. As for yourselves, one of the warships revictualling or refitting in the Canaries may be able to transport you to Gibraltar or Portsmouth, where there are facilities for dealing with you. If not, you will have to wait under guard until one who can drops her anchor.'

'And Miss Dawson?'

Adam had not looked her way. He stood tall and proud between two beams, refusing to admit to others the feeling of defeat Miranda sensed behind the stern mask of his face. How had she come to know him so well that she could read his despair in the set of his firm mouth, the distant look in his normally keen, watchful eyes?

'Should there be a warship cruising to Barbados whose captain is willing to transport her, I shall be glad to arrange for Admiral Dawson's daughter to join him there,' said Captain Ferris, 'though I collect that most destined for the West Indies will be under orders to make their best speed and will not choose to lose time with unnecessary watering and wooding. Otherwise, I fear she will be obliged to return to England and again await suitable passage. But these arrangements are no concern of yours, Captain.'

Adam bowed. 'Except that I would not have her abandoned or distressed, Captain.'

'No, no, of course not—very chivalrous of you, I declare, but there is no question of that. Well, now, since your passage with me will be short I am giving you and your officers the use of my dining place. You have given me your parole, but nevertheless I fear I must confine you for the moment under marine guard. Do not attempt to leave the cabin without my express permission. Mid-morning, we will lay to for burial services to be held. No doubt you would wish to return briefly to the *Seafire* to conduct your own ceremony, Captain.'

Again Adam bowed. 'Your consideration is appreciated, Captain Ferris.'

'Meanwhile, gentlemen, if you would be kind enough to go through. . .? I will show Miss Dawson to my sleeping place, where she can be assured of privacy in which to refresh herself.'

The men turned to troop out, Adam urging the others before him. While watching them depart, Captain Ferris was reminded of Daniel's presence.

'Your servant may wait upon you, Captain; he may join mine in his pantry. Breakfast will be served at eight bells.' He raised his voice, calling his servant, and Daniel, reluctantly, Miranda thought, since his eyes followed Adam as he disappeared, went off with the small man who saw to Captain Ferris's personal needs.

'Now, Miss Dawson! I fear I am a tardy host! Will you take a glass of wine? You must be in need of refreshment.'

'Thank you.' Miranda accepted the drink rather than appear ungrateful and took a large gulp. It did warm her and restore some of her confidence. But it could not lift her from her fit of the dismals. Here she was, back in a restricting gown, and in all probability destined for a speedy return to Portsmouth. She would have to begin her journey all over again and without any prospect of enjoying the freedom she had been allowed by Captain York. That must be why she felt so depressed. After all, whatever had passed between them aboard the frigate, whatever fragile friendship had been established, she and Adam York had nothing substantial in common, just some kind of unwelcome, unacknowledged, physical thing.

She found this so difficult to understand, because she still loved Peter Stannard. That must be why she felt so low—because Peter was dead, killed in an action Adam York had begun. She wondered that she could even begin to imagine that she liked the *Seafire*'s captain. They were still enemies.

The gown she wore was the most sombre at her command and so she kept it on to join the ship's company as the warships hove to in the morning sun and the burial services were read.

The sail-makers had been busy sewing the dead men into their hammocks with a couple of round shot at their feet to make sure they sank. The crew stood uncovered while Captain Ferris's sonorous voice recited the words and, one by one, the bodies slid over the side from beneath the union flag.

In the distance she thought she could hear the echo of Adam's voice performing a similar ceremony on his old command, but using the American flag to cover each corpse before it plunged into the depths. How much returning to the *Seafire* for the burial of his men must wrench at his emotions she could only imagine, for in the end they had died for nothing. Nothing? They had sunk an enemy warship.

She met Adam again at dinner, taken in the early afternoon, when Captain Ferris graciously entertained Adam and all his officers, including the midshipmen, in his dining place. Since they were already in occupation he had little choice. Midshipman Stirling found a moment before they were seated to tell her where Will Welland and the other ex-prisoners were.

'They're still aboard the *Seafire*,' he informed her importantly, 'acting as members of the prize crew Mr York saw them there.'

'Will should be all right, then.'

'He would rather have come with us,' said James. 'He wanted to remain on the *Seafire*, but not under British command.'

'But James, you would not want him to desert. The punishment is death.'

'He knew he couldn't do it, but that didn't stop him from wanting to.'

That Will had felt at home, among friends, aboard Adam's command Miranda already knew. That he wished he could remain with Adam came as no surprise. But he could not, any more than she could. Her sympathy for Will held a strong element of fellow-feeling.

At the table, she found herself sitting at Captain Ferris's right hand, with Adam opposite, on his left. They spent awkward moments trying not to catch each other's eye.

Since he had studiously avoided looking at her ever since he had come aboard the *Victorious*, Miranda had deduced that Adam no longer wished to pursue their acquaintance. Disappointed, mortification added bitterness to her embarrassment. His previous courtesy, even amity, must have come purely from a sense of duty. Conversely, he must imagine that now she was rescued she wished to forget her enforced stay aboard his frigate, forget that they had in the end almost become friends. She had thanked him for his consideration and had meant it, but perhaps he had thought her gratitude a mere matter of form, like his kindness.

Of course, there had been that distressing time when he had punished her and threatened to do so again if she did not conform to his wishes, but nothing had come of that and subsequently their relationship had eased. She had been stupid enough to imagine that he was coming to care for her a little, just as she was for him. Now he was simply ignoring her. Well, she would not attempt to gain his attention. She turned to Zachary West, sitting on her right attempting to eat with one hand.

'Would you permit me to cut your meat for you?' she asked.

He gave her a grateful smile. 'Thank you. It's damned awkward without the use of one's right arm.'

'How is the wound?'

'Not throbbing too badly. The surgeon cauterised it before stitching it up.'

Miranda inspected his face and eyes. 'I can see no sign of fever. I trust he did not bleed you—you lost quite enough blood.'

Zack grimaced. 'No, he did not. He's a good surgeon with advanced ideas. Not just a butcher, knows what he's doing. He chose to remain with his patients.'

Miranda had already formed a favourable opinion of the man. Despite all the mayhem going on around he had found time to tend young Billy in his hammock.

Of course, Captain Ferris, as host, was supposed to initiate any conversation, and Adam glared across at Zack, who lifted a sardonic eyebrow and relapsed into silence. Since no one wished to talk about anything but the recent action and their likely fate and Captain Ferris studiously avoided both subjects, the meal was eaten largely in silence except when an occasional discussion arose over the food or wine. All looked relieved when the ordeal was over.

Later, Miranda went up on deck. The larger warship had a poop deck at the stern, which stood above the far end of the quarterdeck, and, looking up, she could see a lonely figure standing at the taffrail gazing broodingly at the frigate towing behind.

Should she ignore him as he was ignoring her? Miranda stood undecided for a moment and then, making up her mind, mounted the ladder to join him. He must be feeling low. That probably explained his mood. Perhaps she could do something to cheer him. In any case she wanted to know exactly why he was ignoring her. It might not be ladylike to thrust herself upon him, but in some matters Miranda was no lady.

'May I join you, sir?' she greeted him, moving to the rail. From the height of the poop the frigate appeared even smaller than it did from the stately two-decker's stern lights. It looked far too small to house as many men as it did.

Adam turned, startled, her arrival on the poop taking him by surprise, so lost had he been in his own thoughts, turning over plans to recover his beloved *Seafire*, plans that had become more wild and improbable the more he brooded. Especially since he had given his parole and therefore tied his own hands. But he had given it knowing there would be no chance of escape under present circumstances and he had not wished to condemn himself and all his officers to spending the next hours in irons.

The wind was blowing steadily from the north-east, catching the side of their faces, but even so the fellows behind were having trouble keeping the sails filled as the towed ship yawed on the end of the line. Only small sails had been set, hoisted to prevent the dead weight of the disabled frigate from slowing the *Victorious* unduly. That same wind now took Miranda's curls and whipped them into a halo around her anxious, fragile face. He had noticed at dinner that she'd washed her hair. He always noted everything about her.

The devil! Why did she have to come and disturb him with her sweet-smelling, seductive presence? He was quite certain in his own mind that she must now hold him in contempt, since he had struck his colours—an action she had made it very clear she despised when Mr

Piper had done so—so he had avoided contact with her. His loss was painful enough to bear, without having to endure her scorn, however unjustified. But there was another ground, too. Had she not recognised that any sign of friendship between them might cause his captors to doubt her loyalty?

He took his eyes from her face and concentrated sternly on the massive hawser, so large that no man could span it with his hands, as it grew taut and slackened again between the two vessels. 'You should not be here.'

Hurt, Miranda drew slightly away. 'Why not? Am I to ignore you as you are ignoring me?'

'I have my reasons.' He offered one of them. 'Captain Ferris may think you disloyal.'

'Nonsense! And if he does, what can he do but watch me? And since I shall do nothing to concern him he will soon decide that our speaking together is harmless.'

'I wish I could be so sanguine! He will most likely think we are plotting some coup—'

What had made him suggest that ridiculous idea? His frustration at knowing himself helpless to regain possession of his frigate?

'Adam, you have your sword. You must have given him your parole. Do you think he doubts you are a gentleman?'

He stirred at that, turning to look at her again. He was not wearing his cocked hat and tendrils of black hair not held by his queue whipped across his sombre face despite the bandage round his brow. 'In English eyes I am probably not. I may have the second son of an

English baron as a distant forebear, but that is the only aristocratic blood I can boast.'

'But your father is a rich plantation owner, is he not? Considered to be amongst the cream of American society? And you are an officer and therefore a gentleman!'

'I am a sea-bred officer, my promotion was gained by merit rather than by interest or influence in high places, as it so often is in the British navy. I come from rebellious stock, my dear. He may not trust me.'

'Then he would be a fool! Adam, do not torment yourself. In any case, we shall be off this warship later today and Captain Ferris's opinion will not matter a jot.'

'But he will report to whoever takes over responsibility for you.'

'What can he say? That you were gentleman enough to treat your prisoners of war with respect and consideration? That, against your own inclinations—' she still remembered his tirade concerning having women on his ship '—you accepted a female aboard and treated her with courtesy?'

'Courtesy?' he jeered. 'First I used you abominably and then treated you with scant respect.' He glowered at her. 'And now. I surrendered my ship. You must despise me for that.'

She drew a deep breath. The fool! He did not understand her at all! She didn't understand herself much better. But she must confess to the truth.

'Do not torment yourself, Adam. I forgave you your treatment of me before ever this happened.'

He stared. 'You did?'

'Yes, I did. And, as for your surrendering, I know you could have done nothing more to stave off eventual defeat.'

He straightened up to face her, his expression quizzical. 'You were not so understanding of Mr Piper when he struck.'

'I behaved in the stupidest fashion! I was full of romantic, heroic ideas! What did I know of war, death and destruction? He lost his ship and will have to face a court of enquiry. But he saved lives, American as well as British.'

Adam's expression lightened. 'So you do not think me a coward? That I should have forced the men to stand to their guns until most were dead and the ship sank under them?'

'Death or glory? No, Adam. My father never advocated such a stupid notion, and now I know why. Every man must strive his utmost to do his duty. But bravery must be tempered with common sense. Perhaps I still suspect that Mr Piper failed to do his utmost. But you did not.'

He took her hands in his. 'You've grown up,' he said, marvelling, and wanting her more than ever.

He dropped her hands again and turned impatiently to stare back at his frigate. 'We shall be parted for good soon,' he predicted harshly.

A hail came from the lookout above. 'Land on the starboard bow!'

They turned to peer forward. The smudge which was Lanzarote had already slid by on their left with Fuerteventura to its south. The captain emerged from the companionway to take a look, although he must have known what to expect.

Adam pointed. 'Look, the volcanic peak of Tenerife. You can see it for some fifty miles when visibility is good. We shall drop anchor off Gran Canaria before nightfall.'

'And be put ashore?' wondered Miranda anxiously.

'Ferris has not said. Perhaps not tonight—accommodation would take too long to arrange. They can provide cots or hammocks for us to sleep in and mount a guard. But tomorrow. . .'

He allowed his speculation to tail off. Miranda cursed the interruption. She felt certain Adam had been about to say something important to her. But the moment had passed. He was all seaman again, intent on navigation and the fate of his frigate. Their own fates too, she supposed, but to Adam they rated a poor second.

Miranda was taken ashore without seeing Adam again, for he and his officers had been locked in the dining place long before the ship dropped anchor at Las Palmas.

They, it seemed, would spend the night aboard. But there was an English military liaison officer ashore, a Lieutenant Cunningham, who commanded a small detachment of soldiers, and he offered her the hospitality of his house. Captain Ferris took a courteous farewell, after which Miranda was made welcome by the official's stout, matronly wife, looking incongruously girlish in white muslin, who offered a bath and the services of her maid, which Miranda accepted with gratitude. At supper she was regaled with questions regarding her adventures and did her best to answer cheerfully, but her mind would not shift from the predicament of Adam and his men and the strong likelihood that she had seen him for the last time.

Until the actual moment had come she had not realised just how unhappy the final parting would make her. He might be brought ashore the next day but the last thing he had told her was that he intended to withdraw his parole in the hope of escaping on the repaired *Seafire*. He was determined to regain his ship if humanly possible. So he would be locked up.

It was a beautiful island, she discovered the next day, but the new sights and smells—the terraces of vines, the innumerable pannier-laden donkeys, the Spanishness of the people—were of only marginal interest as, from the balcony of the Cunninghams' house, she watched the ships' boats plying back and forth between the two British warships, transferring men and provisions. She even caught a heart-wrenching glimpse of Adam as he and his men were rowed ashore, guarded by marines. Their sea chests were also put ashore and lashed to the backs of donkeys. Then they were marched off under military guard, the donkeys following. The marines returned to their ship, and the two men-of-war bound for the Cape weighed anchor on the ebb.

But the *Seafire* was still in the harbour. Men, looking like ants, swarmed over her deck repairing the masts and rigging while another party removed the shattered rudder and prepared to replace it with a new one fashioned from timber purchased locally. Her own trunks, containing all her possessions and stored in its hold, were ferried ashore and brought to the house.

'When will Captain Godfrey be taking the *Seafire* to England?' Miranda asked Lieutenant Cunningham that night. Strain her eyes as she might, she had seen no sign of the *Osprey*'s captain on the deck while the work was being carried out.

'Didn't know, eh?' wondered the lieutenant. 'Poor fellow was severely wounded in the action—lost a leg. He lies in hospital. If he recovers, it will be weeks before he is fit to travel.'

'I'm so sorry. My father—he lost a leg.'

Cunningham grunted. 'Lucky to survive.'

'Yes. So who will command the American frigate?'

'The senior lieutenant left here, no doubt. Several of'em went off to the Cape with the *Victorious* and the *Argus*. I've been assured that there are enough of the *Osprey*'s people left to form a prize crew and take her back, where she'll be condemned by an Admiralty Court and the prize money decided. She's a useful ship, I'm told, and will probably be bought in for service in the navy.'

The *Seafire* being sailed and fought by a British crew? The prospect would devastate Adam. 'Shall I be going with them when they sail?' she asked. The ship would be familiar but she would hate sailing in her without Adam.

Lieutenant Cunningham, stout like his wife, with a florid complexion not improved by the hot climate, which had turned it almost as red as his coat, shook his head.

'No. Too many American prisoners aboard. I can't accommodate'em here—not enough men to guard 'em all even if I had a lock-up big enough to hold 'em. But they can be battened down on board, so fewer marines can do the job.'

Battened down. Miranda shuddered, thinking of the stinking conditions the otherwise innocuous expression implied. Poor Seafires! They had been such a cheerful, willing crew. With them all being volunteers there had been none of the gutter and jail scrapings one found aboard a British man-of-war. Not that they'd all been saints, for some had undoubtedly joined the navy to escape justice, just as others had run away from shrew-ish wives. But, sorry as she felt for them, her own fate was all important to her at that moment.

'Then when. . .?' She left the question hanging.

'Don't 'ee worry your pretty little head, m'dear. You're welcome here; my wife likes company. Don't 'ee, Mrs Cunningham?'

'Yes, indeed,' wheezed his wife comfortably, giving Miranda a nod and smile.

'That is most kind of you, sir,' responded Miranda. 'I do not like to impose.'

'Not imposin', m'dear. But you may be lucky. A brig came in today, said he'd seen a sail o' the line comin' up from the Cape which signalled its intention of callin' in for wood and water. Should reach here tomorrow if the wind holds. Her captain'll probably take you.'

'Oh,' said Miranda. One part of her wanted to be away, to leave Adam and her memories far behind so that she could forget him. Another part of her bled at the thought of abandoning him to his fate as a prisoner. No man enjoyed being confined, but a man like Adam York, used to the freedom of command, of roaming the seas unfettered by restrictive orders or convention—he must be suffering abominably. It was like putting one of the wild sea birds swooping overhead in a cage, she thought.

She clenched her fingers together in her lap, hoping her hosts would not notice her agitation. 'Would it be possible for me to visit the officers of the *Seafire*, sir?'

Cunningham puffed out his cheeks and let the air escape through his lips with a soft pop. 'What the deuce for?'

'They were kind to me. I should like to take them some fruit and wine,' she added on sudden impulse. She still had a small supply of money with her.

'Can't promise. See how things turn out. Could let you, I dare say. Wait until tomorrow.'

With that half-promise Miranda had to be content.

It seemed strange, sleeping in a bed instead of a swinging cot, not to hear the constant creaks of the ship working about her but to have her ears filled with the buzzing of insects instead. However, with the window open it was undoubtedly cooler than it had been in the enclosed cubicle aboard the *Seafire*. She wondered how comfortably Adam and his officers had been housed. Not very, if the lock-up in which they were confined was in any way typical of such places.

She should have been considering herself fortunate. But she did not. The prospect of sailing away and leaving Adam in prison, perhaps never knowing what had befallen him, kept her sleepless, so that she rose heavy-eyed but still determined to visit the Americans.

'They are prisoners of the British, not the Spanish,' Cunningham informed her testily when she broached the subject again. 'You need have no fear of their being ill-treated.'

'But it can do no harm for me to take my leave of them before I sail,' she argued.

'The *Virago* is reported to be in sight. She will be dropping her anchor soon after noon. Naturally, I have no idea how long her captain intends to remain. He may delay weighing until tomorrow. I suggest you wait until I have spoken with him before anticipating your own imminent departure.'

Miranda decided not to press the matter further. She turned to Mrs Cunningham, who was presiding over the breakfast coffee pot. 'Ma'am, would it be possible for me to borrow one of your maidservants for the morning? I should like to explore the town but shall need an escort. Preferably one with some knowledge of English.'

'Of course, my dear! I would come with you myself but —' she made an expressive gesture '— I fear the exertion would be too much; I get so short of breath. . .'

'I shall manage perfectly well, I thank you, ma'am,' Miranda assured her.

An hour later, as they left the house, she asked the dark-haired, dark-skinned girl detailed to accompany her, 'Do you know where the British confine their prisoners?'

The girl understood some English but spoke little. She looked puzzled. 'Preesoner?' she asked.

'Sailors—men from the sea,' Miranda tried again, pointing to the *Seafire*, 'from that ship.'

The girl's face lit up. 'Ah! Sí! You want go there?'

Miranda nodded.

'Come!'

It proved a hot, dusty and unpleasant journey. At the Cunninghams' residence she had been upwind of the stench of the town, the strong smell of rotting fish and tar emanating from the harbour. But the lock-up was on the inland edge of the town and Miranda pressed her handkerchief to her nose as she passed through the narrow, foetid streets, picking her way around donkey droppings and the piles of refuse decaying in the sun.

Besides suffering a distasteful journey, she had wasted her time and energy, she discovered on arrival. The maid pointed triumphantly at a small blockhouse above which flew the British union flag but two sentries stood guard at the only entrance to the surrounding compound, in which a squad of soldiers was drilling and raising clouds of pipeclay as the men presented arms. Of the Americans there was no sign. There would be no point in begging admittance. She had no authority, they would never allow her past the gates.

She did not know quite what she had hoped for. A word or two through the fence or gate, possibly, or perhaps the ability to persuade a friendly sentry to admit her. Both ideas had proved childish, stupid.

But at least she knew where they were. Could she help them to escape? The idea that she wanted to shocked her, her conscience pecked at her, yet she felt a thrill of excitement at the thought. But the little block-house looked impregnable, the lobsters in their red coats solidly menacing. A rescue, even if possible, would take much thought and planning.

And in truth, her rational side told her, she must abandon the Americans to their fate. An English admiral's daughter, however sympathetic to their plight, simply could not assist enemy naval officers to escape.

She noted thankfully as she reluctantly turned away that the stench here was greatly reduced, the British military keeping their isolated surroundings scrupulously clean. She saw that the small windows were set high in the whitewashed walls and some of them were barred. Adam would never escape from there.

Depressed, she retraced her steps, the Spanish girl pointing out sights Miranda scarcely glanced at, let alone took in. She should not have come. It had served no other purpose than to make her more miserable than ever.

CHAPTER SEVEN

THE *Virago*, yet another warship like the *Othello*, came to an anchor in the early afternoon. Her captain, one Alban Judge, joined the Cunninghams for dinner.

The tall, spare, greying captain had the lantern-jawed, lugubrious face of a Puritan preacher. Miranda met his hard, unfriendly brown gaze as he made a formal bow and her heart sank. Captain Judge would not welcome her presence aboard his ship. If he agreed to take her it would be on sufferance.

'Good day to 'ee, Miss Dawson.' He spoke in an abrupt, hectoring tone. 'You are looking to find passage to Portsmouth, I am told.'

'I would have preferred a passage to the West Indies, sir,' replied Miranda pointedly. 'But since Lieutenant Cunningham informs me that there is little likelihood of a convenient vessel calling here in the near future I have agreed to return to England. I fear I must begin my journey to join my father in Barbados all over again.'

The captain nodded, dour-faced. 'Very well, I will oblige Admiral Dawson by giving you passage, miss. I intend to weigh in—' he fumbled under his coat, withdrew his chronometer and glanced at it '—three hours. I will arrange for your trunks to be loaded without delay. They are ready packed, I trust?'

Miranda's heart sank. She would never see Adam

127

again. 'I will go and lock them immediately, sir,' she
said stiffly.

'Dinner will be served in ten minutes,' Mrs
Cunningham reminded her.

'I shall not be long, ma'am.'

As she departed the room Miranda heard Captain
Judge say, 'The others will be aboard in time,
Lieutenant?' and Cunningham's reply. 'The matter is
being attended to now, Captain.'

'The American frigate—'

She could not linger, so heard no more and was left
wondering. What were they saying about the *Seafire*?
And who 'the others' referred to were she could not
imagine, but hoped they might be other civilian passengers. Any buffer between herself and the undivided
attention of the austere Captain Judge must be
welcome.

Her unfavourable impression of the captain grew
during dinner. Despite his looks he was no Puritan,
drinking copiously of the wine on the table. But drink
made him the more dour, while his host became more
convivial, laughing and talking loudly to cover his
guest's silence.

Miranda was glad when Mrs Cunningham rose at the
end of the uneasy meal and the men were left with the
port decanter. The next couple of weeks loomed uneasily ahead. While the *Virago* headed north and finally
entered the chops of the channel she would be obliged
to eat at Captain Judge's table. She wondered what his
officers were like.

*   *   *

Having taken a cordial farewell of her hosts, Miranda accompanied Captain Judge to the quay. where his barge awaited him.

The pull of some half-mile to where the man-of-war was anchored was accomplished in silence, apart from the rumble of the rowlocks and the synchronised splash of the oars dipping into the comparatively calm waters of the anchorage. As she grasped the ropes and was helped to climb aboard the *Virago* behind the captain, who was piped aboard with due ceremony. Miranda mused on the rigid faces of the impeccably turned-out members of the barge's crew. Not once had one of them dropped their gaze from over her head to look at her, or at their captain. for that matter. Only the coxswain, at the tiller. had given Judge a glance as they'd boarded, respectful but wary, awaiting permission to cast off. The men now sat like marionettes. waiting to ship their oars and climb aboard with drill-like precision.

The men of the marine guard, led by their captain, stamped their feet and presented arms, raising a cloud of pipeclay particles to dance in the sun. Captain Judge's officers touched the peaks of their hats and then stood motionless by the entry port. Only the bosun, whose silver call piped him aboard, had expression on his face — one which Miranda instantly distrusted.

As she glanced round the assembled men her eyes suddenly widened in glad surprise. Her mouth opened to cry out, Dicky!

But the word never left her lips. Her brother. stiff as a ramrod, stood to attention. his desperate eyes on her face, the veriest suggestion of a negative shake of his head begging her not to speak.

Captain Judge must have known she would recognise her brother. Perhaps Dick's presence accounted for his reluctance to ferry her back to England. But Dick's not daring to greet her needed some other explanation. Was Judge waiting for the midshipman to breach some rule?

Miranda turned a limpid, guileless smile on the captain, who had made a motion for her to follow him to his cabin.

'I see you have Mr Midshipman Dawson on board, Captain. Have I your permission to greet my brother?'

Judge gave an abrupt nod. 'Mr Dawson, you may exchange greetings with your sister.'

Dick stepped forward, his eyes full of emotion. Dear Lord, thought Miranda, he looks ill! He was thin-faced, drawn, cowed, the merest shadow of the cheerful lad who had left home two years since, full of his chances of passing his exams with flying colours and being appointed a lieutenant the moment he was twenty.

'Dicky,' she cried, kissing him. 'How wonderful to see you!'

He returned the kiss, whispering as he did so, 'I'll be on the deck during the second dog watch.'

'Come, Miss Dawson,' said Judge impatiently. And then to his first lieutenant, 'Where are the prisoners?'

'Already below, sir.'

'Have them brought to my cabin in fifteen minutes. And signal the *Seafire* to be ready to weigh.'

'Very well, sir.'

Prisoners! Were the 'others' he had referred to prisoners of war? Recaptured deserters? Or men being returned to face trial on some charge? Her heart began to thud in her chest, for she had a premonition that the prisoners would be the *Seafire*'s officers. She had heard no mention of any other men under arrest awaiting transport to England.

Enemy officers, as long as they had given their parole, would be treated with courtesy. It also seemed that the captured frigate was to travel under the *Virago*'s escort. The ship would not be signalled to prepare to weigh anchor if she were not to sail in company.

Seething with impatience, Miranda followed Judge to his cabin, where she soon discovered that her guess was correct.

'I have had my desk and charts moved in here,' Judge told her, indicating the furniture squeezed into the corner of the great cabin. 'My clerk's office has been divided into two. You will have one half and the captain of the captured American frigate will be accommodated in the other. His officers will have to sling hammocks in the wardroom—there are no free cabins. The master and midshipman will mess in the gunroom.' Greg Merrick would not mind that, Miranda thought. Frigates were too small to have wardrooms as well as gunrooms and the midshipmen's quarters were squalid to say the least. 'I believe you are acquainted with the gentlemen?'

'Since I was on the *Othello* when it was taken, yes, Captain, I know them. I was their guest aboard the *Seafire*.'

'Then you will have company while you travel, provided they are prepared to give me their paroles. If not, you will have the entire cabin to yourself, for they will be taken below and clapped in irons. I must ask you not to seek conversation with any of my officers, Miss Dawson. They have no time for dalliance if they are to attend to their duties. You may report to your father that I run a tight ship.'

'My brother,' said Miranda, ignoring the captain's general instruction. 'I may speak with him, I trust?'

'As long as you do not interfere with his duties. He is undergoing punishment for insubordination, Miss Dawson. I will not tolerate slackness, indolence or insolence aboard my ship. He is working double watches at the moment.'

The blood fled from Miranda's face. She stared at him, incredulous. No wonder poor Dicky looked weary and drawn! He'd have to snatch a few hours' sleep whenever he could.

She had heard tell of men like Captain Judge but until now had not, mercifully, been brought into contact with one. His attitude explained why the quarterdeck was silent, why no laughter or quip echoed from the main deck as the seamen went about their duties. The only sounds were those of activity, the shouted orders, the yelp of pain as a bosun's mate struck a man with a knotted rope's end or a cane — 'started' him, as the navy had it, because he had not moved quite fast enough. Dear God! How could she remain silent in the face of injustice and brutality? But she must, for Dick's sake. If she did not, Judge would only vent his anger on him.

'I do not entertain at supper,' he was saying. 'A tray will be brought to you in your cabin, as will all your meals except for when I issue an invitation to dine in my cabin. Your sea chest is stowed there already.' He nodded his head in a slight bow. 'God give you a good night, Miss Dawson.'

She could do nothing but leave. Her only comfort was that she would not often have to be civil to the man while eating at his table.

A tiny triangular lobby had been constructed off the walkway by the quarterdeck ladder. As she entered it by its longest side, angled doors forming the other sides faced her.

'This be your door, ma'am,' said the steward detailed to show her the way. 'That one—' he indicated the door on the right '—that one's fer the American captain.'

Her cabin was small, but larger than the one aboard the frigate, and it did have one half of an opening skylight set under a wooden grating. The other half was on the other side of the newly erected partition.

She sank down on her chest to await developments. To think unwelcome thoughts and at the same time feel a growing excitement at the realisation that she would be near Adam York once more.

Her heart thumped when she heard the marine sentry announce Adam and his officers. Since the partitions were thin she could even hear the rumble of the men's voices as they spoke, but found she could not distinguish what they said, for the captain's dining place separated her from the great cabin, where they were gathered.

Before long she heard Adam enter his cabin, on the other side of the dividing partition. Daniel was with him but did not remain long, leaving to seek his own berth below. Miranda took a deep breath and scratched on the canvas separating them.

'Adam!' She kept her voice low, for she did not want Judge to hear.

'Miranda?' His voice held a pleased note which sent her pulses racing anew.

'Yes. Did you know I was here?'

'By inference, yes. How are you, Miranda?'

Her heart beat even faster, taking some of her breath. The familiarity of the use of forenames, begun under the stress of parting, came easier now. 'I am well enough; I was made welcome and comfortable ashore. But you, Adam, shut up in that blockhouse! You must have roasted!'

A quiet chuckle greeted these words. 'Not quite! It was primitive, but they did their best. How did you know. . .?'

'I walked out hoping to speak with you,' Miranda admitted, feeling shy about it, 'but it proved quite impossible. I am so glad we are together again!'

'Are you?' Adam's voice took on a grim note. 'I think both of us might regret being aboard this particular warship before long.'

'You have noticed it too? Adam, my brother, Richard, the midshipman, is serving on the *Virago*. He was in the welcoming party when Judge and I boarded. He was scared to even smile in greeting when he saw me! He looks ill; he's standing double watches as punishment for some misdemeanour.' She lowered her voice to a mere whisper. 'Can you still hear what I say?'

'Yes. A moment.' As she waited she heard the rattle of the skylight overhead as Adam used the tackle, on his side of the partition, to close it. 'What is it, Miranda?'

'He is on duty during the second dog watch. I imagine he'll be snatching a couple of hours' sleep during the first. I shall go up on deck and speak with him. I must find out what is going on!'

'We shall meet on deck in due course, I promise you. Meanwhile, take care, Miranda. Do nothing to displease Judge.'

'It is such a comfort to know you are here, Adam.'

'For what little it is worth, I am at your service. I have given my parole rather than condemn myself and my officers to travelling in irons in stinking conditions below. I have, however, only undertaken not to attempt to take the ship or to escape in any other way. There would be little chance in any case. But I would not rule out the possibility of mutiny among his own men—the atmosphere positively reeks of it and Judge seems oblivious. In that case the mutineers would probably try to kill all of us as well as the captain and his officers. We should most certainly defend ourselves under those circumstances.'

'Surely the men would not—?'

'Once the blood lust takes hold they will not care which navy the officers belong to, or which of the British ones were used as badly as themselves or treated them well. They will kill anyone in authority who could identify them.'

Miranda swallowed, quelling the panic threatening to rise up and choke her. 'Are all the others still with you, Adam?' she asked huskily, cursing the shake in her voice.

'Aye, Zack West, Abe Windsor and Tom Crocker, plus the senior midshipman, Greg Merrick, and the marine lieutenant, John Fenton. And Daniel, thank the Lord.'

'Seven of you, Adam. I'll warn Dick to be on his guard.'

'Do that, for what such a warning is worth!'

At around seven o'clock, in the middle of the second dog watch, Miranda ventured out on the quarterdeck, cursing her skirts as she climbed the ladder. But she did not care to upset Captain Judge by donning her midshipman's outfit, tucked away in her chest.

The officer of the watch touched his hat to her and, since the captain was nowhere to be seen and he was still a young man, ventured a half-smile.

'Mr Dawson is by the larboard carronade on the poop, miss,' he murmured, keeping his voice low because of the great cabin's open skylight.

Miranda beamed at him and nodded her thanks, not speaking for the same reason. Dear Lord! What a ship! Everyone afraid to even speak for fear of the captain! And he held absolute authority. He could rule his ship, deal out punishment and death exactly as he liked and no one could or would interfere.

In the twilight, she climbed the ladder to the poop and walked to the stern, where she found her brother curled up by the gun, dozing. She dropped to her knees beside him and touched his shoulder.

Dick woke with a start, a look of fear crossing his face before he realised who had woken him.

'Mirrie! Thank God it is you!'

'I don't think the officer on duty would mind you sleeping, Dicky. He sent me to you.'

'No, he's a good sort, all the officers are—even Mr Winchester, the first lieutenant—but if the captain discovered me sleeping Mr Jackson would be in trouble too, so he would wake me if he knew I was neglecting my duties.'

'Which are?'

As Dick scrambled to his feet he raised a wan smile, a shadow of the merry grin she remembered. 'Light, thank God and Mr Jackson!' He held out a hand to help Miranda up. 'I'm supposed to be keeping an eye on the lookout in the mizzen and on the American frigate to make sure she's on station. It's merely an excuse to keep me on deck, where I must remain until midnight.'

'The lookout will be coming down soon, surely?'

'No. Captain Judge keeps men aloft all night. And all hands have to be at quarters to greet the dawn.'

They stood at the taffrail. Dick, she noted, as she turned and rested one elbow behind her on the gleaming teak in order to look at him, did not support himself as she did, but stood back, swaying with the motion of the ship.

He made a gesture. 'No one, even officers, are allowed to lean on any of the rails.'

Miranda frowned. 'Does that include me?'

'Don't suppose so. You're not a member of the ship's company.'

'Thank goodness! Dicky, what ever is the matter with the *Virago*? The atmosphere aboard is so tense, one could cut it with a knife.'

'Shush!'

Dick looked anxiously around them but no one was near and the skylight to the chart room beneath was closed and dark. The master was below, eating his supper. as were all the crew except for those on duty. Miranda had hastily eaten her own meal before coming on deck.

'The captain has very sharp ears, and eyes in the back of his head,' he muttered in rueful explanation of his urgent behest to lower her voice. 'I'm being punished because he overheard me criticising the harshness of a flogging he'd decreed. Four dozen lashes for grunting at a bosun's mate, I ask you! I know it was a disgruntled grunt, if you know what I mean, but still!'

Miranda gasped. 'But according to naval rules the maximum imposition, without a court martial, is supposed to be a dozen, isn't it?'

'Most captains ignore that. But Judge punishes harshly for the slightest thing,' Dick said unhappily. 'The crew is assembled to witness punishment almost every day.'

'I knew there was something wrong! Will the men mutiny?' asked Miranda, remembering Adam's foreboding.

Dick sighed. 'I don't know. Mirrie. I'd not blame 'em if they did.'

'But they'd kill all the officers.'

'Aye.'

'If only Papa were here!'

'Even he could do little unless the captain was insane. or incapable in some other way. He is insane, of course, but not certifiable.'

'You'll be in Portsmouth in a couple of weeks or so,' pointed out Miranda. trying to hand out encouragement. 'You must endure until then.'

'But that won't solve anything! I'd wager the crew will be confined aboard—the officers are too afraid the men will desert to allow them ashore—and even if the officers themselves are given a few days' leave and report the trouble no one will do anything about it. Judge is not officially mad. We shall sail again in a few days, weeks at the most, and be back where we started.'

'There must be something someone can do,' murmured Miranda. 'Did you know there were some American officers aboard, being taken back as prisoners of war?'

'From the *Seafire*? I'm not surprised,' said Dick, glancing across to where the American frigate was sailing two hundred yards to the larboard of the *Virago*. 'Glad to see she's still on station,' he said with a grimace. 'I'd forgotten her. We are escorting the prize and its crew back to Portsmouth. But tell me, Mirrie, what were you doing on Gran Canaria?'

'I was on the *Seafire* when she was taken. It's a long story,' she added hurriedly as she saw the incredulity on her brother's face, and proceeded to give him an edited account of her adventures. 'If Captain York can help, I'm certain he will. He immediately sensed something was wrong.'

'I doubt he could stop a mutiny,' said Dick gloomily.

A shudder of apprehension shivered down Miranda's spine. She asked him again, '*Will* there be one, Dicky?'

Dick shrugged. 'I wonder they haven't taken things into their own hands long before this. All they lack, I imagine, is a leader ready to risk his neck.'

At that moment they heard footsteps on the ladder and Dick stiffened to attention. But it was Adam.

Miranda stepped forward eagerly. The last of the daylight was almost gone, yet the radiance which lit her small face at sight of the American made Dick stare and Adam almost to lose his stride. He had not realised. . .

'Adam!' Miranda greeted him softly. 'This is my brother, Midshipman Richard Dawson. Dicky, this is Adam York, captain of the frigate *Seafire*.'

'Former captain, I'm afraid,' said Adam ruefully, shaking the younger man's hand.

'Glad to make your acquaintance, sir,' responded Dick. 'Mirrie has just been telling me of her adventures. But I must not dally here any longer. The second lieutenant is already risking severe reprimand for granting me so much leeway.'

The noise of wind and water, the sound of the ship's timbers and rigging, was all about them when the human silence was suddenly rent by a hail from the quarterdeck.

'Mr Dawson!'

'He thinks I've had long enough,' sighed Dick, 'and has found another job for me!'

'But the watch is almost ended.'

'But not mine!' came Dick's gloomy response as he shot down the ladder.

Miranda leaned on the rail with Adam beside her, watching the wake and the flashing sea-fire. It reminded them both of the last time they had stood so, aboard the *Victorious*.

'We have met again,' she murmured.

'Fate, or providence,' said Adam. 'But we should not appear too intimate. The same reasoning applies as it did aboard *Victorious*. Judge may think you unreliable.'

Miranda snorted. 'He informed me that the prisoners would provide me with company! I am forbidden to speak to his officers!'

'Really? I thought him stupid, now I know it! I gather your brother is exempt from this ban?'

'Only so long as our speaking together does not interfere with his duties!'

'He calls you Mirrie. I like that.'

'It's an old, childish shortening.' Miranda was not keen on taking the diminutive into adulthood. She became suddenly serious. 'He is suffering, Adam. He used to be such a lively boy!'

'He seems a bright lad. Did you discover anything further?'

'No more than we knew already—that Judge is what is known as a flogging captain. And Dick does fear a mutiny.'

'He does, eh? Interesting. Confirms our fears. But they are very near home now. They've suffered this long, why not suffer a little longer?'

'The men know the navy, Adam. They'll not be allowed ashore and in a few days, weeks at the most, they'll be back at sea again in the same ship under the same captain.'

'Hmm. Perhaps that's why things are threatening to come to a head.'

'Yes.' She moved closer and lowered her voice to a breath. 'Dick thinks Judge is mad but, of course, no one would be able to prove it. So nothing will be done unless they take the law into their own hands.'

'And suffer the consequences. To be shot down by

the marines, or, if they survive that, to be hung from the yardarm if they are caught.'

'Some of them,' said Miranda seriously, 'might prefer that to leading such a hellish life. But it is difficult to know where they could go to be safe.'

'The United States would offer them refuge.'

They stood for a moment in silence and then Adam's hand covered hers as it rested on the rail. Miranda's nerves tightened in a delicious frisson which finished in the region of her thumping heart. The incipient panic which had held her in its grip retreated as she turned her face to look up into his.

He was very near, his features just visible in the darkness. The two double strikes of four bells echoed along the decks, signalling the change of watch, but neither of them moved, even when one lot of silent men went below and another took their place.

'I fear for you,' said Adam simply. 'If anything happens I and my men will try to look after you but it may not be possible. Ask your brother for a pistol. You can use one?'

'Papa taught me years ago, though I'm not much of a shot.'

'You do not need to be to turn it upon yourself, my dear. For if the people gain possession of this ship you would be better dead.'

Miranda, suddenly chilled, shivered. She could visualise just what Adam meant. One female among four or five hundred rough, deprived seamen. . .no, it did not bear thinking of. . .but, even so, could she. . .?

'You would find the courage,' murmured Adam, sensing her doubt, and took her trembling body into his

arms. The only man who might possibly see them was
the lookout at the head of the mizzen-mast, but it was
dark and he was hidden from view by the billowing sail.
And in any case, did it matter?

One of Adam's hands smoothed her hair, the other
rotated soothingly on her back. Miranda buried her face
in his shoulder beneath the stiff, scratchy epaulette, and
gave way to tears.

The feel of her in his arms roused him to an extent he
had not anticipated. But she had come to him trustingly.
He cursed the fire in his loins and concentrated on
offering comfort. She was, after all, an enemy admiral's
daughter, while he was a prisoner aboard an enemy
ship. The sheer frustration of his situation made him
drop his arms, releasing her.

'Don't worry.' he murmured. 'I'll do my damndest to
prevent it happening.'

Miranda raised her streaked face. 'I know, but you
are only one man, Adam. What can one man do?'

'We are seven men, Miranda, six armed with sword
or dirk. As for Daniel. . .' He allowed his thoughts to
trail off. 'He will find something to use, if it is only his
fists!' He pulled her to him again. 'To save you I would
break my oath and take the ship.' Amazingly, it was
true. He would. 'I'd bet any odds the people would not
put up much of a fight to save it!'

'It would be dangerous, Adam. The officers might
feel it their duty—'

'Leave it to me. But get that pistol, just in case.'

Miranda sniffed and wiped her hand across her wet
face. 'All right, Adam. Please kiss me.'

She gazed up at him, her eyes still swimming. For a

fleeting moment he looked taken aback. Miranda flushed, thinking he would refuse.

Good God! thought Adam. I can't! I cannot trust myself— Then he took a grip on himself. A teasing grin spread across his features. 'I thought it to be the last thing you wanted—to be kissed by me! I seem to remember being told—'

She put a finger up to touch the healing wound on his scalp. Then her arms crept about his neck. His mouth was only inches away from hers. 'I changed my mind about that a long time ago.'

'You did?' Adam drew a breath, a steadying breath. The poor innocent did not know what she was inviting. 'Well, then. . .'

First he kissed away the tears lingering beneath her eyes. Then. . .then he took her lips, teasing them apart so that he could feel her welcome his tongue with hers. He did not deepen the kiss further. He was, after all, still offering comfort, not an expression of the forbidden passion that so frustratingly tormented him. And to which she might innocently respond and thus break his control.

Miranda felt dizzy and only the rail digging into her back and Adam's strong arms kept her upright as the ship pitched and rolled its way northwards.

Neither heard a heavy tread ascending the ladder to the poop. Not until he spoke did they realise his presence.

'Consorting with the enemy, I see, Miss Dawson,' grated Captain Judge.

Already shaken to her core by that kiss, Miranda could do no more than gasp as shock waves of guilty

THERE ARE ALWAYS TWO SIDES TO EVERY ROMANCE

...AND NOW THERE ARE TWO SERIES TO SATISFY YOUR DIFFERENT MOODS.

MILLS & BOON *Presents*...
Passionate, compelling, provocative romances you'll never want to end.

MILLS & BOON *Enchanted*
Warm and emotionally fulfilling novels - experience the magic of falling in love.

WITH OUR COMPLIMENTS - A TEAR OUT BOOKMARK SHOWING ALL SEPTEMBER TITLES

FREE GIFTS

TO CELEBRATE THE INTRODUCTION OF

Presents™

AND

Enchanted™

WE ARE OFFERING YOU SOME GREAT

FREE GIFTS

SEE BOOKS FOR DETAILS ON HOW TO APPLY

MILLS & BOON®

apprehension swept over her. Adam kept a steadying arm about her as he faced the man to whom he had given his parole.

'Our nations may be at war, Captain, but on a personal level there is no room for enmity between Miss Dawson and myself.'

'I'll not tolerate immorality aboard my ship, York. If you wish to preserve your freedom you will cease to exhibit disgusting conduct of this nature.'

'You consider a kiss disgusting?' enquired Adam as though interested in Judge's answer. He could feel Miranda's body shaking. 'Tell me, sir, are you wed?'

If possible, Judge stiffened still further. 'A different matter, sir, a different matter entirely!' he blustered. 'With one's spouse such conduct is permitted. But only with one's spouse'

'I could ask you to marry us,' murmured Adam, and heard Miranda's sharp intake of breath. The devil! What had Judge driven him to say?

'Which I should certainly refuse to do! You are an enemy of my country and Miss Dawson is assuredly under age!'

'I thought there would be insuperable difficulties,' sighed Adam, giving Miranda's shoulders a reassuring squeeze as he released her. 'You see, my dear, we shall have to wait. But, once wed, Captain Judge would no doubt bless our disgusting behaviour.'

Miranda realised he had not meant his words as an offer. He had merely been baiting Judge. He had known perfectly well that a union between them was quite impossible. But—marriage, to Adam York? Her pulses raced at the thought while her common sense rejected the idea out of hand.

Adam knew he had caught Judge out but forbore to press his advantage. The man was a bully and a hypocrite but now was not the time to challenge him further. He had already waded into deeper water than he'd intended. He bowed stiffly to Judge.

'Then we shall abide by your ruling, Captain. But you will not, I trust, object to our taking the air together?'

'As long as you do not interfere with the working of my ship,' agreed Judge grudgingly.

Adam saluted the captain, who seemed not to notice the contempt in his prisoner's eyes. 'Your word is my command, sir. We shall, of course, keep to the leeward side of the deck.'

Judge nodded, returning the salute. His chilling gaze rested on Miranda. 'It is time you retired to your berth, Miss Dawson.'

'But—' She felt Adam's touch on her arm and the protest died on her lips. She acquiesced with bad grace. 'Oh, very well, Captain.'

'I will escort you below,' murmured Adam. 'Give you a quiet night, Captain Judge.'

CHAPTER EIGHT

DICK, after a certain amount of demur, handed Miranda the pair of pistols their father had given him for his seventeenth birthday.

'You'll need the powder and shot, the rammer and the priming powder, so you'd better take the whole case,' he said. 'I'll use service issue if I have need of a firearm.' He fingered the chased silver handle of his midshipman's dirk, a short sword, which he had been given upon joining the navy and worn proudly ever since. 'This, or perhaps a cutlass, will be all I need to defend myself with.'

'I'll keep one of these loaded,' said Miranda, weighing the heavy weapon in her hand. 'Then all I'll have to do in an emergency is prime it. I really don't think. . . but Adam was anxious and I promised. . .'

'I don't like it, but I have to agree with him,' said Dick unhappily. 'There's to be another punishment today. The people really are at the end of their tether.'

Miranda shuddered. 'I don't want to watch.'

'Think yourself lucky you don't have to.'

But she did watch. Somehow it seemed necessary for her to join Adam and the other prisoners, mustered on deck with all the ship's hands. She could not shut her eyes to what was going on—she wanted evidence to present to anyone who would listen once she reached England. Or to give to her father, who might be able to wield enough influence to get Judge beached if not dismissed from the service. And she wanted to watch the seamen, to assess their mood. For all their lives might depend on gauging it right.

She found the brutal sight nauseous. After the first few strokes, when the blood began to flow and cover the sailor's already striped back, she tore her eyes away, for the first time in her life wishing she had her mother's vinaigrette to hold under her nose. But she simply would *not* faint! She concentrated her attention on the hands crowding the decks before the main mast, some clinging to the rigging. Their mood, she decided, was sullen. Eventually, as his flayed back became more and more raw, despite teeth clenched on the leather strap placed between them to stop him from biting off his tongue, the man began to whimper.

It was inhuman, thought Miranda, yet part of naval life, a method of keeping discipline that the men understood and tolerated as long as it was not abused. Part of many people's lives, come to that: soldiers, criminals, transportees, slaves. . .even servants and wives. . .were beaten, though not as cruelly, not with a cat-o'-nine-tails. . . She clenched her hands into fists, bit her lip and set herself to endure.

'Thirty-six,' intoned the bosun.

'Cut him down,' commanded Judge, and willing hands ran forward to release the spread-eagled figure from the grating to which he'd been tied, and a bucket of water was thrown over him. The ship's surgeon took a look at the man, who had risen shakily to his feet and squared his raw shoulders, and ordered him below to receive treatment before he resumed his duties.

With the company dismissed, the ship returned to its normal routine. As Miranda swallowed the bile in her throat she felt Adam's hand on her arm.

'Walk with me,' he invited.

She smiled weakly at the other Seafires, who dispersed about the deck or went below.

'We must not appear to be conspiring,' murmured Adam. 'Judge finding us last night may be a blessing in disguise. He will believe we have an attachment which inclines us to seek each other's company—'

'Which, of course, we have not!' snapped Miranda, upset already and now piqued.

Adam's tone hardened. 'That is not what I necessarily implied, but whether we have or not, my dear, it will be as well if Judge continues to think we have. Otherwise we cannot plan.'

Damn being a woman, thought Miranda as tears welled into her eyes. Dick, despite all his suffering, had not gone to pieces at the sight of a man being flogged. He was on the foredeck now, supervising the hands in his division as they did repairs to the rigging. The captain had gone below to eat his dinner. While she. . . It must be because she was so upset that she had snapped at Adam. But she did not wish him to know how weak she was, she'd done enough crying into his shoulder the previous evening. Then he'd healed her tears with his kiss. The temptation to give in and repeat the performance was almost overwhelming, but she resisted it. There were too many people watching and it would not be fair to Adam. But she could apologise. She took a steadying breath.

'I'm sorry, Adam. I should not have jumped on you like that. Of course we need to plan.'

Adam nodded. 'You're upset and so am I or I would have chosen my words with more care. I will talk to Zack and the others when I get the chance. We must be ready to nip any mutiny in the bud. I think we can do it, though I'm not yet entirely clear how.'

'The men are sullen. Even the marines.'

'Yes, and resentful. It would not take much to tip the scales. The marines, with their arms, present the greatest problem for us, for it is their duty to quell any sign of rebellion. Have you acquired a pistol?'

'Two. The pair Papa gave to Dick for a birthday present. I have the box tucked into the foot of my cot. If the ship is cleared for action I will keep the box with me.'

Adam gave a wry grin, one which made her heart jump and did more to relax her than any words could have done. 'Lucky pistols! But don't you find the wood hard when you kick it?'

'Adam!' Miranda's cheeks had become a fiery red. 'As a gentleman you should not say a thing like that!'

'But then,' murmured Adam, 'we are already agreed that I am no gentleman.'

'We are no such thing! You are descended from the English aristocracy and can behave as a perfect gentleman when you wish!'

'Such a pity that I do not always wish! Instead, I enjoy teasing you, my dear, for you rise so beautifully to my bait. And I do envy that box of pistols.'

Her face could scarcely become hotter, but the heat spread to the rest of her body.

'Oh! You!'

Miranda pretended outrage to cover the frisson of awareness that engulfed her. Adam was saying that he wanted to share her bed and instead of being dismayed and fearful her whole being longed quite shamelessly for him to do so. Quite apart from his being an enemy officer, the conventions surrounding a female who aspired to be considered a young lady of breeding bade her quell any such desire. But did any of that really matter? She only had one life to live and she might be dead tomorrow.

The thought heightened her responses. If only he could join her in her cot! But it would be far too small and the marine sentry might hear something... Shame swept over her that she was even entertaining such a dreadful idea!

As her emotions see-sawed they were reflected on her expressive face, in her wide blue eyes. The confusion he saw there shook Adam. How could such an intrepid spirit be so vulnerable? It made him regret teasing her, even in so lightly flirtatious a way. Made him realise that protecting this child—no, he had to be honest, not child but desirable young woman—from harm, even from confusion, had become the mainspring of his life. Even the recovery of the *Seafire*, normally dominant in his thoughts, had been demoted to second place.

How was it possible that she had become so important to him in so short a while? He, who had forsworn the prospect of committing himself to one woman for life, because he was already wed to the navy. Had he been foolish enough to fall in love? And with an English admiral's daughter?

No, certainly not! It was indubitably his duty to safeguard Miranda Dawson, because without his interference she would have been halfway across the Atlantic, safely on her way to the West Indies by now. What he felt was simply protectiveness allied to a desire which would soon pass, but meanwhile her presence was deuced uncomfortable, for she roused all his male instincts.

His fingers lightly brushed her jaw. 'Don't be vexed, Miranda. I will not tease you so again.'

But he should not have touched her, he realised as she shied away like a startled horse. Her trembling could be fear, but he thought not. He had enough experience of the opposite sex to know when his own desire was reciprocated. But this was an innocent young girl, emotionally immature, who did not quite know what to make of the sensations assailing her. And was probably feeling as guilty as he was for reacting as she did. He must tread warily.

'I'm glad you've got the pistols,' he told her prosaically. 'Keep them loaded and at the first sign of any trouble prime them and keep them handy.'

Them? Surely one would be enough. . .? Yet it would be stupid not to try to defend herself first. She nodded.

They had come to a halt by a gun near the master's chart room. There had been no one near to overhear their conversation, for the master stood by the great double wheel watching the helmsmen, checking their course.

'Shall we continue to walk?' suggested Adam.

Miranda nodded. 'The wind has eased. It is quite pleasant on deck now.'

'And we are still too far south for it to be chilly.' Adam crooked his elbow. 'Will you take my arm, ma'am?'

'Thank you, sir!'

That was a mistake too, but the feel of her small hand resting trustingly on his arm gave Adam such pleasure that he could not regret it. That startled reaction had been what he'd suspected—awareness, not fear. The knowledge gave him satisfaction. But of what use was that when he knew he dared not kiss her again?

After eating her solitary supper, Miranda decided to go up on deck. She could watch the sunset and maybe find someone to talk to. Dick would be on watch during the evening. She might find a chance to speak with him again.

She might find Adam on deck, too, unless he was visiting his officers in the wardroom, for he was not in his cabin.

Feeling lonely and abandoned, Miranda emerged to discover herself in the midst of a hive of activity. The most able of the seamen, the nimble topmen, were swarming up the rigging like monkeys to furl the topgallants—the third tier of square sails, whose yards—the horizontal spars crossing the masts from which the sails hung—swayed high above the deck. Up there they would look like ants as they shuffled along the ropes to space themselves out at intervals in order to furl the sails and lash them to the yards. The men had scarcely begun to climb before the captain's voice rasped after them.

'Smartly, now!' He waved the watch in his fist. 'I am timing you! The last man down will be flogged.'

Miranda could feel the wave of animosity which swept towards the quarterdeck from the men tailing onto the ropes which controlled the sails and yards. As for the men climbing the rigging, one or two faltered but most doggedly continued their swift upward progress.

Her heart seemed to be in her throat. Someone must be last down; the threat of punishment could not be fair. She looked round anxiously but there was no sign of Adam. Dick, she saw, was with the men at the foremast, stationed partway up in the top, directing operations from there.

The lieutenant's voice sounded tinny and strained as he shouted the necessary orders through his speaking trumpet. Tension had gripped the entire ship, or so it seemed, although those off watch below could not know what was happening.

But the news spread through the grapevine of the ship's company faster than lightning. Heads began to appear at the hatches and all the officers not actually sleeping came up. The Seafires were with them. Miranda saw Adam's head appear through the companion hatch and, careless of what anyone thought, moved swiftly to meet him.

'A damnable thing,' he growled as he led her to one side out of the way. 'By all accounts he did the same thing a couple of weeks ago. The man who came in for the punishment then is in this watch.'

Miranda lifted anxious eyes. 'He's up there now?'

'Aye, so I'm told. On the main mast.'

They both gazed up. The massive timbers reduced in size the higher up they were, but, even with the mast vertical, which it never was since it constantly gyrated with the movement of the ship, men would be hanging out over the sea. One false step and someone would drown.

'They'll all be clumsy with nerves,' muttered Adam. 'Him especially.'

The billowing canvas was beaten and pounded into submission, the lashings tied. Naturally, the smaller sails fore and aft were finished first and, on the order, those hands clambered down the rigging. Shortly afterwards those up the main mast began to return to deck. Down they came, swinging through the rigging, hands and feet sure as they found their holds. But then, suddenly, the *Virago* was no longer a silent ship. An agonised groan, more like a roar, rose up as one of the tiny figures above missed his grip and, because of the way the ship was heeling with the wind, plunged, not into the sea but to the deck.

Miranda's fingers flew to her mouth but an instant later she found herself gripping Adam's arm with both her hands as the flailing figure bounced off the solid lower yard to land spread-eagled on his back across one of the boats stowed upside down on the main deck below.

The surgeon had come up from the gunroom. He surged forward, the only man to move in the awful silence which had followed the initial gasp of horror.

'Get about your duties, you bastards,' thundered Judge. 'Anyone caught idling will earn punishment!'

'The fool,' muttered Adam. 'Is he asking them to mutiny?'

They had instinctively gone forward to peer down to the main deck. The surgeon finished his examination.

'Broken neck,' he proclaimed laconically.

'Heave him over the side,' ordered Judge.

The silence deepened, if that were possible. Such an unceremonious burial was acceptable in the heat of battle but not in these circumstances.

'He was incompetent,' proclaimed Judge harshly. If his words were intended as a justification of his edict they cut little ice with anyone who heard them.

''E were one of our best topmen 'till you 'ad 'im flogged,' came a brave voice from amongst the other topmen gathered about the foot of the mast. ''E still weren't fit—stiff as a board, 'e were—'

'Arrest that man for impudence!' thundered Judge. 'I shall decide his punishment, which will be administered tomorrow.'

The bosun had hold of the man and a couple of the marines came forward in response to an order, reluctantly as far as Miranda could tell, to escort the man down to the lock-up. He would spend the night in irons.

'Now,' went on Judge in an awful voice, 'disperse! Get about your duties or, by God, I'll have the lot of you flogged! Captain Goddard,' he shouted to the captain of marines, 'have your men dispose of the body.'

Having issued his orders, Judge stalked from the deck.

Even Adam was white-faced. Miranda forced her fingers from his arm—she must have bruised him with the strength of her grip—and grasped the rail instead as they watched four marines pick up the broken body.

'I'll sew him in his hammock,' said the sailmaker grimly. 'Smith,' he addressed his mate, 'get it laid along, and a couple of round shot too.'

'A man of some sensibility,' murmured Adam as the mate passed on the order and seamen raced eagerly to do the sailmaker's bidding. 'Not leaving the body for the sharks will help to mollify the men.'

'Until tomorrow,' said Miranda grimly.

'Aye. I think we can expect trouble when punishment is administered tomorrow. I can't tell you what I intend to do, because I don't know until it happens. But be ready.'

Miranda nodded. Her knees seemed weak and she was trembling but panic had passed, the calmness of inevitability had settled on her. By this time tomorrow they would all either be dead or not. She could do nothing to alter the course of events, a course dictated on one side by a cretinous bully with absolute power, and on the other by the ingenuity and swift reactions of a foreign prisoner of war.

Someone had brought out the Union flag and laid it over the body. As the marines slid it gently over the bulwark their captain's lips moved in what she suspected, by his bowed head, was prayer. The seaman's erstwhile shipmates stood around with bared heads. So the poor creature would have a half-decent burial after all. The captain of marines went up in her estimation. Possibly the marines would not pose as much of a problem as Adam feared.

A collective sigh seemed to rise at the sound of the

splash. Then the officer of the deck shouted an order and the ship returned to its normal routine.

Before long Dick came aft for a word with his sister, something the other officers tolerated unless the captain happened to be on deck. He saluted Adam.

'There'll be trouble tomorrow unless I miss my bet,' he muttered.

'Could you do something to calm them?' asked Adam. 'Pass word round the ship, anonymously if possible—is there a hand you can trust?'

'Aye, sir. If I tell him and he gossips with the orderly. . .'

'Right. Tell them to bear up and not to be surprised whatever happens, but don't mention me.' Seeing Dick's questioning look, he grinned wryly. 'I can't tell you more, because I don't know myself. Anything I do will be dictated by Judge's actions and how I can expect the marines to react.'

'Captain Goddard is unhappy, sir, like all the sea officers are, and his marines are restless. There isn't a man aboard, except the bosun, who doesn't hold the captain in the deepest dislike.'

'Capital. But don't repeat that in the hearing of anyone else, for it is mutiny, my lad!'

Dick shrugged. 'If that constitutes mutiny, then the whole ship is already guilty!'

'Be that as it may, pass the word for everyone to wait. Let no one risk his neck or his future until he's absolutely certain there is no other way. Mutineers usually end up dead or wishing they were.'

Dick lifted his cap from his head, ran his fingers

through his cropped hair and put it back on again. 'If there's anything else I can do—'

'Absolutely nothing, except start that rumour. Keep your powder dry, Mr Dawson. You may need it later!'

Dick grinned as some of the tension drained from his face. 'I'll be required to muster to witness punishment,' he observed. 'More broken sleep!'

But he sounded cheerful for the first time since Miranda had come aboard. And if he was cheerful perhaps the man he entrusted with the message might be infected and so enthuse others.

So much depended on Adam. As Dick took his leave she glanced up at that face she had come to know so well. The harsh lines had become harder, his brows gathered into a frown over those slate-grey eyes. He was, she realised, lost in his own thoughts, unaware of anything around him, including herself. But that did not trouble her. If he was planning the release of all these men from daily torture she was happy to fade into the background for a while. But, watching the concentration mirrored on his face, she relished anew his powerful personality, the leadership qualities which came so naturally to him. His officers and Daniel would do his bidding without question, even in a lost cause. As would she. American he might be, but how much she admired him!

How different he was from the effete fops and dandies who idled about the assembly rooms and drawing rooms of Bath! His strong personality had almost erased the memory of Peter Stannard. She had loved Peter with all the ardour of a first love but even those feelings had done little to prepare her for the devastating effect Adam York had upon her. Almost, she resented the hold he had gained over her emotions, for it could not be right or proper. Yet—had that kiss last evening meant the same to him as it had to her? The signalling of an emotion welling between them that only death could destroy?

But tomorrow death might in fact destroy it. She slipped quietly away and Adam did not notice.

She heard him retire to his cot. Heard Daniel leave. Lying so close beside him with only the canvas partition between them, she allowed her imagination to run riot. But only for a while. Until she was certain that Captain Judge, too, had taken to his cot and that the marine sentry was most probably dozing at his post.

Then she swung her feet to the ground, took up her silk wrapper and covered her simple lawn nightgown. She did not bother with slippers but padded barefoot to the door, opened it quietly and slipped out into the tiny lobby.

There she paused, gathering her fast diminishing courage. Guilt almost overcame her as she hesitated on the threshold of Adam's cabin. But she had decided on a course of action and she would not allow guilt, nerves, modesty or any other of the dozens of emotions racking her to prevent her from carrying it out. She pushed open the door.

He was not asleep. As the door moved he sat up sharply in his cot, making it swing against the motion of the ship, causing the bolts to groan against the timbers holding them. The skylight let in a little starlight and

Miranda caught the glint of steel as he snatched a knife from beneath his pillow.

'Adam!' she whispered urgently, afraid he might throw it, a skill she knew he possessed. She had not known he had the weapon with him. 'It's me.'

He relaxed. 'Miranda? What the hell are you doing here, scaring me half out of my wits?'

As Miranda trod the two steps which took her to his side, he replaced the knife and sank back against the pillow. For answer she took her courage in both hands, leant over and kissed him on the mouth.

For a moment his lips accepted hers. Then he was pushing at her shoulders, thrusting her back as he struggled up.

His voice came out as a harsh whisper. 'Miranda! Don't.'

Miranda drew back, shamed and mortified by his rejection. 'I thought you liked me,' she mumbled.

'I do! Oh, Miranda, my dear, don't you understand? I am intolerably tempted but I can't. . .we can't. . .' Devil take it, he was stumbling like a guilty adolescent boy! 'We cannot make love here,' he went on more firmly. 'We'd be heard—the cot would rock—'

'Would it?'

They were both whispering and for a moment Adam was tempted to laugh at their ridiculous predicament. But not for long. 'My dear innocent,' he murmured, his voice a trifle unsteady, but not with laughter, 'I'm afraid it would, rather noisily, and if Judge found us I'd be in irons before you knew it and unable to lift a finger to help tomorrow!' Anticipating a rare undisturbed night, he had undressed fully and was in his nightshirt. He swung his legs from the cot and gathered her shivering figure into his arms. 'Besides,' he went on gently, stroking her hair and sternly controlling his own responses to the soft nearness of her thinly clad body, 'when — if — I ever make love to you, sweetheart, I do not want to do it in a narrow, swinging cot in a cubbyhole on a foreign ship where I am not a free man. Once I am back in my own cabin —'

'Aboard the *Seafire* ?' In her astonishment Miranda's voice rose slightly. 'But she is a prize of war! Could you get her back?' she continued, whispering almost soundlessly in response to Adam's hissed warning.

He shrugged as her hands crept up his chest and her arms encircled his neck. 'I don't know. It may be possible — but it all depends. I have the glimmering of a plan but it's best you don't know anything of it.'

'We may not have a chance after tomorrow. That's why I came,' breathed Miranda, her fingers digging up under his pigtail to bury themselves in his hair. 'Adam, I couldn't bear to die without. . .' She allowed her barely audible words to tail off, unable to express her deepest desires.

So it was the prospect of death which had brought her. That certainly explained her astonishing behaviour. Yet to meet the threat headlong was characteristic of the young woman who had challenged him, changed into convenient boy's clothes regardless of decorum and borne herself with courage in the midst of battle. This was his Miranda, the girl he — loved? Adam leashed his own desire and kissed her tenderly. 'Sweetheart, if we indulge ourselves now there may indeed be nothing after tomorrow. But trust me and the other

Seafires to do our best and God willing we shall all survive.'

'Of course I trust you, Adam. I love you. I want to belong to you.'

Adam groaned, resting his face on her hair. 'You cannot mean it, my dear. An enemy officer, sworn to damage your country's interests? I would delight to think it so, but how can either of us be certain of our deepest feelings under these conditions?'

'You don't want me,' muttered Miranda flatly.

'Did I say that? I could believe I love you too, sweetheart, but neither of us can be certain until we are out of this mess and looking to the future with hope. Hope of an end to war, of a peaceful life together. . .and I shall still be a naval officer, at sea for long periods. . . not exactly good husband material, my dear.'

'I didn't say anything about the future, or marriage,' protested Miranda, sounding the more fierce because she was denying her dearest wish. 'I just said I loved you and wanted to belong to you. If only for this one night.'

'And I. . .' Adam breathed a rueful laugh '. . .must conquer my own longing for the sakes of everyone on board the *Virago*. Go back now, my dear, and try to sleep. Tomorrow will be a demanding day.'

He kissed her again, restraining his impulse to kiss her silly, to rouse the passion he knew to be burning just under the surface of her innocence. God grant there would be time enough for that another night. Though— but he thrust the fears, the doubts, the guilt aside. He'd deal with them all when the time came. If it did.

Miranda felt his body move against her and an

uncontrollable shiver of desire took the strength from her limbs. She clung weakly to the cotton of his nightshirt, felt the hard flesh beneath, shut her eyes and gave herself up to the rapturous feel of his lips on hers. He did not deepen the kiss, just as he had not last night, yet the tumultuous feelings invading her body could not have been more shattering.

Voices from the quarterdeck above, a bustling about the ship as the watch changed, brought them back to reality.

'You must return, my dear, but quietly. The new sentry will not yet be asleep!'

Reluctantly, Miranda extricated herself from Adam's arms, surprised to find that her legs would bear her weight. He took her hand and, after kissing the palm, led her to the door, opened it and then hers. The last he saw as he beat a retreat was a wistful, slender shadow closing the door between them. He retired to his cot to lie fighting the frustration gripping his body. To take his mind off Miranda he concentrated on his nebulous and rather dubious plans for the morrow. Zack and Abe had been enthusiastic; Tom Crocker, a cautious man as became a sailing master, had pointed out all the difficulties. Greg Merrick had been eager, Lieutenant Fenton determined to show what the military could do. Daniel he could rely on to back him whatever harebrained scheme he might dream up. In the end, success or failure would be in the lap of the gods. But to save Miranda from the clutches of mutineers he would risk almost anything. Damn and blast! He was back to thinking of Miranda again!

The sight of Adam's stalwart figure, albeit shrouded

in white linen, remained in Miranda's vision long after she returned to her cot. A sense of grievous disappointment, of having been cheated of something beyond price, kept her wakeful. But he had kissed her hand. She fell asleep at last with the palm nestled beneath her cheek.

CHAPTER NINE

MIRANDA could not settle. All morning she paced the quarterdeck, accompanied in turns by most of Adam's officers, who seemed more in evidence than usual, though this did not appear to disturb the marine sentries posted about the decks. Adam himself was lying low, although he did take a turn just before noon.

Each day the master, several midshipmen under instruction and the captain, if he felt like it, took a sight as the sun reached its zenith, measuring its distance above the horizon. This enabled the master to fix the latitude—the ship's exact position relative to the equator—and to turn the glass to correct the ship's time to noon. Miranda suspected Adam wanted to know the *Virago*'s location—a suspicion confirmed when he remarked that they had already left Madeira to larboard, though the island had been too distant for even the masthead lookout to sight.

Passing on this information allowed him to address her without undue awkwardness, though both were conscious of the events of the previous night. Miranda's embarrassment had become acute the more she'd considered her forward conduct, while Adam had a ridiculous sense of guilt for rejecting her, albeit in the best interests of herself as well as everyone else. So his casual announcement of their whereabouts covered the difficult moment and they were able to resume an easy relationship without further fuss.

After a few turns about the deck Adam prepared to go below again.

'Do not stand near me or the captain later,' he murmured as he bent over her hand in farewell. 'The surgeon reckons that a sentence of more than a dozen lashes will kill that man, who already has a raw back from previous punishments. He was a fool to speak out as he did, but a brave one. I'll not allow him to be killed for speaking the truth.'

'So if the punishment is severe—'

'I intend to intervene anyway, since I've sent word round the ship for the people not to make a move themselves but to expect action from another direction, but brutality of that magnitude would vindicate my decision.'

'Adam.' Miranda's fingers clung to his hand. 'Take care.'

He smiled, that buccaneering smile she had glimpsed before when he'd scented action. 'If I die it will be in as good a cause as any I can conceive. But I will take care,' he added quickly, seeing the dismay written on her face and turning her away so that others would not observe it. He bent his mouth near her ear. 'I have no wish to lose my life before I have savoured the delights you so generously offered last night, sweetheart.'

Miranda hid her face now, for it was poppy-red. 'I shouldn't have. . .' she muttered.

'I'm glad you did.'

He kissed her fingers, reminding himself that her life was more valuable to him than his own, and that he'd better remember that when the time came, otherwise he might act less decisively than he should, afraid to die now that he had discovered life to be more precious than it had ever seemed in the past.

Punishment would be administered in an hour's time. Miranda remained on deck after Adam left, afraid that she would not be able to swallow her dinner, which Daniel was due to serve soon. She hoped he would understand and not be offended if she failed, for he went to great lengths to obtain decent food from Judge's cook to serve to her and Adam.

She did follow him below, though, when Daniel came to fetch her.

'You must eat, missie, you'll need all your strength,' he told her in a gruff whisper. 'The cap'n will be all right. Ah'll take good care of him, never you fear. You could surely manage some stew?'

There was no sound from the other side of the partition. 'Is he eating in the wardroom?' asked Miranda. Daniel nodded. Miranda grinned despite herself. 'Making friends and influencing people?'

'Talking to Mr Winchester and sharing a bottle with him and Lootenant Goddard.'

Daniel's colonial inflection was always more noticeable than that of the other Americans and now his Southern drawl had become more pronounced than usual. He was, she guessed, as anxious for Adam's safety as she was.

Miranda sniffed at the salt pork and chicken stew, thickened with dried peas, and decided it did not smell too bad. One tentative spoonful was followed by another as she discovered the concoction to be both tasty and filling. And her stomach had been feeling hollow. Yes, she could manage some. If the routine of the ship was disturbed it might be hours before she would be able to eat again.

She had scarcely finished her meal before the drum began to beat and the bosun's pipes to twitter, calling all hands to witness punishment. Miranda stood up, drew a deep breath and reached into the foot of her cot. She took out the box Dick had given her. She had already loaded both pistols with powder and shot, ramming it down the barrel and then adding a wad of cotton to keep it there. Now she checked the flints and poured priming powder into the pan before tucking them into her reticule. Luckily it was capacious, but the weapons dragged it down; it was obvious she had something heavy in there and she hoped no one would notice. Or wonder why she had chosen this particular occasion to carry the cumbersome drawstring bag up the companion ladder to the deck.

But no one was concerned with her. Adam gave her a brief smile as he lounged against the breech of a gun waiting for Captain Judge to appear. He and all his officers wore their swords, Midshipman Merrick had his dirk. These weapons were accepted, since this was a ceremonial event, and the Americans were on parole. Daniel, she discovered after some searching, was half-way up the main rigging, hanging on with one hand and idly swinging a heavy belaying pin in his other fist.

Yes, as usual on such occasions, every English officer had a sword at his hip, for it was, after all, the visible sign of his status and authority. As Judge stepped on deck, Captain Goddard stood in front of his main body of marines with his sword drawn and held with the blade vertical between his eyes.

Marines were posted along the quarterdeck rail, their loaded muskets pointing at the seamen beyond. One was stationed in the main top above Daniel's head, manning a swivel gun. So that was why Daniel was where he was. Zack, his right arm still in a sling, stood near Mr Winchester, the first lieutenant; Abe had taken up position close to the marine manning a swivel on the starboard bulwark, while Tom strolled casually over to stand between Zack and the soldier stationed by the larboard gun. Lieutenant Fenton stood to attention near the main body of British marines. Young Greg Merrick hovered behind Zack and near the master, the only Seafire to look anything other than casual. He appeared excited, but no one was looking. No one ordered the American officers to stand in a group; it did not seem necessary—the seamen were the danger and they were glaring sullenly but doing nothing, covered by the marines' muskets and swivels. None of the officers suspected the Americans of an intention to interfere; why should they? This was a purely domestic matter of a kind they had witnessed before.

Miranda supposed it would have been too obvious for Fenton to actually join Captain Goddard, standing to attention before his marines. Or perhaps Adam felt able to disregard any threat from his direction. But Goddard could shout an order and the well-drilled soldiers would react like puppets and fire without thought. And they would aim at Adam.

She crossed the deck to stand as near to the marines'

captain as she dared, which put her in the line of fire between Adam and at least half the soldiers. No one told her to move, although Fenton beckoned her to join him, a worried frown on his round face. She did not think they would shoot with her in the way and if the moment came her presence might cause confusion. She ignored him.

Surreptitiously, she loosened the strings at the neck of her reticule. She would shoot Goddard herself if she had to, despite quite respecting the man.

Captain Judge stepped forward and Adam straightened up, at the same time gaining a couple of paces in Judge's direction. Judge read the relevant Articles of War and pronounced sentence.

'The prisoner is sentenced to receive five dozen lashes.'

An audible sigh went up from the mustered crew but no one moved.

'Silence!' roared the captain. 'Bosun, carry on.'

The prisoner had been brought up in manacles. These had already been removed and he'd been tied to the grating erected for the purpose, so a flogging had been anticipated. Only the number of strokes had been in doubt. The leather strap was now placed between the victim's teeth.

'Captain. . .' began the surgeon anxiously.

'Silence, sir! I have already listened to what you have to say! You are too soft. The man has persistently offended and must receive his due punishment. I consider five dozen lashes a lenient sentence.'

'But he may not survive. . .'

'Then he will be entered in the muster book as discharged dead! Bosun!'

The evil grin on the bosun's face made Miranda's stomach turn. 'Do your duty, Spencer!' he snapped.

The mate picked up his lash and ran the tails across his palm as the marines' drum rolled. Nervously, he moistened his lips with his tongue.

Everyone else's eyes were fixed either on Judge or the man at the grating, whose back was already a mess of half-healed weals. Miranda's were on Adam. She could sense him gathering himself, waiting for exactly the right moment to act.

In one sweeping movement his sword was drawn and pointing unerringly at Judge's throat. As he moved he shouted, 'Belay that order! Seafires!'

The mate, looking relieved, lowered his cat-o'-nine-tails. Adam continued talking over the sound of short, abrupt scuffles on the quarterdeck and in the main top.

'A single shot,' he warned in ringing tones, 'a move by anyone, will ensure your death, Judge, and that of anyone who attempts to come to your aid. You will notice that all the swivel guns are under the control of my officers. Mr Winchester has been relieved of his sword.'

Zack held the first lieutenant at the point of his own sword. Abe and Tom had knocked out the marines at the swivels and had the guns aimed, Abe at the bunch of officers, including Dick, standing to one side of the captain and Tom at the three lines of marines behind Goddard. Greg Merrick was waving his dirk threateningly at the master. Daniel was behind the swivel in the top.

The helmsmen were keeping the warship on the designated course, apparently uninterested in what was going on around them. But Miranda noticed a tension about their shoulders, the whiteness of their knuckles on the spokes of the wheels.

As for the men of the lower deck, it was difficult for her to see most of them, but some stood on the raised foredeck and others clung to various parts of the rigging. Their expressions were universally ones of expectation. But they had made no move themselves. No one could ever accuse them of mutiny.

'Parole!' thundered Judge. 'You have broken your parole, you pirate! Bosun, ignore him, carry on!'

'If he does, you die, he dies, and many others with you! And I am not breaking my parole. I do not intend to take this ship, although clearly I could, but merely to prevent you from meting out any more inhuman punishments to your people.'

'You cannot stop me, York. Neither you nor anyone else can dictate the way I run my ship. Aboard the *Virago* I am as God! I can do as I please. Under God, I rule here!'

'Under God, aye. God is merciful, Captain Judge. You have no conception of mercy. If you refuse to moderate your tyrannical rule I will see that you are certified unfit for command. In the meantime you will be relieved of this one.'

'Whoever dares to do that will be brought before a court martial and sentenced to be hanged!'

'But I am not in your navy, Captain.'

Adam was taking a great risk, Miranda realised. Judge had only to acquiesce in order to recover com-

mand of the ship and he could then have Adam and the
other Seafires thrown into chains or even hung from the
yardarm, and carry on exactly as before. Except that
were that to happen the Viragos would probably
mutiny.

Adam knew the risk, and held his breath, praying
that his gamble would come off. Judge, he had assessed,
was not a devious man but a stiff-necked tyrant who
could never be seen to give in. It would be beneath his
dignity to surrender his authority. If Judge did choose
to use guile, if he promised to mend his ways, then
Adam would have to chance his arm and rouse the men
to mutiny. Under those circumstances, the Seafires and
Miranda might be safe. But he desperately did not wish
to test the theory.

'My officers will all be charged if they follow your
orders and fail to come to my aid!'

He was trying intimidation still. It seemed to be the
only way he knew of retaining any kind of authority.

'Look round,' offered Adam, sweeping his unoccu-
pied arm but not allowing his sword to waver from
Judge's throat for an instant. 'They are helpless,
Captain. They are incapable of assisting you. Only you
can help yourself, by confessing your error in treating
your people with such insane brutality and promising to
mend your ways.'

'You demand the impossible! Captain Goddard,
shoot this man!'

Relieved that he had assessed the fellow's character
correctly, Adam pricked Judge's throat with the point
of his sword. 'You are inviting a blood bath!'

Captain Goddard was still standing as though cast in

stone. Miranda had seen the shock on his face at Adam's original action, seen him open his mouth to shout a command and then close it again. But Judge would not be easily subdued and Goddard had his duty to perform. He hesitated, glanced anxiously at the nearest swivel and then issued a gruff order.

'Corporal, execute Captain Judge's command.'

Miranda had her hand on the pistol in her reticule but she did not wish to start the shooting. Abe and Tom, grimly determined, were sighting their swivels. They must not fire! Chaos would result.

'No!' she screamed, and flung herself behind Goddard to collide with the corporal—a man renowned for his accurate shooting.

She was conscious of the click of the flint, the splutter of the priming powder as the spark ignited it, of a deafening bang above her head. Despair took her. She had not reached the marine in time to spoil his aim. She had hit him a split second after that deadly report. But so far it had been the only shot fired.

An enormous cry went up from the ship's company but Miranda did not heed it. She clung to the man, regaining her balance, afraid to look to see if Adam had been hit. Of course he had; the corporal would not miss.

A firm hand pulled her off. 'Now look what you've done!' came Captain Goddard's grim voice in her ear.

She looked up. He was under threat from John Fenton's sword and pistol, but was ignoring both. And was that a grin he was attempting to suppress? Chaos had broken out all round, but it was a slightly hysterical chaos which sounded as though people were attempting to subdue a desire to cheer. Then she heard Adam's clear tones addressing the company and relief swamped through her so that she almost fainted. She did not know what had happened, but Adam was alive!

'Hear me, lads!' came his confident, ringing tones. 'We Seafires have not broken our parole and taken your ship! We were intent only on preventing an injustice.' A ragged, spontaneous cheer rose at his words and Adam held up his hand for silence. 'Your captain is dead, therefore Mr Winchester is your commander! Hear him!'

'Well, my lads,' called Winchester, his youthful, long face showing complete confidence despite the strain he must be under, his left hand resting on the hilt of his sword, now restored to its scabbard. 'Discipline aboard this ship must be maintained at all costs. Make no mistake about that. I will not tolerate slackness or disobedience. A King's ship cannot fight when called upon to do so without the strictest discipline. However, you may cut that man down, he has already suffered enough.'

'But, sir,' began the bosun indignantly, 'you must execute the captain's last order! And you must arrest the American prisoners of war! They caused his death!'

'Must, Bosun? Must? You are in error. I now command the *Virago* and my word is law! Cut him down!'

The bosun's mates were ready with their knives. The prisoner was soon standing up rubbing his wrists.

'Thank you, sir,' he called. 'Three cheers for Captain Winchester! Hip, hip—'

The huzzahs rang around the deck. Winchester stood gravely acknowledging the accolade. For a young man of less than thirty summers he had managed the change of command with commendable authority and coolness, considered Miranda, though Adam must be even younger, and look what he had done! She hoped that if Winchester took the two-decker home successfully the Admiralty would see fit to promote him to a ship of his own. The bosun's had been the only dissenting voice. The rest of the ship's complement knew their lieutenant and would follow him.

'Dismiss,' ordered Winchester when the last cheer had died. 'Be about your duties. Doctor, see that Captain Judge's body is dealt with having due regard to his rank. I shall conduct a funeral service tomorrow morning at six bells. We do not have the means to preserve his remains in order to transport them back to England.'

They could have used what was left of the rum ration, Miranda supposed, but no one even suggested wasting good spirit on the carcass of the detested Judge. He would be consigned to a watery grave and all evidence of the cause of his death would be lost for ever.

Adam turned to Winchester. 'I should be glad of a few words with you below, Captain.' Like the man released from punishment, he gave the lieutenant the courtesy title his new command warranted. He indicated Abe, Tom and Daniel, still manning the swivels. 'My officers do still control the ship. They will not, of course, interfere with its normal running. But they will remain at the swivels until our own futures are decided. And that of Miss Dawson. Perhaps she could accompany us below?'

Winchester nodded. 'Very well. Carry on,

Mr Jackson. Oh, and Mr Dawson, go and get some sleep. You are relieved of your double watches.'

'Aye aye, sir!' grinned a delighted Dick. 'Congratulations, Captain York! You did it!'

Leaving the second lieutenant in charge of the deck, Winchester led Adam and Miranda down to the great cabin. It would be his now and once in its privacy he relaxed, though as yet he had not smiled. He knew Adam held the trump cards and was wary.

'So young Dawson was in on the plot, was he?'

'He knew I planned something to prevent an injustice being done, and kept the men quiet, that is all. But his passing the word saved this ship from mutiny and a blood bath.'

'Quite. I wonder the men stood for it as long as they did,' admitted Winchester with a sigh. 'I did what I could to relieve their misery, but Judge's brutality grew steadily worse the longer the voyage lasted.'

'The men knew they had your sympathy, Captain. That is why they will follow you now.'

Winchester nodded and the first glimmering of a smile touched his narrow face. 'What can I do to be of service to you, Captain York?' he asked without further preamble.

'Restore my ship and men to my command and allow us to return to America, where we were headed when we ran across the *Osprey*.'

Winchester pursed his lips. 'I thought that might be your price for freeing this ship from the rule of that tyrant. Is that why you did it?'

Adam grinned. 'No, although I confess the possibility of regaining my command did enter into my calculations. No, I could not stand by and watch that man's merciless punishments at the merest suggestion of an offence, real or fabricated. That topman's death finally decided me. In my opinion, and that of Mr Dawson, who had contact with his sister and informed her of the situation, a mutiny was imminent. All our lives would have been forfeit and Miss Dawson would have been at the mercy of hundreds of crazed seamen.'

'The commander of the *Seafire* would have come to our assistance.'

'Lieutenant Piper? Yes, he might have done. And instigated a sea fight if only to refute any charge of cowardice over the way he surrendered the *Othello*. He might have saved the ship, but he could not have saved us. However, as it happened he was too far off to be disturbed, especially by a single musket shot. May I suggest that you hoist a signal to have him close with us?'

Winchester called for a midshipman and gave the order.

'What of Miss Dawson?' he demanded, turning to Miranda, who had been sitting quietly listening to the two men, wondering what plans, if any, Adam had for her future. Right or wrong, she knew what she wanted, and held her breath as Adam placed one foot on his other knee, removed a strand of hemp from his trouser leg, and settled back more comfortably in his armchair, facing Winchester across the vast mahogany desk.

'She will return to the *Seafire* with me and join the other prisoners I took from the *Othello*. I have, for all practical purposes, recaptured them. My men will expect their share of the head money.'

'And mine, although they cannot claim prize money for the *Seafire*, for our ship was not in sight when she was captured, would be due a salvage payment for bringing her back to Portsmouth.'

Adam settled even more deeply into his chair, his respect for Winchester growing. The man, narrow of body as well of face, was yet possessed of both the physical and mental strength necessary for the task ahead of him. He had become a different man, relaxed, confident, prepared to bargain even under his present difficult circumstances. How he must have suffered under Judge!

Adam appeared to consider, though his mind was already made up. Piper and the others would be nothing but an embarrassment on the *Seafire* and his men would receive plenty of prize money from other sources. He would be well rid of the prisoners of war. But Miranda was a different proposition. His body quickened at the thought of what could lie in store for them once he was back with his ship. Their relationship was fraught with difficulties, but he would not easily surrender her to Winchester.

'Very well,' he agreed, 'I will release the officers of the *Othello* to you.'

'Together with Admiral Dawson's daughter.'

As Adam appeared to hesitate, Miranda stiffened. What should she do if he agreed? Throw herself at him again, plead to be taken to America? Never!

But she had judged too soon. A smile played about Adam's mouth as he said, 'Captain Judge accused Miss Dawson of consorting with the enemy. He noticed,' he added drily, 'that we had become somewhat attached.

She may return with you if she so wishes, but I would choose to keep her with me.'

'He was not the only one to notice your, er, partiality for Miss Dawson,' responded Winchester, equally drily. 'Or hers for you, Captain.' He turned to Miranda. 'What are your wishes in this matter, Miss Dawson?'

Miranda swallowed the lump in her throat. Adam had not let her down. Nevertheless, she was mortified to find herself put to the blush by the exchange.

'My father is stationed in Barbados,' she reminded both men. 'I should be nearer to my family in America. It might take me many months to find another warship agreeable to giving me passage out to join them. I would rather cross the Atlantic with Captain York.'

Adam had a frown between his eyes. He had admitted his partiality for Miranda but the only reason she had given for wishing to sail with him was her eagerness to cross the Atlantic! Yet, sitting there with hands tightly clasped about the reticule in her lap, her confusion was obvious. The sardonic smile on Winchester's face told that he had noticed it too. She was, understandably, too shy or too ashamed to admit her desire to be with him.

'I see,' murmured Winchester. 'But I believe I must insist that you return to England. I shall have to face a court martial upon my return, when I shall have to account for all my actions, and describe the circumstances leading up to Captain Judge's death. I shall also have to account for the loss of a captured enemy frigate. To be forced to admit the loss to the enemy of a British admiral's daughter as well might stretch the tribunal's credulity. My position will be difficult enough—'

He broke off as Miranda rose to her feet and he saw the pistol pointed steadily at his breast. It was a desperate expedient, yet she felt she had no alternative.

'You may say, sir, that you had no choice. If necessary I will hold you at gunpoint until I am safely off this ship!'

Adam almost burst out laughing at the comical expression on Winchester's face. Surely he realised the gun wasn't cocked?

'Madam!' the commander exclaimed, climbing carefully to his feet and holding out his hands in a warding-off gesture. 'Please be careful with that weapon! I presume it is loaded?'

'Loaded and primed, sir, and I have another in my reticule. I was prepared for every eventuality, you see. But do not be unnecessarily alarmed. I am an excellent shot, taught by my father.'

'I have only to raise my voice and call the marine sentry—'

There was a click as the pistol was cocked. 'For us all to be killed!'

'My dear,' murmured Adam, rising slowly to his feet, 'I do not think you need threaten Mr Winchester. I am certain he will accept your decision—'

'I am taking no chances! Besides, I am giving him a defence at the court martial! The death of Judge he can blame on you! No one will contradict his version of events—'

'Could I not blame that on you as well, Miss Dawson? It was, after all, you who spoiled the marine corporal's aim!'

Miranda opened her mouth to deny the truth of this

accusation, but closed it again. That had been her purpose in barging into the man—only he and she knew that he had deliberately aimed at his captain, and although this mitigated her own sense of treachery for acting against a British officer, she could not condemn the corporal, who had done everyone a good turn, to the hangman's noose. She temporised.

'But the prisoners of war had already taken the ship, Captain. Such accusations will not concern Captain York and his officers once they are back aboard their own ship. As for my actions in connection with Judge's death, I leave your account of those to your instincts as a gentleman! This is another matter. No one, I conceive, will blame me for wishing to cross the Atlantic as soon as possible in the company of Captain York.'

Winchester bowed. 'Your action at the time of Judge's death confirms your regard for Captain York beyond doubt, ma'am. It is unfortunate that you are on opposing sides in this war. But I wish you well. Since you are so determined, I will not oppose your sailing in the *Seafire*.'

Miranda beamed, lowered her weapon and uncocked it, though she still held it in her hand. 'Thank you, Captain.'

'What,' asked Adam mildly, 'did Miss Dawson do that so spoiled the corporal's aim?'

He had been too occupied with keeping his sword pointed at Judge's throat to see anything going on more or less behind him. He had accepted that Judge had been shot by mistake without knowing why.

'Miss Dawson,' drawled Winchester, seating himself again, 'threw herself at the marine to deflect his aim and save your life, Captain. It was perhaps incidental that she also prevented your Lieutenant Windsor from spraying my marines with canister! It was sheer bad luck that the man hit the captain instead.'

'Or good luck—depends which way you look at it,' said Adam, but his eyes had sought Miranda's to verify the truth of Winchester's statement. The fact that hers were lowered in embarrassment confirmed the truth of the matter. She had been prepared to attack her own side to save his life.

Miranda felt dreadful. No wonder Fenton had beckoned her to move to his side! She realised now how carefully he had sited himself out of Abe's line of fire! Yet, unwittingly, her action had saved the British marines from devastation even if it had not actually saved Adam and caused Judge's death.

'Will you be able to convince the court martial?' asked Adam once they had all resumed their seats. It would take the *Seafire* a good hour to come up with the *Virago* for she had dropped a long way to leeward. Zack and the others would have no trouble on deck, he was certain, apart from, perhaps, the bosun. 'Will the bosun cause a problem?'

Winchester smiled. 'I doubt he will survive to bear witness. He has made too many enemies aboard this ship. He will simply disappear.'

Adam did not seem surprised, thought Miranda, herself shocked. 'You mean he will be murdered?' she demanded. 'And you will do nothing to prevent it?'

'What can I do?' asked Winchester with a shrug. 'He has done nothing to warrant his arrest, so I cannot confine him for his own safety. And I cannot act as nursemaid all day and all night. There are plenty of opportunities to slip an unpopular man over the side, Miss Dawson, the seamen have their own form of justice and are quite merciless.'

'It's true, my dear. Do not concern yourself over it. The man deserves to die.' Adam had accepted a glass of Judge's wine and he twirled the glass between his fingers. 'I am puzzled as to why Judge treated young Dawson, an admiral's son, so harshly. One might have thought he would toady to the youth, hoping to influence the father.'

Winchester snorted his scorn. 'Not Judge! Nothing he did could possibly be wrong! A man without mercy himself, he would suppose that the admiral would admire his devotion to duty without fear or favour! But your brother will make a fine officer one day, Miss Dawson. He will pass his examinations with flying colours. I am short of an officer and shall appoint him as temporary lieutenant for the remainder of this voyage. Not long, I grant you, but the appointment will go down on his record.'

'You are very kind, Captain. I trust you will obtain a command of your own soon.'

'A frigate, like yours, York! That would make me very happy.'

'Then here is to your achieving your ambition!' said Adam, raising his glass.

'You know, for an enemy, you are a most congenial fellow,' smiled Winchester, acknowledging the toast.

The two men had much in common, thought Miranda. All Winchester lacked was Adam's charisma.

CHAPTER TEN

THE *Virago* had shortened sail to enable the *Seafire* to claw her way back to her escort. As the smaller ship approached, Winchester ordered the two-decker to heave to.

While this manoeuvre was being carried out the lookout suddenly yelled a warning.

'Deck, there! Her gun ports are opening, sir!'

Adam and Winchester had already spotted the black holes appearing along the frigate's side, followed almost immediately by the sight of the muzzles of her guns as they were run out.

'Confound it! What the devil is the man thinking of?' exclaimed Winchester. 'Has he run mad? Can't he read our signal to heave to and come aboard?'

Adam had snatched a telescope from the hands of a nearby midshipman and was studying the quarterdeck of his frigate.

'Mr Piper is not on the deck, Mr Winchester.' A smile of sheer delight lit his face. 'The Seafires have recaptured their ship!'

'What?'

'Afraid so.' He scanned the gun ports before lowering the glass. 'Can't you see the US marines? And they are my men behind the guns. Midshipman Lightfoot, the bosun and a master's mate appear to be in command and they're handling her well!'

'Confound it!' exclaimed Winchester again, peering intently through his telescope. 'You're right. How could the dolts allow that to happen?'

'We shall no doubt discover. My men have come to rescue their officers and anticipate having to use force, so they have manned the guns. They will think us still prisoners. I suggest we find a white flag and mount the bulwarks together, Mr Winchester, before they decide to fire! Unless you wish to engage in battle?'

Winchester shook his head and snapped an order. As they leapt up on the bulwarks, clinging to the rigging, he assured Adam, 'We came to an agreement, Mr York. Nothing I shall do will break it.'

'Nor I. We want no unnecessary bloodshed at this stage.'

A midshipman ran to Winchester with a large piece of white bunting flapping in his hand. Winchester snatched the flag and waved it as Adam flourished his sword and hailed his ship. They were too far away still to hear what he said, even with the aid of a speaking-trumpet, but he hoped someone over there would get the message.

Once the *Virago* was hove to Winchester ordered the men of the watch to line the bulwarks and make friendly gestures, but others, on the lower deck, were quietly preparing their guns to fire. 'Don't run them out,' he'd ordered his officers, 'and on no account fire without my express command. But be ready, just in case. They might think this is a ruse.'

Adam feared that too. With the warship's crew prepared to obey their new commander's orders without demur, and having come to an agreement with a man he instinctively knew he could trust, Adam had told his own men to stand down from their captured swivel guns. Now he shouted to the Seafires to wave and cheer from the deserted poop, which they raced to do with such enthusiasm that Daniel almost fell overboard in his eagerness to be seen and understood.

Once again cursing her skirts, which prevented her from climbing up on the bulwarks with Adam, Miranda followed his officers to the poop and pushed her way to the rail. The *Seafire* was slowing down, spilling wind from her sails, hesitating, approaching with caution.

Lieutenant Fenton, whose stentorian voice as he drilled his marines was a joke among the seamen, had captured a speaking-trumpet. 'Sergeant!' he bellowed, his round face red with effort. 'Stand down from your arms! We are free and returning aboard, bound for home!'

Miranda wondered whether his voice had carried, but the distance between the two ships was diminishing fast. She could just about recognise the rotund figure of Fenton's sergeant without the help of a telescope now, could see him hesitate, confer with the bosun and midshipman and then order the soldiers to lower their muskets, which had been levelled at the *Virago* across the hammock nettings and from the tops. Everyone breathed a sigh of relief, although the cannons still pointed menacingly at them. Mr Midshipman Lightfoot, no doubt revelling in his first taste of command, was not about to relinquish his advantage easily.

'I don't blame him,' observed Zack. 'I'd be cautious in his position.'

Greg Merrick, almost in tears, groaned. 'Why didn't

they leave me behind? That could have been me commanding the *Seafire*!'

'I'm glad to see the boy has learnt some of the lessons I've been trying to teach him,' remarked Tom Crocker drily, eyeing the midshipman's course and sail handling with approval.

Abe, his tension somewhat relaxed, laughed as he answered Merrick's moan. 'Penalty of being the senior midshipman, Mr Merrick. But you played your part in preventing a mutiny here. Don't be greedy.'

'The cap'n's going to speak,' said Daniel.

'Listen!' ordered Zack.

Adam's distorted voice echoed over the two hundred yards of sea still separating the ships. 'All is well, Seafires, we are no longer prisoners! We'll lower a boat and I'll come across. Stand down from your guns and heave to.'

The bosun answered, presumably because Mr Lightfoot feared his newly broken voice might not carry. 'Aye, aye, sir, but we'll keep the quarterdeck carronades trained, just until you gets here safe.'

'A good compromise,' came Winchester's rueful voice. 'You have your men well taught, Mr York.'

Adam acknowledged the compliment with a grin. 'Accepted,' he shouted back to the bosun. 'Prepare to receive your captain!'

Miranda quickly descended to the quarterdeck and Adam.

'Let me come with you,' she pleaded.

'If Mr Winchester agrees. And it would reassure my men if you would allow my servant, who is also my coxswain, to cox the boat, Captain.'

'Very well,' said Winchester, who was watching the lowering of the quarter boat. 'My own boat crew will row you over.'

Details of the exchange had already been decided. Once Adam was back aboard the *Seafire* and his men reassured, the operation could proceed as planned. Her trunks, Miranda noted, had already been brought up from below, and at that moment were joined by her sea chest and those of Adam and the other Seafires.

A yawning Dick had appeared on deck, wakened no doubt by the shouting and the noise made as the quarter boat was lowered on its davits. Miranda ran across the deck to him.

'I'm going over to the frigate with Captain York,' she explained. 'Here are your pistols, Dicky, thanks for lending them to me and be careful—they are both loaded and primed. The box is hidden in the foot of my cot; you'd better rescue it quickly.'

'You're going?' asked Dick ruefully, accepting his pistols back and tucking them into his belt. 'You're not returning to Portsmouth?'

'No. Captain York is releasing all his other captives, but not me.'

'Of all the—' He drew a breath. 'I'd thought better of him. I'll have a word—'

'No, Dicky. I could have refused.' She hesitated, then confessed, 'I wish to return to the *Seafire* with him.'

Her blush confirmed Dick's growing conviction as to her feelings and he shook his head. 'Are you certain, Mirrie? He's a fine fellow and I have cause to be eternally grateful to him, but he's an American!'

'I know, and an enemy. Somehow, Dicky, it doesn't

seem to matter any more. You see. . .' She lowered her voice and admitted something she had scarcely dared to even think. 'I love him. If possible I want to spend the rest of my life with him.'

'Good Lord! What will Father say? He'll never allow it!'

'I don't know. That's what worries me most. But he may not find out until after the war is over and I am free to leave America, unless you decide to betray my confidence when you write.'

'I shan't do that, Mirrie, I promise you. In fact I don't often write, you know.'

'Mama looks for your letters. Be a dear, Dickie, do write, but only say I'm safe and that I've been taken to America; give no details.'

Dick drew her to him and kissed her cheek. 'Be happy, Mirrie. God go with you.'

'And with you, Dickie; keep safe. Mr Winchester says you'll pass your exams with flying colours. I'll expect to hear you've received your commission and become Lieutenant Dawson before long!'

'How?' Dick grimaced.

'Once I reach America the Admiralty will be informed of my whereabouts, I imagine. You could write via them and with luck I'll receive it eventually.'

'Are you ready?'

Adam came up, looked enquiringly at Miranda and held out his hand to Dick. 'Good luck, and thanks for your help. The men behaved supremely well. I guess they approve of you, young fellow.'

'I'm glad to have met you, sir.' Dick hesitated, then, 'Look after my sister,' he said rather gruffly.

Adam placed an arm about Miranda's shoulders. 'I intend to. But the boat is waiting. We must go.'

Final farewells to Mr Winchester and all those they knew were made as they crossed the deck ready to descend into the waiting boat. 'See you later,' Adam called to his officers, still gathered on the poop.

They knew what was happening. Once Adam had reassured his crew, a boat with them aboard would cross with others ferrying British captives to the *Virago*. 'Aye, aye, sir,' they called, saluting.

Adam caught Miranda as she followed him down into the heaving boat and held her a moment longer than was strictly necessary, sending messages of awareness winging along her nerves. Together, they sat on a thwart in front of Daniel, who sat at the tiller with the boat's usual coxswain beside him. Daniel gave the orders to the British seamen, who cast off and rowed across the swell to the *Seafire*. At times, as the small boat dipped into a deep trough, Miranda lost sight of the frigate apart from the tops of its masts and sails. But her spirits were so high she could have shouted for joy just knowing it was there and that she would soon be back on board. With Adam.

The bosun's squealing pipe was drowned by a spontaneous cheer as Adam climbed aboard, the first up the side, as tradition demanded.

Close behind him, Miranda's eyes reached the level of the entry in time to see Midshipman Lightfoot salute smartly and cry, 'Welcome back on board, sir!'

Miranda, followed by Daniel, stepped onto the deck. Adam gave Miranda a brief smile and turned back to the midshipman. He looked around the deck, which showed signs of recent conflict. A pile of discarded weapons lay near the mast and a dark stain on the scrubbed planking looked remarkably like blood.

'Congratulations, Mr Lightfoot! You had to fight for possession?' he enquired.

'Aye, sir. But we outnumbered 'em by four to one, they didn't stand a chance.'

'Any dead or wounded?'

Mr Lightfoot looked grave. 'Lieutenant Piper is dead, sir. He fought bravely. I'm afraid the English marine on duty guarding us was killed after he shot one of our men as we took him by surprise. Several other English and two more of our people were wounded as well.'

Adam's brows came together in a frown. 'Mr Piper is dead? He was to go back in the boat in exchange for me. Mr Gander will have to go instead. Bring them all on deck.' He turned to Miranda. 'Wait for me in my cabin.'

She nodded. Adam was in possession of his command again. Her sea chest had been brought over with her and immediately taken below. She would be glad of a moment to freshen up and change.

She had many moments. The ships lay alongside each other for an hour or more as the British prize crew, numbering some fifty men, were ferried across to the *Virago* with all their possessions.

The moment the great guns had been withdrawn, unloaded and lashed down, Daniel had set the cabin to rights, restoring Adam's things as Adam liked them, removing all traces of Mr Piper's occupation. The lieutenant's body had gone across to the British ship with Mr Gander, as had that of the marine. The wounded had been taken across too, once the *Seafire*'s surgeon had attended to them.

Miranda, washed and changed back into her midshipman's clothes, was soon on deck again to watch the operation, emerging in time to bid farewell to Mr Haskett. She had grown quite fond of the master of the *Othello*. She looked about her for Will Welland, but he was not among those still waiting to be taken across. He must have already gone, or not been part of the prize crew.

It did not take her long to reacquaint herself with the Seafires. The seamen grinned, saluted, and told her they were glad to have her back with them.

The last boat was about to leave the side of the *Seafire*. Lieutenant Fenton had the muster book of the prize crew in his hand and was marking off the British seamen as they went down the side. As the last boat prepared to cast off, he called a halt.

'There's a midshipman missing,' he told Adam. 'William Welland.'

Miranda stiffened. Will missing? How could that be?

'He was in the prize crew?' Adam demanded.

'Aye, sir, he's listed here. Seems as though Piper and all the old Othellos were; it was a way of sending 'em back to England to give an account of themselves before being posted to other ships, I guess.'

'Very well. Ask our people if they saw what happened to Welland.' As the marine lieutenant moved off Adam leaned over the side and called down to the bobbing boat below, 'Do any of you men remember seeing Midshipman Welland recently?'

After a short conference the call came back from Tony Keeper. 'Last seen on deck with his dirk in his hand.' There was a slight sneer in the boy's voice which Miranda resented on Will's behalf. 'One of the escaping prisoners picked him up and set him aside. No one remembers seeing him since.'

'Rather than kill the lad, I expect,' mused Adam to no one in particular, returning to await Fenton's report. 'He'd become quite popular with the hands.'

When questioned, the man who had picked the boy up vowed he had not hurt a hair of the lad's head and had most certainly not tossed him overboard, though after that he seemed to have disappeared.

'Mr West, have the men search the ship,' ordered Adam. 'He may be lying somewhere wounded.'

It took no more than five minutes for a team of men to sweep through the ship. Will Welland was nowhere to be found.

'Check that he's not already gone across, his name might not have been marked off,' Adam instructed Tony Keeper. 'Signal the result. One arm raised if he's there, two if he's not. If he's not, Mr Gander will have to enter him in the muster book as dead. He must have gone overboard during the fighting.'

Miranda felt sadness at the thought that Will was dead. He'd been a lovable child. As the boat pushed off without him she looked across to where James Stirling was standing gazing steadfastly at the planks beneath his feet. He must be mourning too.

They waited while the boat rowed across and enquiries were made on the *Virago*, then saw Winchester raise both arms above his head, signalling that Will had not been taken across.

'Very well. A pity,' remarked Adam. 'Prepare to make sail and to fire the salute.'

A gun roared out from the *Virago*, followed immediately by one from the *Seafire*. Six times the blank shots were exchanged before Adam gave the order to proceed. 'Right, Mr Crocker,' he said, 'you were given our exact position by Mr Winchester's master. Set a course for Madeira, if you please.'

Tom grinned. 'Aye, aye, sir. By my reckoning we should sight the island by tomorrow morning.'

He gave the helmsman the bearing. Sail orders were bellowed, men leapt to obey, the ship heeled and steadied on its new course. Behind them, the *Virago* had resumed her progress to Portsmouth. Already, the distance between the two ships was widening. Soon the *Virago* and her dead captain would be no more than an unpleasant memory.

But not just yet. The remembrance of that almost paralysing fear as the marine had aimed his musket was still with Miranda. She could not quite believe that the ordeal aboard the *Virago* was over, that the menace of ugly mutiny had gone, that she was safe with Adam.

He, meanwhile, turned to Zack. 'Have the cook light the galley fires and serve a meal. And see that every man receives a double ration of spirits. Carry on, Mr West. I am going to my cabin.'

Miranda remained where she was, in her favourite spot at the taffrail. Adam had forgotten her, she imagined, in his eagerness to resume command and to settle in below. He managed to forget her all too easily, she thought gloomily. Sailors! He was just like all the others she knew. His ship stood head and shoulders above everything else in his affections. While she could think of little else but him.

But they were safe, safe, safe, and even Adam's neglect paled into insignificance when she remembered that. Besides, it was stupid to be jealous of a ship.

A rumble in her stomach reminded her that they'd missed dinner again but it was some time before Daniel appeared at her side. Time Miranda had spent in worried speculation.

'Cap'n sent me to tell you a meal is served, missie.'

'My thanks, Daniel.' Miranda smiled up into his face. 'You must be glad to be back on the *Seafire*.'

His grin widened. 'We all are, missie. Worse than a sea fight, that was, watching things go from bad to worse, feeling helpless. But the cap'n, he wasn't goin' to let any bunch of mutineers get the better of him!'

'Thanks to him they never became mutineers,' Miranda reminded him as they crossed the deck to the companion ladder. She shivered. 'I reckon I shall have nightmares about that ship for a long time to come.'

'Not you, missie,' said Daniel confidently.

Miranda didn't know what to expect from Adam now he was back in command. She had spent the last hour fretting about it. He'd implied that once in his own cabin—but maybe that had only been a sop to pass over the awkward moment when he'd refused to—

She still went hot and cold all over when she thought of her unbelievably forward behaviour the previous night. Behaviour that, were it known, would ruin her reputation and brand her a traitor. Yet one part of her could not regret it. If only Adam had meant what he'd said! It was because of their improved relationship that she'd dared to go to him, and he'd been roused, she knew, but by all she'd heard men were easily stirred, especially by ladies of easy virtue, which was how she must have appeared to him. She could never bring herself to throw herself at him again and, if he did not care for her, now they were safe he might simply revert to treating her as he had before the disastrous engagement with the *Osprey*.

Yet he had kept her with him. Because he truly wanted her with him, or because he sought favour with his admiral and she was a valuable hostage?

One minute she was full of hope, the next sunk in a fit of the dismals. Her uncertainty kept her on an emotional see-saw, her feelings in constant turmoil. Supposing Adam simply thought her easy and took what she had offered without serious commitment himself? Could she live with that?

She didn't know. She'd protested that she hadn't been thinking of marriage, but that had been when she'd believed that day might be her last and before she'd realised the true depth of her feelings for him. Now the future stretched ahead, a glorious future if Adam loved her as she loved him, but if she gave herself to him and he did not care it would become a wilderness through which she would have to wander without hope or direction once this passage to America had been accomplished.

But she still had the best part of a month before they reached their destination. Lack of wind or storms might delay the ship further. Or they might run into another enemy. That thought made her shiver. But if she could not win Adam's love before they reached Annapolis she would at least have something to remember for the rest of her life. Taking a deep breath, she came to the conclusion that she might just as well live for the day and not fear for the future. Tomorrow might never come.

She was still on a see-saw of emotions when she reached the great cabin, but of one thing she was certain. She would not beg again. Her innate dignity would not allow it. Adam must make the next advance. If he made it she would give herself up to him. Meanwhile, she would behave as though that embarrassing incident had never occurred.

The table was set for two, a simple meal, lit by candles in a darkening cabin. One could have called it an intimate setting. Her hopes lifted slightly.

'I should have changed,' she apologised, with a little laugh to hide a new embarrassment.

'I've heard it said that clothes maketh the man, but men's clothes could never make you less than a woman, Miss Dawson. Here—' he pulled out a chair with a flourish '—do sit down.'

Miranda supposed that was intended as a compliment despite the formality of his address but she did not blush as she might have done a few days ago. Blushing was for stupid chits and she seemed to have aged years over the last eight and forty hours. She could scarcely believe that she had become a watering pot and wept into Adam's shoulder because her brother was unhappy and a mutiny threatened. Or even that, in order to satisfy her own immature urge to know what it was like to be loved by Adam before facing an ordeal which might end in their death, she had gone seeking a union he was not willing to consummate. The memory of that escapade and his refusal to accommodate her could still mortify her.

She was hungry, but scarcely noticed what she was eating while maintaining a flow of small talk designed to ease the tension which had sprung up between them now they were alone together. She managed to make him laugh as she related tales of her experiences at the Academy. Adam, prompted by her, spoke a little of his family and his early days at sea. He drank rather more wine than usual, she noticed, and appeared ill at ease, but who could blame him, when she had so far forgotten herself as to behave in such an outrageous manner? Neither of them could forget her intrusion into his cabin. Things could never be the same between them again.

Hot soup was followed by cold meats, fresh vegetables and fruits from Las Palmas. Finally, wiping her sticky fingers on a napkin, smiling brightly, she pushed back her chair.

'I'll leave you to your port. God give you a good night, Captain.' If he wanted to retreat into formal forms of address, she would oblige. 'Thank you for taking me off the *Virago*. I am glad to be back in my cabin here once more.'

Adam had been listening to Miranda's chatter with wry resignation. She was nervous and he did not blame her. That was why he'd opened up a little, spoken of his family, of his early life. At least they knew each other better now.

What the devil was he supposed to do? Did she still want him to take her to bed? He doubted it. She'd said she loved him, but now she was doing her best to keep him at a distance. Her visit to him had been born of desperation out of fear. And as a gentleman he must forget her advances, subdue his own raging desire, for she was not to be taken lightly. Hence his defensive need for formality. Yet, were she willing... He had never wanted a woman so much, and her boyish garb only added to his titillation, for it could not hide the voluptuous curves endowing her body. No, not an exaggeration, for although small she was strong and beautifully formed. And had a mind and spirit to match. She had cried for her brother and for them all, had shown fear, but reacted with courage. Her rash action had saved his life. He owed her. He wanted her, was willing to risk his honour for her sake, but if she wanted to go he must let her, whatever the cost to himself.

'I thought you might have preferred to remain with your brother,' he remarked, and awaited her response with well-concealed tension.

She could not confess her need to be with him, it would be too lowering. 'I shall be nearer my parents in America,' was the only excuse she could think of.

His brows lifted. Remembering all the difficulties, not entirely fabricated, with which he had once attempted to deter her, he was not entirely convinced by her thin pretext. 'I see. Will you not have another glass of wine?' he asked in an attempt to delay her departure. He could not bear to lose her company yet.

She shook her head as she stood up. 'No, thank you, Captain.' She dared not stay. Being so near to him was torture. If she did not get out soon she would lose her resolve, break all her vows and throw herself into his arms.

He stood too, walking round the table to take a studiously polite leave of her. But, the devil, how he wished she were staying! His frustration threatened to deprive him of his senses, of his fragile hold on honour. All he wanted was to have her in his arms, to prove that she was still alive, to lose himself in her, to forget the appalling events of the last couple of days, have them wiped from his consciousness in the joy of knowing she was safe. And his.

They met near the cabin door. Adam took her fingers in his and bent over them, meticulously correct. Yet even that impersonal touch agitated Miranda, who would have snatched her hand back except that to do so would show lack of conduct. Lack of control.

Perhaps because they were both distracted, the sudden corkscrew motion of the ship took them by surprise. Even Adam lost his balance for a moment though he recovered instantly, but as Miranda, who had not, staggered into him his arms automatically closed about her.

It was as though a charge of powder exploded between them. Miranda actually gasped with the shock of his embrace, while Adam's arms tightened and his head came down and his mouth found hers.

Miranda had flung her arms about his neck and when he lifted his head momentarily to take a gasping breath she pulled it down again, her lips seeking his, her fingers digging into his thick hair. As their passion rose she grasped his queue, and, in her abandonment, tugged at it.

As the frigate corkscrewed again Adam instinctively kept them both balanced, though they staggered back to collapse on the settee. She was underneath him now, her fingers untying the ribbon on his queue, teasing out the plaits, releasing his long hair to hang down around her face.

He had unbuttoned her jacket. His lips were still on hers, his tongue exploring the sweetness of her mouth, as he searched for the buttons on her shirt so that he might feel the satin skin beneath.

He had just succeeded in freeing one generous breast, which fitted so perfectly into his palm, when the sentry knocked on the door.

With a smothered imprecation, Adam leapt to his feet. 'What is it?'

'Mr Merrick, sir. Message from Mr Windsor.'

Miranda had sat up and quickly fastened her jacket. There could be no restoring his hair to its queue, but he must see what Windsor wanted.

'Send him in,' he said, striding to meet the lad by the door. With luck, he would not notice Miranda's dishevelment.

Greg Merrick entered, saluted. 'Mr Windsor's compliments, sir, but the wind has risen and veered so he proposes to shorten sail and alter course a point or two. With your approval, sir.'

Only now did Adam become aware of the rain pelting down on the deck above and spattering from the open skylight. 'My compliments to Mr Windsor and I'll come up,' he said, reaching for his tarpaulin.

'Aye, aye, sir.'

Merrick disappeared and Adam went back to Miranda. He touched her cheek, took her hand, placed a kiss in her palm and closed her fingers over it. 'Keep it until I get back,' he murmured. 'I shall not be long.'

CHAPTER ELEVEN

SEEING Adam struggle into his tarpaulin as he left the
cabin brought Miranda's attention to the drops of rain
spattering in through the skylight. Trembling, far from
in command of her mind or her senses, she struggled to
her feet and made her way across a deck which was
pitching and rolling with alarming violence, intending
to shut it. She clung to the table, grabbed at sliding
dishes and glasses.

Daniel knocked and entered.

'Sudden squall, missie,' he informed her, unconcerned, as he closed the skylight. 'I'll light a lantern and
douse the candles, it'll be safer. Then I'll take care of
those things.'

'I'll put the decanter back behind its bar on the
sideboard,' offered Miranda, hoping Daniel would not
notice the unbuttoned shirt beneath her jacket. Or her
neckcloth, lying discarded on the settee. He did not
seem to.

The squall had come at an opportune moment; it had
literally thrown them into each other's arms, removing
at a stroke all the doubts, all the reservations between
them. If they had not been interrupted anything might
have happened. At least she now knew beyond any
doubt that Adam desired her. Dressed as she was, too.

All the same, the interruption had given her a chance
to think again. She stood on the edge of a moral and

social precipice. If she jumped off there could be no turning back. In the eyes of the crew and the world at large she would be the captain's doxy, mistress of a man her father and brothers were sworn to fight. Was that truly what she wanted?

Yes. For she loved him and did not care what anyone else thought of her. With still shaking fingers, she unbuttoned her jacket again. He could, if he wished, finish what he had begun and she would help him.

A thrill of urgent, almost alarming excitement rushed through her at the thought of Adam's return. Wicked, ruinous, against all the rules of conduct it might be, but she did not care. She'd had a foretaste of rapture and here on the high seas convention did not exist. At least, it did not for her!

True to his promise, Adam was not long on deck, returning to drip pools of water all over the cabin's sailcloth-covered deck. Daniel appeared to relieve him of the streaming tarpaulin and hand him a towel, and was promptly dismissed for the night.

Rubbing at his wringing-wet hair, Adam looked at her sideways and gave a rueful laugh. 'What a downpour! But it has rinsed the salt from my hair!'

'Let me rub it dry for you.'

Adam paused, standing as though paralysed. 'Would you?'

'Come here,' ordered Miranda with new-found confidence, patting the settee beside her.

As he sat, Miranda knelt up, took the towel and began to use it with a slow, rhythmic motion which both found almost unbearably stimulating.

'You waited,' murmured Adam at last, his breathing

somewhat ragged, his voice muffled, although that might have been because of the towel and his luxuriant, tousled hair.

Miranda tried to subdue her thumping heart as, throwing aside the towel, she ran her fingers through the tangles the drying had caused. 'Yes, Adam, I waited. Do you have a comb?'

He ignored the question of a comb. 'Then you still want—?' He seemed afraid to go on.

Miranda hugged his dark head to her, damp hair and all. 'More than ever.'

At that he turned and dragged her into his arms. 'Miranda, my little love!' His voice was little more than a groan.

It happened all over again, the explosion of feeling, the reckless abandon. They'd both had time to think, but the parting had only fuelled their need for each other.

For Adam it was so unexpected, this wanting of a small, seemingly fragile creature he had come across by chance under circumstances so unusual as to be almost impossible. Yet she, for all her youth and innocence, was meeting his fierce demand with an abandon which astonished him. But he needed more; he needed to lose himself in her, to know that she belonged to him, at least for now. In the throes of passion, he was incapable of contemplating the future, the end of the *Seafire*'s cruise, the inevitable parting. Or of considering that, for the first time in his life, he would be depriving a young girl of her virginity. Guilt had no place in his emotions at that moment.

While Miranda had thrown any such considerations

aside, together with caution. Why be cautious when, so many times in the past few days, her life had hung by a thread? Might do so again at any time? No, she loved Adam and wanted, longed to give herself to him, to be part of him, to feel they belonged together. Even if that belief should prove to be an illusion. For they came from different worlds and Adam did not want a wife.

But the tiny spear of pain that thought brought was quickly swamped by other, more immediate, more urgent sensations as Adam swiftly removed her garments and she, her innocence tempered by growing up with two brothers and listening to girlish gossip at the Academy, became equally involved in removing his as fast as she was able.

They had not quite finished—both still wore shoes and stockings and Adam his breeches too—when the ship gave another lurch and they were deposited on the floor in a tangle of limbs. Adam's response was to pick her up and stagger through to the darkness of his sleeping place.

The feel of his skin against hers, the soft tickle of body hair against her cheek, thrilled Miranda. He laid her in his swinging cot and stripped off her stockings and half-boots.

The cot was much larger than any other she had seen. She had a moment to notice this while he removed the last of his own garments. Then the bed lurched as he climbed in, landing partly beside and partly on top of her.

She shifted a little to give him more room. 'Lucky you have a large cot,' she murmured, wondering a little jealously why.

'I sprawl,' he explained, pulling up a cover, for the night had turned chilly with the storm.

But they were both talking for the sake of it, to cover the slight embarrassment of actually going to bed together. There had been too many interruptions, otherwise, surely, she would no longer be a virgin, Miranda thought as Adam began his wooing all over again.

The initial, explosive urgency had died. Now he took his time, stroking, kissing, murmuring words of love as he nibbled at the lobes of her ears. She seemed to be drowning in his flowing hair, in the clean scent of him as he bent over her. And then he lowered his lips to caress her breasts. Spears of fire shot through to her vitals and Miranda gasped aloud as her hips moved in response. As he took her nipple into his mouth the sensations multiplied. She moaned her pleasure.

She didn't know how to respond at first, then simply followed her instincts. Now it was Adam's turn to gasp. And then he parted her legs and hovered over her for a long, breathless moment before he whispered, 'Miranda?'

'Yes,' she whispered urgently, her hands pulling him to her. 'Yes, Adam, yes!'

He was so gentle, probing carefully before plunging into her, that the pain barely registered. For Miranda, surrendering herself completely to the exquisite sensations, responding with all the ardent passion and love of youth, time ceased to exist as she rejoiced in the rhythm of their union. The cot, rasping and creaking on its tackle as it swung, became a small island of delight. For the two people in it it represented their entire world. Adam gave no thought to who might hear and speculate, for aboard his own command he ruled supreme.

Adam, roused almost beyond reason, taken beyond endurance by the sweetness and warmth of her, by the sheer exuberance of her response, had to let go. But he had held out long enough to take Miranda with him. And the joy this knowledge gave him added to his own completion. After long moments in the limbo of his little death, he returned to awareness to find that Miranda was lying beneath him, her fingers playing idly with his hair, taking strands to her lips and kissing them.

'My sweet,' he murmured, touching her mouth gently with his own.

She clasped him to her fiercely, afraid that it might all turn out to be a dream. But it was not. This had been her true awakening to womanhood. To her, it was her wedding night. No one could regard her as a green girl now. And Adam had been wonderful. She spared a moment from her euphoria to feel jealous again—of all the women who had contributed to his experience. In view of Zack's remark that first evening, she doubted there had been many. But there must have been some.

'I shouldn't mind dying now,' she murmured, stroking his smooth, muscled shoulders.

He rolled off her and gathered her into his arms, holding her tightly against him. 'You are not going to die,' he asserted fiercely. 'You are too precious. Besides, I promised your brother to take care of you!'

'So you did. He wondered what Papa would say and wished you were not captain of an enemy warship.'

'So do I, believe me! But this war cannot last long. And then...'

'And then?' whispered Miranda.

'We shall have to see.'

No promise of lasting love. No proposal of marriage. But why so disappointed? In that moment she felt far older than Adam. Whereas she was prepared to give her entire life to him, he was not yet ready to make any such commitment. A naval captain had to be young, carefree, prepared to risk his life time after time. How could he shoulder the responsibilities implicit in marriage?

She did understand. How could she fail to, when her own mother had more than once ruefully remarked that her father should not have wed? His duty to the navy would always come first with him, she'd said. Not until he'd been made Vice-Admiral of the Blue and posted to Barbados had he managed to spend more than short, infrequent periods with his wife and family. Communications being what they were, he'd not even known she, Miranda, was on the way until he'd arrived home one day to find her staggering about clutching a rag doll and asked who she was!

Now, of course, with a port posting, it was different; he could have his family with him. Her mother and younger sister, Chloe, were already in Bridgetown, where she had been meant to join them.

She snuggled closer to Adam. 'You know, I've no wish to reach Barbados at all. All those gossipy women, the eternal tea and dinner parties, the evening soirées and balls. I'd rather remain at sea. I used to be so envious of my brothers!'

'Aren't you still?' he asked in a teasing voice, with a subtle caress that sent an ecstatic shudder running through her.

'Well, I no longer wish I was a boy, if that's any comfort to you! You, my dearest captain, have made me realise just how wonderful it is to be a woman! If I could somehow remain at sea. . .'

He was too busy kissing her to answer at once. Then he said, 'Some captains allow women on their ships, but to my mind women aboard a warship must only be a liability, my love—even women as intrepid as you. Have I thanked you for saving my life?'

He kissed her again, his hands wandering deliciously about her body. Miranda fought down an inclination to let him go on thinking he owed her his life. She could never live with that kind of lie.

'I didn't save it,' she told him when she could speak again. 'The marine aimed at Captain Judge, not you.'

He shot up on one elbow to look down at her and the cot swung violently. 'But you threw yourself at him and spoiled his aim! Everyone saw you!'

Their eyes were used to the dark now. He saw her shake her head. 'I was too late. He fired seconds before I hit him. But I didn't say anything earlier because I didn't want to get him into trouble.'

'A musket is not terribly accurate at that distance,' muttered Adam. 'Are you certain, Miranda?'

'As sure as I can be. He had the reputation of being the best shot, after all; that's why he was ordered to shoot you. No one expected him to miss, least of all Captain Goddard, who hated giving the order.'

'So,' mused Adam, sinking down again, 'it was

mutiny, after all. And the fellow will get away with it, thanks to you.'

'Aren't you glad? I am!'

'I don't know. It could become a dangerous precedent. The marines are supposed to put down mutinies, not collude in them! The man may think he can do it again.'

'He was driven, like everyone aboard the *Virago*, us included. But let us forget all that, Adam. It is over now, you have your ship back—'

'And shall not have to face an inquiry when I reach port!'

'Or spend months or years in a British prison!'

'From which it would have been my duty to escape.'

'Huh!' said Miranda. 'Fat chance! And how would you get back to America?'

'Via France, perhaps,' he said, knowing that would annoy her. 'She is an ally.'

She pounded his chest with her fists. 'Don't talk to me about France! Thank goodness Napoleon lost the battle of Leipzig! He surely cannot raise yet another army. We must defeat him soon.'

Adam pinned down her fists and lay on top of her again. 'I don't care about Napoleon,' he murmured, 'and the only person I want to conquer at the moment is you.'

Miranda put up no resistance.

By morning the gale had abated, but they'd been forced slightly off course. Instead of sighting Madeira at dawn they saw the conical peak of Porto Santo, altered course and, later, the larger, mountainous, volcanic island of

Madeira itself became a recognisable smudge on the horizon. Miranda watched as they approached, fascinated by its steep green lower slopes and the layer of cloud hovering about the volcano's rugged peak.

The *Seafire* came to an anchor in a sheltered cove to the west of Funchal, avoiding being seen by any ships of the line possibly anchored there by approaching from the north-west, passing by the high cliffs of Cabo Cirao with Miranda's eye glued to a glass so that she could see the strange, grotesque shapes of the rocky outcrops, the caves and inlets worn away by the storms which lashed the coast from the Atlantic. Turning south, they passed the Ponta do Pargo, the most westerly point, and finally beat against the wind into a sheltered anchorage on the less rugged south-eastern shore. Even so Adam ordered a masthead watch to be maintained and sent men to a nearby headland, telling them to fire three warning musket shots if they saw danger approaching.

'I have no intention of being caught anchored in a bay by a British warship,' he explained. 'But we should have an hour or so to slip out if one is sighted.'

Meanwhile the watering party was busy carting empty barrels on deck and lowering them into the water, where they were strung in a long line to be towed ashore, bobbing like corks, by one of the ship's boats.

'While they are filling them from the spring, I'm going inland to purchase some wine,' Adam told Miranda. 'Do you want to come?'

Without a town nearby to put a stench into the air, the delicate perfumes of the land were on the breeze, a persuasive argument for sampling them at closer hand. Besides, she did not want to be parted from Adam.

'Yes, please. Is it far?'

'Up through the terraces of the vineyards. If the warning guns are fired we can be back in less than half an hour.'

They were rowed ashore and Adam took her hand as they began to climb through the arbours formed by the vines sprouting on supports above their heads, which sheltered them and the crops growing in their shade. Sometimes they walked beside irrigation channels. Miranda noticed again, as she had on Gran Canaria, that the ground seemed to heave under her at first. This time, though, the fragrance of warm, moist earth and growing vegetation met her nostrils, not the reek of rotting garbage encountered in a port.

They were not alone, of course. A string of half a dozen seamen followed them, ready to carry the casks of wine and any fresh fruit and vegetables available down to the beach, and a couple of marines had come along to afford protection.

'You know the way,' remarked Miranda as Adam unhesitatingly followed the paths.

'I have been before. Madeira, in all its forms, whether it be the sweet after-dinner malmsey, the medium-sweet, lighter bual or the dry sercial, is the favourite wine at home. It has brandy in it and benefits from the long sea voyage across the Atlantic in tropical climes, particularly if it crosses the equator!'

'Will we cross the equator?'

'Not this time, I fear, even for the benefit of the Madeira.'

'I'd like to cross the equator one day.'

She sounded wistful. Adam smiled. 'Who knows? Perhaps you will.'

It was a cheerful, happy party that arrived at the *quinta*. Miranda luxuriated in the amazing perfumes and colours of the shrubs and trees of the gardens surrounding the stylish mansion and outbuildings while Adam negotiated for his wine and other stores. It was an equally high-spirited group which made its way down again with butts of Madeira and baskets of produce hoisted on all shoulders. Even the marines and Adam were carrying something, Adam a small cask of best French brandy.

Miranda, carrying a net of freshly baked bread, could not have been happier, mostly because Adam was there.

The watering had almost been completed by the time they reached the beach. The boat towing the last string of filled barrels, now lower in the water, though barrels filled with fresh water still floated in the sea, had just hooked on to the frigate.

'No alarm,' remarked Adam as he lifted her into the boat awaiting their return. 'We'll be away within the hour.'

'A pity. It would be nice to stay longer. I'd like to go right to the top of the volcano, up among the clouds.'

He shook his head. 'Sorry; it'd be dangerous to remain long. I'll be glad when the men on the headland are back on board.'

They pulled away from the beach, leaving a smaller ship's boat to transport the lookouts. The moment he had seen the captain on his way back, Zack had given the order for the blue and white flag known as the Blue

Peter to be hoisted—a signal for the lookouts to return to their ship.

Once they were safely aboard, Adam weighed anchor without further delay, setting the frigate on a course far enough west to avoid the Canaries while still travelling south to meet up with the trade winds. Madeira was well behind them when Lieutenant Fenton presented himself on the quarterdeck, stamping his boots in a smart salute.

'Yes, Fenton, what is it?'

'I have to report a stowaway aboard, sir. I have him under guard below.'

'A stowaway? Where the devil did he come from? It is a he, I trust? Who is it?'

'A midshipman from the *Othello*, sir. William Welland.'

'Will!' exclaimed Miranda. 'He's not dead after all?'

'Seems not, ma'am.'

Miranda heaved a sigh of relief. 'Thank God!'

'Where did you find him?' demanded Adam curtly.

'He crept out for air while most of the people were ashore, sir. The bosun's mate caught him emerging from the forward hatch. Seems he'd been hiding in the cable tier.'

Adam's expression was grim. 'And no one thought it his duty to inform me before we weighed?'

'No, sir,' admitted Fenton uncomfortably. 'You were occupied, and we did not imagine you would put him ashore on Madeira.'

Adam glowered. 'It is not for my officers to decide what I should do!'

Fenton's face had gone more red than usual. 'No, sir.'

'The damage is done now. You may inform the other officers concerned in this deception of my severe displeasure!'

Lieutenant Fenton clicked his heels and stamped again in a dignified salute. 'Very well, Captain.'

'As for the boy—he was certain to be discovered when we weighed again! Stupid child! Doesn't he know the penalty for desertion?' It was a rhetorical question which no one answered. 'Have him brought to my cabin in ten minutes.'

'Yes, sir!'

Fenton saluted again and disappeared below. Miranda looked at Adam's harsh expression and shifted uncomfortably.

'They were right, weren't they? You wouldn't have left him abandoned on Madeira. What will you do?'

'I cannot condone insubordination.' He made an irritable gesture, the pleasure of the day's excursion spoilt by the necessity to reprimand his officers. 'It's damned embarrassing! What can I do? Clap the lad in irons? Hand him over to the next passing British warship? Take him back to the United States as a prisoner of war? I'll decide when I've heard what he has to say.'

'He hated the *Othello*.'

'Most youngsters hate life as a midshipman when they first join.'

'Most of the seamen seem to hate life at sea too. Especially those landsmen who have been pressed or who accepted service in the navy instead of a sentence in gaol.'

'You're talking about the British navy when you

speak of pressed men. But even volunteers find it an alien, harsh, overcrowded, evil-smelling environment at first. The ship's boys are probably the happiest—they mostly come from very poor homes or even the gutter; they're used to being cuffed and don't expect much in the way of comfort.'

Miranda nodded and indicated the three or four boys, including Billy Crow, who were skylarking up in the rigging, climbing about like monkeys. 'They seem perfectly happy.'

'And will make first-class able seamen in a few years. But, unlike them, a midshipman is most likely used to a soft life at home and is suddenly thrust into an over-crowded, possibly unhappy berth, with every officer seemingly out to make life as difficult as possible for him!' He grinned down at her. 'I hated it too, but luckily I loved the sea and soon grew used to the conditions. Welland would too, given a chance.'

'That's why you brought him aboard the *Seafire*. You told me so at the time.'

'Aye. Well, I'd better go below and see what he has to say for himself.'

'May I come?'

'Provided you don't interfere.'

'As if I would!'

'No, of course not, my love. I had quite forgot how detached you can be!'

Miranda coloured, both at the endearment and the reminder of previous interventions she had made. But they'd all been for the best, hadn't they? And Adam's whole attitude told her he was funning her.

A dishevelled and rather smelly Will was brought in

by the marine sergeant, whom Adam instantly dismissed. With the sleeping place and storeroom between the cabin and the sentry he was unlikely to hear what was said, and Adam wanted no witnesses to what was about to take place.

'Well, Mr Welland. What have you to say for yourself, pray?'

Will gulped. 'Nothing, sir.'

'Nothing? When you need to explain why you allowed us and the Viragos to think you dead while all the time you were stowed away in the cable tier?'

'I didn't want to fight you, sir. I wanted you to recover the *Seafire*, and I didn't want to go with the others, sir. I've been happy aboard your ship, sir, happier than I've ever been. I wanted to stay.'

'You are a deserter from the British King's navy. If I return you where you belong you will find yourself hanging from a yardarm.'

Will swallowed. 'I know, sir. But I was hoping you'd keep me as one of your midshipmen, sir.'

Adam raised his brows and stared at the lad. Will was showing a remarkable degree of courage at the moment. Gone was the snivelling boy who had been brought aboard as a prisoner of war. Will knew what he wanted and was prepared to fight for it. To risk death for it.

'Supposing the frigate is taken again? You would be discovered as a deserter and hanged.'

'I'd risk that, sir. You said they think me dead. So I could change my name, become an American citizen, and they'd never know.'

Miranda thought it time to interfere at that point.

'What about your family, Will? Have you thought of them?'

'Yes, Miss Dawson. My mother's dead. My stepmother persuaded my father to send me to sea to get rid of me. They'll not be troubled to think me dead. Her son will inherit the estate, which isn't large anyway.'

'I'm sorry, Will. I didn't realise—'

'That's all right, miss. It wasn't that that made me unhappy. And being in action doesn't frighten me any more. At least, not much,' he added honestly.

'You'd be a strange man if you were not afraid sometimes, Welland. By the way, why did we not find you during our search of the ship? Did Mr Stirling help you to hide?'

'James, sir?' Will looked uncomfortable but said, 'No, sir. But he guessed I was down in the bilge, beneath the hold, because we'd laughed about me being small enough to get through the scuttle. He said the cable tier would be safe enough until we anchored.'

'In the bilge? No wonder you stink, young man! James Stirling brought you food?'

'I'd taken some ship's biscuits and cheese down, sir; I haven't needed more yet.' Miranda shuddered as he added, 'The rats were the worst part.'

Adam's response to this was a sardonic smile. 'So I would collect. When were you going to be so obliging as to show yourself?'

'Soon, sir. As soon as we were far enough away from the *Virago*.'

'So when you came up you were expecting to be found?'

'Well, not exactly, sir. I wanted to see where we were.'

'Hmm. I see. What name would you choose were I to grant your request?'

'William Williams, sir.'

'Very well, Mr Williams. I'll have you entered in the muster book and the moment we reach the United States you may apply for American citizenship. Meanwhile, as punishment for evading your true duty and causing me to take a difficult decision, you may climb to the fore masthead and remain there until I say you may come down.'

Will saluted smartly, his face beaming. 'Thank you, Captain.'

'And pass the word for Mr Stirling to come to the cabin.'

As Will left them Miranda went up to Adam and clasped her arms about his neck. 'What will you do to James, Adam?'

'Send him to the main masthead. The young rogues!'

She kissed him. 'Thank you, Adam.'

'What for? Turning young Will into a renegade?'

She shook her head. 'For showing mercy to a rather confused boy. He's too young to feel any allegiance to England when his family have cast him off. And you are his hero.'

'That will not last for long when he has a full taste of my discipline,' asserted Adam grimly.

Miranda rather thought he had underestimated his power to inspire devotion in those he led.

CHAPTER TWELVE

THE days became weeks which passed like a dream for Miranda. The weather held, they picked up the trade winds which swept them westwards at a fine pace, and not only did she spend ecstatic nights in Adam's arms but her days were full of interest and delight, leaving no room for negative thoughts.

The trade wind clouds marched across the sky from east to west like a ranked army of strangely shaped balls of cotton wool. Unfamiliar birds, like boobies and twin-tailed frigate birds, flew past despite their distance from land. Flying fish leapt from the water and even landed on deck, washed aboard by the creaming bow wave. Schools of playful dolphins leapt and dived alongside the ship. Fearsome sharks cruised nearby, hopeful of finding a feast.

Added to all those pleasures was that of joining the midshipmen to learn about the rigging, how to splice a rope, tie a knot, to navigate, and being taught by Adam to read the weather, to trim the sails to suit every condition. In fact, learning all about a ship and how to sail it.

The *Seafire*'s people indulged her. She was the captain's lady, even if she was a foreigner, and if they thought it strange that she should dress like a boy and be interested in seamanship they were too polite to say so.

Adam's reaction passed from indulgent amusement to admiration. He'd thought her worthy of respect and regard before, but this was different. She loved the sea, accepted the discomforts of the life cheerfully, learned quickly and seemed to him the most perfect female he had ever met. As the days went by he was tempted to consider the possibility of making her his wife. He would never, he was certain, meet any other woman to compare with her, who would so wholeheartedly share his interests. She would never desert him while his back was turned. He wanted her for his own.

Yet marriage, even were it possible between them, and he'd need her father's consent, meant more than sailing the seas together and making love, delightful as these occupations were. Marriage meant responsibilities, a family, the obligation to worry about the needs and comfort of others. Of course he did that already, for every Seafire relied upon him for his health, happiness and safety while aboard the frigate. But a wife would be in another class altogether. He would worry about her and his family while he was at sea. As she would no doubt worry about him. They'd miss so much by being separated. No, it would be best in the long run to say farewell when they reached journey's end, painful as that would be, as painful as losing a limb, but men did recover from such an amputation. Look at Admiral Lord Nelson, winning the battle of Trafalgar with one arm and one eye!

And being killed in the doing of it. Still, that had had nothing to do with the loss of his parts.

A nagging voice told him that Lord Nelson had not only had a wife but a much loved mistress as well. Yet he had remained in the British navy, only to be killed, leaving two women behind to mourn him. And Lady Hamilton, it was said, survived on the charity of her friends and the curiosity of others.

He could never condemn Miranda to such a fate! No, if he did not wed her he must set her free. She was young, she would find another, more worthy man to love and cherish her once he was out of her life. A prospect which pleased him not at all. He thrust the pain aside, snapping an unnecessary order to the helmsmen to mind their course.

Their cracking pace was brought to a temporary halt when they ran into a calm. For four days the *Seafire* wallowed in the swell, drifting with the west-running current, for despite setting every stitch of canvas the frigate had no steerageway. The boats could be sent out to tow it along, but this would be hard on the men rowing and scarcely worthwhile, since Adam was in no need of extreme haste.

In these conditions, for the first time ever, Miranda felt the stirrings of seasickness.

'It's the unusual motion,' explained Adam. 'You're normally such a good sailor the sickness is bound to pass off quickly. Certainly the moment we catch a puff of wind strong enough to move us forward again you'll feel better. Do you want to lie down for a while?'

Miranda, sitting in a canvas chair, shook her head, reluctant to leave the shade of the awning spread above the deck. 'It's not bad enough for that. I just feel queasy.'

After twenty-four hours, to her relief, Miranda's sickness did pass off and the next morning she felt well enough to join in the life of the ship again. Some of the men spent the otherwise idle hours scrubbing the decks, polishing the rails and buffing up the brass fittings with brick dust while others hung over the sides, scraping them down before adding a fresh coat to the paintwork. For recreation they fished, and those who could swim frolicked in the water while a lookout kept a wary eye open for sharks.

A small cheer went up when the calm finally gave way to a brisk wind which eased the sweltering atmosphere and allowed the *Seafire* to chuckle through the water again, making a fine bow wave and leaving a spreading wash astern.

Miranda climbed up to the main top, as she often did, and put a glass to her eye. Nothing pleased her better than to sweep the horizon for sight of anything of interest.

The official lookout was on the higher platform, known as the crosstrees, above the topsails, but it was Miranda who called Adam's attention to the dark grey patch on the horizon.

'Squall coming!' he cried. 'Come down at once!'

It was rushing down upon them. Adam ordered most of the sails to be taken in and those remaining to be reefed. Hectic activity up the masts and on deck resulted in his orders being carried out just in time. The last men slid down the rigging as the first of the wind and rain swept across the frigate.

The *Seafire* bucked and swung. Everything shook, banged and creaked. Even with a pocket handkerchief of sail left set, keeping to their course became impossible without risking the masts.

'Alter course to run before it!' shouted Adam and Tom Crocker immediately translated this into directions for the helmsmen while seamen ran to haul round the yards to alter the set of the few remaining sails.

No one bothered with tarpaulins; the officers were all clad in tropical linen, the seamen in little more than duck trousers. Once the squall had passed their clothes, like the decks, would dry in minutes.

The men began to rig sailcloth into enormous basins to catch the rain.

'Why are they doing that?' demanded Miranda. 'We're not short of water, are we?'

'No, we're not, but we may as well fill the empty barrels. It's for washing—both clothes and themselves,' explained Adam. 'You, madam, are privileged to use precious drinking water but if we run short the men often have to use sea water and the salt dries in the clothes and chafes the skin.'

Miranda watched the men, amused, as they unplaited each other's pigtails. 'They're letting their hair loose,' she commented. 'Why don't you free yours?'

'Why not? An extra wash wouldn't do my hair any harm. Perhaps you'd unravel my queue?'

'Certainly, Captain!'

And so, in the midst of a tropical storm, Miranda set about the sensuous task of releasing Adam's hair so that the rain could wash out the salt. It reminded her of the first time they'd made love, when he'd come back to the cabin with his flowing hair dripping water. Queues were a bit old-fashioned, according to her father, but all the ordinary seamen wore them. Dick and many of the other officers kept their hair short, she'd noticed. But she liked Adam with his plaited and clubbed queue. Doubling it up meant it did not dangle down his back but hung tidily at his shoulders. It gave him a distinction no fashionable haircut could have achieved. And she'd have missed the pleasure of running her fingers through its vibrant strands when it was loose.

She removed her boy's cap and shook out her curls. She still wore her hair short, with the help of the ship's barber, it was less trouble to keep in order. Because it was fine and curly she had never been able to grow it long enough to make a decent bun, let alone a pigtail. She envied Adam his luxuriant growth.

The waves grew alarmingly high, each one a huge wall of water towering above their stern before the ship rode up on it and fell back into the trough behind. Sailing the ship became a nightmare which took all Adam's and his officers' skill and the seamen's strength.

'This,' declared Adam eventually, as alert and taut as though he were in action against a human enemy, 'is no squall.'

'It can't be a hurricane—it's not the season,' shouted Zack.

All the officers were quite calm, Miranda noticed as she clung on to the nearest stay, feeling useless, and so were the seamen, although all were on their toes waiting to react to whatever the elements threw at them. The four helmsmen heaving at the double wheel were changed every five minutes, for keeping the bucking ship at the right angle to the wind took all their combined strength.

'Don't worry, this is but a severe storm and the

Seafire could ride out a hurricane if necessary,' Adam reassured Miranda.

Her trust in Adam was absolute. 'I'm not afraid,' she assured him.

He spared her a quick smile. 'Good girl! But we'd better furl the remaining sails if we don't want a mast to go by the board. Give the order, Mr West.'

'Aye, aye, sir.'

Zack used his speaking-trumpet and men swarmed up the rigging to the wildly swaying yards to fight the wet sailcloth and lash it down. Miranda heaved a sigh of relief when the last man returned safely to the deck.

Looking over the stern, Zack remarked, 'With this sea running at us from behind we'll be lucky if we're not pooped. Hadn't the men better make themselves fast?'

Adam nodded. 'Make it so, Mr West. And belay anything movable!'

Zack shouted again and Miranda watched as the seamen took lengths of rope, tied them round their waists and then to any fixed part of the ship within reach.

Adam knotted a rope round her but he had not finished fixing it before he grabbed her, yelling, 'Hold fast!'

A huge wave was curling over them—the stern would never lift in time! She flung her arms around several ropes attached to the mizzen-mast and felt the comforting weight of Adam's body pressed against hers as his arms encircled her and grasped at them too.

The wall of water swept the length of the decks, dragging mercilessly at their bodies, knocking the breath out of them, hurtling anything loose overboard with it. The ship slewed as the helmsmen, like everyone else, were hurled off their feet.

Adam and Zack yelled at the same moment; Zack and Tom staggered up and reached the wheel in time to help the helmsmen's struggle for control. If the ship turned far enough to be sideways on to the waves they would capsize and all would be lost. Moans from the foredeck indicated that someone was hurt but such was the violence of the storm that no one could easily go to anyone else's assistance.

'Probably a broken limb,' said Adam grimly as he finished lashing them both to the mast. 'There'll be someone nearby to see to him and take him down to the surgeon as soon as there's a lull.'

The most violent phase of the storm soon passed. They were not pooped again and after a while the officers and most of the men untied themselves so that they could move about the decks and take the wounded man beløw, though the helmsmen remained fastened to the wheel. At Adam's insistence, Miranda kept the rope about her waist. She knew quite well that she would never be strong enough to resist the pull of the water by simply holding on and there was still the chance of a freak wave.

For two days the officers and men snatched what sleep they could, ready to face any emergency at a moment's notice. None of them undressed. Adam spent most of the time on deck, falling into a deep sleep the instant his head touched the pillow at those moments when he felt he could allow himself a few minutes below, while at night Miranda lay in their cot missing him. She had the utmost faith in his ability to bring the *Seafire* safely through.

In a way she enjoyed the weather, the struggle against the elements. To her it was a far more satisfactory challenge than any action, however successful, against an enemy warship. Sailing was the thing, not fighting. During one of his rest periods she said as much to Adam, for a brief time awake beside her in the cot, who grinned.

'That's the female in you coming out, my love. Of course you don't like fighting! But you love the sea, it's born and bred in you, I guess.'

'But you enjoy a battle.'

'"Enjoy" is not quite the word I'd use, sweetheart. I find an action stretches me; the smell of gunpowder in my nostrils stimulates my senses, forces me to use all my skill and knowledge to defend and attack; it's a challenge like no other. But I hate the bloodshed—the killing and maiming of good men.'

She kissed the new scar on his forehead. 'And I fear for your life, my dearest.' She did not add, How will I bear it, wondering whether you are safe? If only this stupid war would end!

Although it seemed like weeks that they battled with the storm which drove them far south, it had passed by dawn on the third day.

The sails were set again, a rough position estimated and a new course laid. The sun had reappeared from behind the banks of cloud by noon and Tom and Adam were able to fix their position.

'Three hundred miles too far south,' Tom decided gloomily.

Adam agreed with his calculations. William Williams, midshipman extraordinary, had them sailing on the South American continent. He was told to check his sums.

'Do you want me to lay a course more to the north?' asked Tom as captain and master pored over the chart.

Adam shook his head. 'Not yet. We'll take advantage of the trades and current as far west as we can.'

He stood gazing at the chart long after Tom had left him. He'd been intending to leave the Leeward Islands to the south before heading north for Annapolis. Now the *Seafire*'s course due west would take her to Dominica, halfway down the string of islands towards Barbados. If only he had an excuse to divert those extra three hundred miles south! He could land Miranda, leave her in safety and to the devil with what his admiral might say!

And probably never see her again. An unbearable thought. Yet he'd give much to see her safely reunited with her family.

But he couldn't do it. He'd been given an open commission to harass the enemy but his time was almost up. Unless he could justify more delay he must be back in port early in April and as it was, with the time spent in captivity and the bad weather he'd met, he'd have difficulty in complying with his orders. He needed an excuse. . . .

As though on cue, a distant rumble interrupted his thoughts. He shot on deck.

'Thunder?' wondered Abe Windsor doubtfully.

Another rumble had Adam shaking his head. 'Gunfire!' he proclaimed with absolute certainty. 'To the south of west. Tom, lay a course towards it and Abe, we'll set all the sail she'll carry!'

The *Seafire*, already skimming along in a brisk breeze, came alive under Adam's control. She surged through the waves and only moments later a hail from the masthead confirmed his diagnosis. Two vessels of doubtful origin were exchanging broadsides at regular intervals.

'It'll take us an hour to get within range,' Adam declared. 'Have the men piped to dinner. Then clear for action and pipe to quarters.'

As they drew nearer it became clear that one of the vessels, a brig with one of its two masts down, was fighting off the attack of a pirate brigantine flaunting a black flag with skull and crossbones at its masthead.

'No flag on the merchantman,' said Adam, who had joined Miranda up in the top. 'But from the looks of her I'd bet she's a British brig. Lost her main mast in the storm, I'd guess. She carries five guns a side, but so does the pirate. If only we can reach them before the pirate boards her!'

Adam kept both craft in his telescope as the battle ahead raged on. The merchant ship fought desperately, giving a good account of itself, but the pirate was closing on the crippled brig fast.

The *Seafire* was still out of range but Adam decided, 'We'll let 'em know we're coming,' and ordered the bow chasers to fire.

The men took boarding pikes from their racks around the main mast and drew cutlasses and pistols from the arms chest as they went to quarters. Once there, the gun crews loaded their cannon and ran them out.

'We may have to board the pirate,' Adam explained to Miranda as he buckled on his sword and tucked pistols into his belt. 'You'd better have a brace of pistols too, just in case.'

'This could be worse than the trouble aboard the *Virago*, couldn't it?' asked Miranda quietly.

'Not for you, my love. We shall outgun and outnumber the pirate. If he's any sense he'll make haste to get out of our way. If he doesn't, then we'll take him. You'll stay here with Zack, who'll be in command of the *Seafire*.'

'While you, I suppose, will be leading the boarders!'

'Naturally,' grinned Adam, the reckless expression she knew so well back on his face.

She had to accept him as he was—a man who thrived on danger. And not try to hold him back. She nodded. 'We must rescue that merchantman, whatever his nationality.'

'They're holding out well, considering they're so damaged. Ah!'

The glass was at his eye and at Adam's exclamation Miranda concentrated hers on the pirate.

'He's sheering off!'

'Aye. Mr West! Give chase!'

The brigantine had been damaged in the exchange of fire—her largest fore and aft sail was in tatters.

'It won't take long for us to overhaul her,' remarked Adam confidently.

'They're bending on a replacement, sir!'

'They'll not be able to raise it in time.'

The bow guns were still firing at regular intervals and

now their shots were falling close in the pirate's wake. Then one pierced its large square sail.

'Starboard guns ready, rake her stern. Fire as you bear!' shouted Adam. 'Helm hard over! Now!'

The frigate swung round, presenting her side to the retreating pirate. The guns roared out almost together and shouts of triumph went up as several of the balls found their mark.

The *Seafire*'s heavy broadside again crashed into the smaller vessel, whose shots fell short. Half a mile apart, the vessels raced along side by side, exchanging fire. As the pirate's crew found the range, a shot hit the *Seafire*'s side and another punched a hole through her main sail.

As the thunderous roars followed each other in quick succession Miranda found her ears ringing. Deafened, when the great flash came she scarcely heard the sound of the explosion. But a blast of hot air swept across the deck and she staggered to recover her balance as the wash heaved beneath the frigate's hull.

Where the pirate ship had been there was nothing but scattered wreckage.

'We must've hit his magazine,' said Zack quietly.

'May not have been us,' said Adam, aware of Miranda's stricken face. 'May have been carelessness. It'd only take a spark and they wouldn't be trained as we are. We'd better go and search for survivors.'

'Will there be any?' wondered Miranda, fighting not to be sick, not to crumple to the deck. Everything seemed far away, voices came to her as through a thick blanket. Adam's hand gripped her shoulder.

'Take some deep breaths,' he ordered crisply. 'You'll

be all right. It's only the shock. Sit down on this cartridge case.'

By the time they reached the wreckage she had recovered enough to watch the search. There were no survivors and before they left to join the merchant ship the sharks were already gathering. Well, thought Miranda with a shiver, the men would not be aware of their final fate.

Half an hour later Adam had boarded the merchant ship, the *Daphne*. now flying American colours above a British flag. He left Abe and a dozen or so craftsmen, sailors and marines on board her and returned. He was in fine spirits, smiling as he ordered the *Seafire* to make sail, keeping the brig under its lee, and gave the helmsmen a bearing.

Down in the cabin he told Miranda, 'An excellent prize. She's a splendid vessel in good repair except for the mast and some superficial damage inflicted by the pirate's guns. and she's carrying a valuable cargo of necessary tools and equipment from England. The mast went by the board in the storm. and they had just sorted out the mess when the pirate attacked them. Its crew was about to board her when we arrived. Mighty glad to see us, the master was. although we're American. They'd rather be our prize than taken by pirates.'

'I'm sure. Where were they bound?'

Adam's hesitation was fractional. 'Barbados.'

Miranda's eyes widened. 'Barbados? But you'll take them back to America with you.'

He shook his head. 'We've come to a better arrangement. The *Seafire* will escort them to Barbados in return for a ransom. The master thinks his owners will be only too glad to pay to have the ship and its cargo returned intact. They'll recover the ransom from insurance, too, so we shall all gain.'

She'd thought they'd been sailing rather too far to the south. This explained it. 'You're going to Barbados, to an enemy naval station?' she asked disbelievingly. 'Can you do that? What about me?'

'I can enter Carlisle Bay and anchor off Bridgetown, yes, under a flag of truce. And you, my love, will be reunited with your family.'

'You'll put me ashore?'

'Isn't that what you want?'

'Yes—no! I don't know, Adam,' she wailed. 'I want to remain with you!'

'You know that's impossible, Miranda.' His voice was gentle as he took her in his arms. 'A warship in time of war is no place for a woman, however intrepid she may be. You'd see sights far worse than those you witnessed earlier.'

'Yes, I suppose so. But in peacetime—'

That was a stupid thing to say, she realised as a closed expression settled on Adam's face.

'That may be a long way off.'

She lifted her eyes to his, trying to read his thoughts. Her anguish was clearly written in hers, he could not fail to see it.

'So we shall have to part.'

'It will be better so, my love. A few more weeks and it would have happened anyway, but you would have been in a strange land without friends.'

'Zack said I could stay with his wife,' she whispered.

'He did? That was generous of him. But you would

not be able to join your family, Miranda, and that is what you set out to do. I should like to make up for all the inconvenience I have caused you.'

'You arranged this so that I could be with them, didn't you? I do thank you, Adam.' Her voice sounded stiff. She was grateful in one way, but disillusioned and sad in every other. He could not truly love her or he would never let her go!

She would not plead.

CHAPTER THIRTEEN

THE *Daphne*'s crew, with the help of the *Seafire*'s carpenter and his mates, rigged a temporary mast as the brig progressed. That increased the speed they could make, to Adam's relief. He had little patience with travelling slowly when there was a brisk wind to fill his sails.

Now the die was cast he wanted to get the parting over with quickly. It would be less painful for both of them that way. He dared not think beyond putting Miranda safely ashore in Bridgetown. He must face the admiral, he supposed, but could scarcely admit to deflowering his daughter. Admiral Dawson would call him out. If he ignored his own scruples and asked for her hand her father would simply laugh in his face. Parting was inevitable.

Miranda, hiding her quiet despair, gave herself up completely to Adam's lovemaking on the few remaining nights, storing up the memories to live on in the barren years to come.

She knew Adam by now. He was not ready to abandon a career in the navy which had become his whole life, and did not consider it right to wed only to leave his wife for months, perhaps years, at a time.

Many men did. She tried, in subtle ways, to assure him that she would not mind, she was a naval officer's daughter, she understood, that she'd rather have him part of the time than not at all. Of course, she would rather sail with him, but her mother had survived many protracted partings. She could do the same. But Adam did not want to hear. His mind had long been made up and he would not change it easily. And her father would never consent to the match. There seemed little hope of a happy ending to her adventures.

The storm had passed, there were no further emergencies, and he was not once called out at night by the officer on watch. So the last precious hours of sharing his cot were almost perfect, filled with wistful tenderness and a desperate, despairing passion.

To Miranda's disappointment she could not glimpse any of the string of islands enclosing the Caribbean Sea, since Barbados was out in the Atlantic a hundred miles to the east of them. People said they were strung out like a necklace, mountainous, full of beauty and delight.

When Ragged Point, on the east coast of Barbados, hove into sight the brig took the lead, for its master was familiar with the shoals and reefs which surrounded the island.

'We have to sail round the south-eastern coast, pass South Point and then bear up, round Needham Point, to turn into Carlisle Bay,' Adam explained.

Miranda regarded the low slopes of the distant island with dismay. It looked flat and singularly uninteresting.

'Sugar cane,' explained Adam when she asked what the isolated patches of green vegetation were. 'Not much can be grown on this side, facing the Atlantic and catching the full blast of the trades, but I'm told they grow plenty of sugar and some tobacco and other crops on the sheltered side.'

So this was where she was to live, for some years, at least, unless her father got another posting. Or a promotion. Her disappointment in the island, on top of her despair at parting from Adam, kept her quiet and subdued while the ships wove their way through the ever-changing colours of the sea, following the channels between the reefs and sandbanks. Miranda noticed some huge, awkward-looking birds with enormous pouches under their long beaks basking on coral out-crops from which they flapped to dive for fantastic fish, brilliantly coloured and teeming around the reefs.

'Pelicans,' said Adam of the birds. 'And the fish are colourful but tasteless. Always are in warm waters.'

'Oh.' Miranda's interest in the wildlife was surface only, something to take her mind off losing Adam.

'I'd better change back into a gown,' she told him a little later, choking back her tears. 'Otherwise I shall scandalise Bridgetown society before I've even landed!'

'It would be better.'

Adam seemed almost indifferent. His attention was focused on navigating the intricate channels. A lookout in the foretop, who had experience of what the different colours of the sea indicated lay beneath the surface—coral or sand or deep water—shouted directions and warned of trouble ahead, while the leadsman's chant came with monotonous regularity as he sounded the depth. Even with the merchant ship leading the way they might ground, for the frigate needed a greater depth of water to keep afloat. Besides, although Adam was inclined to trust the master of the *Daphne* and Abe was aboard her to see he got up to no tricks, there was always the possibility that he might get past Abe's guard and try to trick the *Seafire* into grounding herself.

By the time Carlisle Bay hove into view Miranda was respectably gowned as a young lady should be, in sprigged muslin. She even wore a bonnet, tied with blue ribbons beneath her chin. The fact that she had not been wearing bonnets for some time would be obvious to anyone looking at her face, which was most unfashionably weather-beaten. Being fair skinned, her nose and forehead had burnt and peeled at first, but that phase had passed during her first days on the *Seafire*, before Adam had been forced to surrender it. He liked her the colour she was, he kept telling her, stroking the roughness where her skin still peeled slightly. She doubted whether anyone else would.

The brig flew the American colours above the British, and had a white flag at its masthead. The *Seafire* flew its own colours together with a large white flag. It was a tense moment, for if the British shore batteries ignored or doubted the flags of truce they could be bombarded as they approached. And once inside the bay they'd be under the guns of the flagship and any other British warships at anchor there.

The watch-tower would have reported the arrival of the two strange vessels. Both Adam and Zack had Charles Fort and the Beckwith Battery in their glasses, looking for the first wink of a red eye or any other sign that they had been, or were about to be, fired on. The *Seafire*'s guns were loaded and ready to be run out, but the ports were closed and most of the crew was either up in the rigging or lining the bulwarks, all the men on show and obviously making no hostile moves. The marines were drawn up in a parade-ground square at the stern.

Adam was taut as a bowstring, more strung up than Miranda had ever known him before, even in the heat of battle. As tense as she was. She realised it was not sailing into possible danger that had him so strained. Parting must be as painful for him as it was for her. So why was he forcing it upon them? From some quixotic but implacable notion that he was doing the right thing! How foolish men could be!

The grand sweep of the bay curled from east to west, the land a grey smudge with a scattering of cloud above which would afford no shade. As they drew nearer she could see low, rolling hills covered in vegetation and make out Bridgetown at the western end of the bay. Palms fringed a long line of glaring white sand which merged with a pale green sea. In its way, it was beautiful.

Ships of all descriptions rode at anchor before the town. As they drew nearer—no one had fired on them yet—Adam pointed out the admiral's flagship, flying the blue ensign with a white ball.

'That must mean he's on board,' murmured Miranda, excited despite herself at the prospect of seeing her parents and sister again.

'Aye,' said Adam, 'and they're already lowering a boat.' Seeing the brig signalling him to anchor, he gave the order. 'And smartly, now, my lads! Let 'em see what the United States navy can do!'

The anchoring ritual was carried out with faultless accuracy and speed. Adam ordered a party to the entry port ready to greet the admiral's emissary with due ceremony.

A lieutenant climbed the side and stepped on deck, holding the hilt of his hanger to prevent the sword from getting between his legs and tripping him up. As the bosun piped him aboard he saluted Adam, who returned the courtesy. The lieutenant took a quick look round before introducing himself and addressing the frigate's captain.

'I am Admiral Dawson's flag lieutenant, Captain. You have anchored under a flag of truce. What is your purpose?'

'Twofold, Lieutenant. First, to escort my prize, the brig *Daphne* yonder, into port and to arrange the details of its ransom. Second, to deliver Admiral Dawson's daughter into his safekeeping.'

The lieutenant had noticed her standing behind the captain, his eyes had lingered on her face. Miranda stepped forward.

'Good evening, Lieutenant.'

'But you were supposed to arrive on the *Othello*, Miss Dawson! We have been expecting her arrival these several weeks.'

'Unfortunately the *Othello* will not be arriving at all,' put in Adam with a show of regret. 'She should, by now, be in Annapolis, taken there by a prize crew under the command of my first lieutenant. Most of her original crew are aboard her as prisoners of war.'

'Well,' said the lieutenant, somewhat stunned, 'perhaps you had better both accompany me across to see the admiral. Where is the master of the brig?'

'Still aboard his vessel. The owner is in Bridgetown at present?'

'I believe so. I have not heard of his travelling elsewhere. We will collect the master and take him with us. If that is convenient to you?'

The question was perfunctory. Adam had little choice but to agree.

Miranda's trunks and sea chest were being hoisted on deck. She motioned towards them.

'Can you arrange for my things to be taken ashore, Lieutenant? Or may one of the *Seafire*'s boats take them? Captain York will, I am certain, have no objection to that.'

'No, Miss Dawson, but the admiral might! Do not fret, your dunnage will be collected and conveyed to his residence as soon as he gives the order.'

Miranda turned to say goodbye to all the officers, who were gathered around the entry port. Will, so much more self-assured now, nevertheless looked ready to burst into tears. But he'd be all right with Adam. She sent her regards to Zack's wife and thanked Daniel for looking after her. Then, as she cast her gaze around the massed seamen and marines, one of the older hands stepped forward.

'Permission to speak, sir?' he asked Adam, who nodded.

'Carry on, Scott.'

'Well, miss, the lads have asked me to tell you that we've enjoyed having you aboard and hopes as how you'll be happy here in Barbados, ma'am. We wants you to know that we wishes you well.'

Tears misted Miranda's eyes. She would miss all

these men, who had been unfailingly courteous and helpful, rough and tough as some of them were. 'Thank you, Scott.' Her voice almost broke and she cleared her throat before looking again round all the grinning faces. 'Thank you all.'

For the last time, Miranda climbed down the side of the frigate, to be helped to a seat in the British boat. British sailors, smartly turned out in blue and white striped duck trousers, white shirts and round black hats with striped bands, bent to the oars.

As they were escorted to the admiral's cabin it seemed strange to be surrounded by British voices, English, Scottish and Irish dialects amongst them, after the weeks when only the accents of the New World had struck her ears. Strange, even, to see her father. He had become rather corpulent since the loss of his leg and been made more so by his advanced age, for he owned to sixty years. He wore an admiral's dress uniform — a blue frock coat, dripping gold lace and festooned with gold rings, above white breeches and silk stockings — and his lined, astonished, sweating face beneath his tricorn hat suddenly broke into a smile of joyful relief.

'Miranda! My dear girl! How did you get here?' he asked as he drew her to him to kiss her cheek, adding, 'Your mother will be so relieved to see you!' He held her away to gaze at her with fond eyes. 'You look well enough.'

Miranda introduced Adam, who presented the brig's master, who was asked to wait in an antechamber. Then Miranda gave her father a brief and discreetly edited version of the adventures aboard the *Othello*, the *Seafire*, the *Victorious*, the *Virago* and finally aboard the

Seafire again which had led up to her belated arrival in Bridgetown.

'So, young man,' the admiral began when she had finished, 'I have you to thank for the safe delivery of my daughter. But you have been responsible for the loss of a valuable seventy-four-gun line-of-battle ship which should have been under my command, and of the British frigate *Osprey*. I will not ask how many supply ships and other prizes you have deprived us of but I congratulate you on the destruction of the pirate. They are the scourge of the seas to all nations. And, although I am certain it suited your own purposes to do so, you saved the *Virago* from almost certain mutiny. I compliment you, sir, on a successful commission. Your admiral should be grateful. I should delight in having such an enterprising officer under my command.'

'Thank you, sir.' This was generous praise from a senior officer of an opposing navy. He went on, 'But the period of my commission is fast running out. As soon as I have settled matters regarding the ransom for the brig *Daphne*, I must return to my station with all possible speed. At the latest, I must sail on tomorrow's first ebb.'

Adam was behaving with great rectitude. He no longer seemed to be the Adam she knew and loved. He was so withdrawn. Her father's voice boomed out again. 'But you'll dine with us, I hope, Captain? My wife will be anxious to thank you in person for delivering our daughter to us.'

Would he? Miranda studied the toes of her shoes. She did not wish to influence him in any way but she hoped he would refuse the invitation; his presence would be too awkward with him in his present mood and no one allowed to guess what their real relationship aboard the *Seafire* had been. And, although he had once engaged to discover how she went on once the war was over, more recently he had made no such commitment. On the other hand she hoped he would not refuse. A few more hours of his company. . . Oh, she didn't know what she wanted. Except for Adam to take her with him when he left. But there was no chance of that.

In fact, Adam had little choice but to accept the admiral's invitation. To refuse would be thought unforgivably bad manners. And he was intrigued to meet Miranda's family. He would be able to picture her living among them when he was back at sea without her. Missing her.

'Thank you, sir; I appreciate the honour.'

'Good. My lieutenant will escort you wherever you wish to go and bring you to the house at six. We dine in the cool of the evening here.'

Adam saluted smartly. 'Thank you, sir. Miss Dawson.' He bowed over her hand. 'Until six, then.'

The admiral took Miranda ashore in his barge, rowed by sixteen of his uniformed seamen. As a post captain he had been accorded every courtesy but she was amazed at the added deference his promotion had earned him.

Bridgetown was much like any other port, though it lacked the large shipyard of many British naval stations. If any of the warships in his squadron needed a refit or much in the way of repairs they had to go up to English Harbour on Antigua. But the victualling agent could supply stores and spares in plenty: flax, thread and beeswax for the sailmaker; rope and light cordage for the bosun; shirts, trousers and shoes for the purser. Not to mention water and salt meat, fresh fruit and vegetables—and fresh meat if a captain liked to purchase it for his crew. Along the shore a powder coy waited to come alongside at the gunner's request. And almost anything else anyone might wish to purchase could be found in the town.

A pervading smell of tar, stale fish, rotting vegetation and sewage filled the air around the bustling jetties but the admiral had a residence well away from that crowded area. He hired a kind of one-horse gig with a fringed canopy slung above to take them home.

It would have been a long walk to the residence—a typical colonial structure with, to Miranda's astonishment, light internal partitions which did not reach the ceilings. This, she discovered later, was to encourage the air to circulate. But it would be somewhat like living aboard a ship. Everyone would hear everything that went on.

Her mother, a stylish figure in a light muslin gown which, despite her forty-odd years, suited her, clasped Miranda to her bosom with a cry of joy.

'My darling! We had quite given up hope! When the *Othello* failed to arrive we naturally thought you were lost.'

'I did not,' rumbled her father. 'Stephen Blackmore is a fine captain—'

'Was, Papa,' interrupted Miranda quietly. 'I did not tell you earlier, but he was killed, together with his first lieutenant. Lieutenant Piper, his second, surrendered the *Othello*, and he was killed later, aboard the *Seafire*, when Ad—' she caught herself up quickly '—Captain York's men retook it from the British prize crew.'

'You have had an adventurous time, Mirrie,' said her sister, Chloe, a demure, pleasant-faced young lady due to be let out of the schoolroom to come out in society on her sixteenth birthday, in July. She needed no encouragement to behave as a young lady should. She would escape banishment to some academy. 'I should have died!'

'No, you wouldn't,' said Miranda fondly. 'You would have had a fit of the vapours and all the gentlemen would have rallied to your assistance!'

'Didn't they to yours?'

Miranda's hesitation went unnoticed but memories of Adam's attitude during her first days aboard the *Seafire* no longer rankled; in fact they rather amused her. She had guessed long ago that he had been fighting his attraction to her. 'I was always treated with the greatest respect.'

'Here comes your dunnage,' boomed the admiral as several seamen noisily dumped her trunks in the cool, shaded entrance hall where they were still gathered.

'I'll take you to your room, my love,' said Delia Dawson, linking arms with her daughter. 'I think you'll like it. It is on the cool side of the house, facing north-east, and you have a fine view of the bay.'

'Mine's next door,' said Chloe. 'I'll come with you.'

After a while they left Miranda to settle into a delightful room done out in pastel colours and transparent drapes. The furniture here, as below, seemed to be mostly made of wickerwork, or rattan as it was called. And the feet of the chairs and tables stood in small bowls of water to prevent the ants and other insects from climbing up. Well, it was different, and preferable to the Academy in Bath.

Delia Dawson's maid would unpack her trunks later. Meanwhile a black servant brought a can of hot water so that she could wash and change.

The girl's grin reminded her of Daniel. She refrained from making the mistake she had made with him, for despite Mr Wilberforce's Act there were still slaves in the colonial territories. She merely asked her name.

'I'se called Lilah, Miz Dawson, ma'am.'

'What work do you do here?'

'I works in de kitchen and fetches an' carries.'

'How old are you?'

'Don' rightly know, Miz Dawson. 'More'n twenty, accordin' to ma mammy, who done come from far, far away on de slave boat. But I done bin born here right 'nuff and we's free now.'

So that answered that question. 'Would you like to learn to serve me? I'm sure the master and mistress would have no objection to your becoming my personal maid.'

'Oh, yaz, ma'am, I sure 'nuff would, Miz Dawson.'

Miranda smiled. 'Call me Miss Miranda.'

'Sure 'nuff, Miz Mandy.'

Well, that would do.

By the time she was ready for dinner Miranda felt slightly better. She was back with her family, all of whom she loved, especially her mother.

Gauze at the windows prevented mosquitoes from entering the house, but on the terrace it was a different matter. They began biting the moment she set foot outside.

'Come in!' called her mother, seeing Miranda smacking at the insects. 'It is much more comfortable!'

'You did say you liked it here, didn't you, Mama? I cannot imagine why!'

'Oh, it is delightful once you are used to the minor discomforts, my love. And I can be with your father at last. That is such a blessing.'

'Yes,' agreed Miranda. 'It must be.'

'And there are so many sea officers here!' put in Chloe. 'You are certain to find a husband, Mirrie!'

'I would not wish to marry a sea officer. I should be left so much alone.'

'Oh, pooh!' Chloe looked disgusted. 'What of that? Think of the homecomings! It must be like getting married all over again! What was your Captain York like?'

'You'll see for yourself soon, since he is coming for dinner.'

'He's an American, Chloe, dear,' protested Mrs Dawson. 'Most unsuitable!'

'Why?' demanded Chloe.

'Oh, do be quiet, Chloe! I want to forget all about Captain York and my dreadful journey here,' Miranda lied. But she could not discuss Adam with her family. Their relationship was too precious, too private to be bandied among others. And what had made her protest that she did not wish to wed a sea officer? She did. Even if he was American. Her protest had been a kind of self-defence. For she knew no other man would interest her now, at least not for a very long time, and she did not want her mother matchmaking on her behalf.

'Here comes our guest,' announced the admiral, entering the sitting room where his womenfolk had gathered. 'Admirable fellow, m'dear, even if he is a foreigner. Ah, there you are, Captain!' he said amiably as a servant announced Adam. 'Come in, my dear sir, come in! Allow me to present my wife. My eldest daughter you already know and this is Chloe, our youngest. She is not officially out yet but we gave her special permission to dine with us to meet you.'

Adam did the pretty all round but Miranda knew he was as uncomfortable as she. They dared not look at each other for fear of giving their feelings away. Or at least Miranda feared that she would, but could no longer make out what Adam's feelings were. He was not himself, but was it discomfort he was feeling or merely irritation at having to spend the evening socialising when he would rather be dining with his officers aboard his frigate?

Dinner was served and the meal wore on. The admiral dominated the conversation, talking to Adam as a fellow sailor. Chloe, Miranda noticed with secret amusement, could not take her eyes from Adam's face. She was about to develop a *tendre* for the dashing captain. Well, she could scarcely blame her.

At last the meal was over, the men had joined them and Adam was about to take his leave.

'Once this little fracas is over you must come and visit us again, young man,' invited the admiral, who seemed to have taken to Adam. If only everything had been straightforward, thought Miranda miserably.

'Thank you, sir. I will if I am able. Your servant, ma'am.' He bowed to her mother. 'And yours, Miss Chloe. Miss Dawson.' He held her hand in his warm clasp and for the first time looked into her eyes. 'I shall be glad to renew our acquaintance when it becomes convenient. But for the moment I am happy to have been of service.'

'And I thank you for bringing me safely to Barbados, Captain. I shall always remember the *Seafire* with affection.'

Did he guess she had meant him, not his frigate? He kissed her hand and then let it go, quickly. Next moment he had gone, the admiral following to ensure an escort back to the jetty. After all, an enemy officer, however congenial, could not be allowed to roam freely around a British naval base.

Miranda fought down a compulsion to burst into tears.

Chloe burst into speech. 'Don't you think Captain York just perfect, Mirrie?' she cried. 'So dashing and handsome! I declare I am in love with him already! Oh, Mama, do you think he will really come to visit us when the war is over?'

'Stop your foolish chatter, Chloe,' ordered Mrs Dawson, noting the fixed expression on her elder daughter's face. 'You are far too young to be talking so!'

'I'll wager he is not more than ten years older than me,' declared Chloe petulantly. 'If he does come back, I shall attempt to engage his interest!'

'It is quite time you were in bed, my child! Go upstairs at once!'

When Delia Dawson spoke in that tone, her children did not argue. 'Yes, Mama,' said Chloe meekly. 'I shall go to bed and dream of Captain York,' she sighed as she trailed languidly towards the door.

The moment her sister had gone, Miranda stood up. 'If you will excuse me, Mama, I will go to my room. I am very tired. Oh, and by the way, I have asked the servant Lilah if she would like to be my personal maid. You will not mind?'

'Not at all, my love, if you are certain. Come here.'

Miranda walked over to where her mother sat by the tea-tray, wishing her legs did not tremble so. She felt shaky all over. She had not realised how severely the final parting with the man she loved would affect her. Her mother grasped her hands and pulled her towards her.

'So Friday-faced, my dear,' she said softly. 'Chloe is right—he is an attractive young man. But it would be better if you were to forget him. He seems quite wedded to his profession.'

How had her mother guessed? Miranda shook her head helplessly. 'I shall not repine over him long, Mama. He was kind to me, we became good friends.' And that was the truth, if only half of it. She scraped up a smile. 'He taught me to sail his frigate, you know. I shall miss the life at sea.'

'No wonder you are so weather-beaten! Sailing his ship, indeed! That is no sensible occupation for a young lady! Did you learn nothing at the Academy?'

'Oh, yes, Mama. But I did not regard it at sea. I have always envied my brothers. Now I do so even more. Being a young lady is so boring!'

Mrs Dawson smiled. 'My love, I fear there is no help for it, since you are one! Unless, of course, you prefer to be regarded as a hoyden without manners or address and quite unsuitable to marry a gentleman?'

Miranda sighed. 'Do not concern yourself; Papa's money will not be wasted on me. I shall comport myself impeccably in Barbados society.'

'I may be prejudiced, but I believe you are quite beautiful, my love, despite your burnt face, which will recover if you will only protect it. You will undoubtedly be a success with all the gentlemen. You do have a choice, for besides the officers there are plenty of planters' sons who will wish to fix your interest.'

'I do not think,' said Miranda soberly, 'that I should wish to remain on Barbados for the rest of my life.'

'Perhaps not, but, you will see, you will not lack for suitors here! You will soon forget Captain York.'

'Yes, Mama.' She bent forward to kiss her mother's cheek. 'Goodnight, Mama.'

'Goodnight, my love. You must tell me all about your adventures tomorrow.'

'I will.'

With that promise Miranda retired to her room and, to her surprise, fell asleep the moment her head touched the pillow.

The next morning, the morning of Adam's departure, Lilah presented her with a note.

'It done come by a boy from de town, Miz Mandy,' she explained.

'Thank you,' said Miranda faintly. That bold scrawl was quite unmistakable. 'Leave me now.'

Adam had written! Eagerly, she removed the wax seal and unfolded the paper. He had not written much. 'If you should ever need me, write care of the following address.' The US Admiralty's direction followed. The note was signed simply, 'Adam'.

Why had he written? Because she might have his child. The reason came to her with blinding clarity. He would not desert her were it to prove so.

She had been so caught up in the spell of love that she had given the possibility of conceiving a child scant consideration. The possibility must have stirred at the back of her mind, but she had disregarded it. Hadn't wanted to face the likely consequences of her uninhibited behaviour. Now she tried desperately to remember back, back to the time she had last seen her courses. They should have come during her last days aboard the *Seafire*. And then her arrival in Barbados had taken such mundane matters from her mind. But she might just be late.

Adam had seen and faced the danger. He would not abandon her were she indeed pregnant. How she loved him! But would she wish to tie him down against his true inclination to be free? She thought not.

The following days were so full of social visits, meeting her parents' friends and acquaintances, that Miranda found little time to speculate or mope, although she felt so generally upset in herself that everything she did seemed an effort. And her period did not appear. But all her strange symptoms could be accounted for by her precarious emotions and the heat, which would have been intolerable without the relief brought by the trade winds from the east. When they died out, as they did from time to time, the discomfort became insufferable.

She tried to put a brave face on her misery, to recount amusingly the story of her adventures to all who asked. Tongues were clicked at the torment which could be inflicted upon an entire ship's company by an unworthy captain. Her father in particular wanted to know every last detail of her experiences aboard the *Virago*, while her mother wept over the suffering of her youngest son. She allowed them to think that it had been her fault entirely that Captain Judge had been killed. She could not implicate the marine corporal.

'Write a report,' said her father gruffly. 'The Admiralty must be told. Your evidence may save some of the ship's company from disciplinary action.'

'But there was no mutiny,' protested Miranda. 'What could they be charged with?'

'You don't know Admiralty courts martial, my child. If they are looking for a scapegoat... No, if I send them your account it may help Winchester—especially over his allowing York and his officers to go free.'

'Very well, Papa. And I shall emphasise that Dicky played an important role in preventing a mutiny.'

The report took her some time to write and brought back such vivid memories that her pain was intensified. But when it was done and had been dispatched to London by a fast frigate she tried hard to put the past behind her.

But it was not to be. Within a month of her arrival her vague forebodings were confirmed. For the second month in succession, she had not bled. The conclusion was inescapable. She was pregnant.

She had to tell her parents. Her mother would understand. If she told her, she could pass on the news to the admiral, who would be deeply shocked and extremely angry.

'You really must be increasing,' murmured her mother faintly, having been informed of her daughter's symptoms. 'Miranda, you have always been headstrong, but how could you so far forget yourself as to allow that creature to possess you? Had you no thought for sin? For propriety? For your future?'

'I love Adam, Mama. We were at sea, in danger every day. I wanted to know. . .to live. . . I might easily have died before I arrived in America, which was where he was taking me until we captured the brig, as you know.'

'Does he love you?'

'I think he does, in his own way. He certainly wanted to make love to me.'

Her mother made a derisive noise which was almost an undignified snort. 'So will most men you meet! Miranda, you have been extremely gullible and foolish, and now you will have to suffer the consequences. You will bring disgrace upon the entire family. What your papa will say I fear to think!'

Miranda, in the long watches of the night, had already agonised over her desperate situation. Since she did not wish to call on Adam for help, she suggested the only other solution which made any sense to her.

'I could tell everyone that we were married at sea. We could have been. And that because Adam is an American and engaged in fighting us we decided to keep it a secret until after the war. But with me expecting his baby I have no option but to admit to my union with an enemy.'

'And what of Captain York?' demanded Delia Dawson. 'Has he no sense of responsibility? If he comes to visit us after the war and finds himself spoken of as a husband and a father...'

'He must understand,' whispered Miranda, wondering whether he would. 'If I wrote, he would come when he was able. He is not irresponsible, Mama. But I will not force him into marriage. His mind is set against it. The navy is his life.'

'But you must write! And the moment he presents himself here he will wed you, my girl. Your father will see to that!'

'I will not trouble him, Mama.' Miranda's firm tone belied her inward quaking. 'He has no obligation to me. What I did I did of my own free will. I shall call myself Mrs York, but I will not have him compelled to marry me. What sort of a life could I hope for if he were?'

'He may not come back. What will you do then?'

'No, he may not. And if he does it will be awkward to explain things to him. But I will neither trick nor force him into marriage. Deserted wives are not uncommon, I believe. I shall survive—provided you, dearest Mama, do not turn your back on me.'

Suddenly, Delia Dawson took her errant daughter into her arms. 'That I would never do, my love, you know that. We must face this together. I am persuaded that your father will come round to our way of thinking.'

'You will ensure that he does not write to Adam care of the US navy, won't you, Mama? I could not bear for

Adam to be made to feel guilty for what was not his fault.'

Delia did snort this time, and her arms dropped away as she stood back to glare at Miranda. 'Not his fault, you say? Then whose child is it, if I may make so bold as to ask?'

'His of course! But he did not seduce or rape me, Mama. I wanted him to make love to me!'

Her mother sighed, making a helpless gesture. 'You should be repenting, child, not throwing defiance in my face!' She shook her head and asked despairingly, 'How did I come to bear such a wayward child?'

CHAPTER FOURTEEN

PREDICTABLY, the admiral raised the roof, threatening to thrash Miranda if she did not write to Adam, vowing to call 'that young puppy' out.

'And to think I judged that renegade honourable!' he roared. 'To defile my daughter! Fellow deserves to be flogged!'

Miranda discovered previously uncharted depths of courage and determination in the face of her father's wrath.

'I will not write, Papá, and nor will you. Neither will you call him out, for, I declare, if you do you will suffer humiliation at his hands. He is an accomplished swordsman and a prime marksman.'

'I can still aim a pistol, young lady!'

'Yes, Papa, but not with the accuracy you once possessed.' She glanced pointedly at his unsteady hand. 'Besides, duels are illegal. And whatever you may protest, you were not mistaken when you judged Adam York honourable. It was a misconceived sense of honour and duty which prevented his asking me to be his wife. He did not wish to abandon me for long periods while he was at sea. He thought it tragic that his lieutenant had not seen his daughter yet, and she almost a year old.'

Her father's head went back as though she had hit him. That thrust had found its mark.

'But that is a sailor's lot!' he roared.

'Quite. If he marries.' Miranda clenched her fists. She would not allow her father to think badly of the man she loved. 'Adam has chosen his career and, unlike you, cannot bring himself to condemn me, or any other woman for that matter, to such a fate. Sailors, he believes, should not wed.'

She thought her father might have an apoplexy but could not regret her words, for they were true.

'Ask your mother,' seethed the admiral, 'whether she would prefer not to be wed!'

'Of course she would not,' said Miranda quickly, before her mother, who was sitting twisting agitated fingers in her lap, could intervene. 'Just as I would prefer to marry Adam. But your long absences were difficult times, Papa, especially when we children were young and Mama had so little money to manage on.' She ignored her mother's muted cry of distress and went on, 'Adam has money, and I should not lack for funds, but I will not condemn him to suffer the pangs of conscience during his long cruises which must have been yours during those years.'

Had she managed to make him understand? She glimpsed the uneasy look in his eyes and thought that perhaps she had. She relaxed slightly, unclenched her fists and smiled.

'Papa, I promise I will be as discreet as I possibly can, will be a model of decorum from now on. Please, Papa, grant me your understanding, as Mama has done. I cannot manage without it.'

The choleric colour faded from Admiral Dawson's

face. He emitted a deep, heavy sigh and slumped into a rattan chair.

'Y'know I only want the best for you, m'dear. Don't care about the disgrace. Only your happiness.'

Miranda went over and kissed his cheek. 'Thank you, dear Papa. If I cannot have Adam, I shall be content to have his child.' Her mind went back to Adam's taunting and flippant suggestion that Captain Judge should wed them. It gave her an idea. 'And there will be few to prove that Captain Judge did not marry us aboard the *Virago* before he died.'

'But what if you wish to wed someone else?' asked her mother anxiously.

'That is unlikely. But I should confess the whole of it. After all, I could scarcely marry a man without telling him the truth.'

Both her parents looked sceptical.

'It will take an extraordinary man to wed you after such a confession, Miranda,' her mother pointed out.

'I know. I have already said that I doubt I shall marry.'

'Have it your own way, then. What will you tell Chloe and your brothers?'

'What I tell everyone else. Even Dicky cannot prove that such a ceremony did not take place, though he may strongly doubt it. If necessary, I would tell him the truth. But no one else.'

Her father struggled to his feet again. 'Well, I've had my say,' he rumbled. 'Shan't mention it to anyone. Let you do the explainin'. Must get back to my flagship.'

As the door swung to behind him Delia heaved a sigh of relief. 'I thought for a moment he would not come round. But he has always been soft where you and Chloe are concerned.'

Miranda gazed at her mother, astonished. 'You call that being soft?'

'Imagine if it had been Ned or Dick!'

'I suppose so,' admitted Miranda with a grimace. 'He would have cast them off after horse-whipping them!'

'Well, perhaps not quite that.' Delia gave a soft, rather breathless laugh. 'His bark has always been a lot worse than his bite, but he is used to naval discipline and finds any show of leniency difficult. When will you begin to explain?'

'When I cannot put it off any longer.'

'When you begin to show, you mean? In July?'

'Probably, yes.'

'Very well, dear.'

But Miranda noticed that her mother behaved in a way that made everyone think she was hiding a secret. She looked conscious whenever her daughter's future was mentioned, whenever a suitor hove on the horizon and was gently rebuffed. And Miranda, taking her cue from her mother, did not attempt to hide her blushes whenever Adam's name was mentioned. Which, considering he had met few people outside the family while he had been in Bridgetown, was quite often. But then, everyone still wanted to hear Miranda describe her adventures.

She had become quite a celebrity in Barbados society.

Her eighteenth birthday, on the seventeenth day of April, passed almost unnoticed outside her family. Even there, all attention was focused on Chloe's sixteenth anniversary in July, for which Mrs Dawson was planning a grand reception to be followed by informal dancing. Making the arrangements for this, and ordering new gowns and bonnets, kept her mother occupied.

Miranda did her best to appear enthusiastic. But it was difficult, with Adam's child growing inside her. In the privacy of her room she sewed baby clothes. Lilah became her confidante. The girl would, considered Miranda, make an ideal nurse for the baby when it came. She wanted a boy, of course, but a girl would be nice. A girl was unlikely to run away to sea and leave her!

In the third week of May a British frigate came tearing into Carlisle Bay, flying a string of flags signalling that it carried dispatches and that there had been a victory.

Miranda had taken to watching activity in the bay from her bedroom window, using the telescope Adam had given her aboard the *Seafire*—her most prized possession. Even before the ship was properly at anchor a boat had been lowered and her captain had embarked to carry the bag over to the admiral.

Everyone aboard the frigate appeared to be excited and soon she could see cheering aboard the flagship.

She rushed down to the sitting room to find her mother.

'Dispatches have arrived and there's been a victory!' she cried. 'Papa's barge has been brought round to the entry port; he must be coming ashore!'

'A victory? I wonder what it can be?'

'Could it be a defeat for Napoleon? He's been on the defensive on all fronts for months now. Lord

Wellington is already in France! Napoleon has to give up sooner or later.'

'Oh, I do hope this terrible war is over!' cried her mother. 'It's been so long! Ned and Dick will be safe at last!'

'Safer, anyway. I wonder if America will carry on. . .?'

Miranda trailed off. She dared not think that the war with America might be over too.

A couple of hours later, the admiral, having relayed his news to the governor and those others who must be told, arrived home.

'Henry!' cried Delia, running to him the moment he entered the house. 'What is the victory? We are so excited!'

'There is a letter for you from Richard,' said the admiral, handing his wife the missive. 'As for the victory—' He kept them in suspense while his ruddy face broke into a broad grin. 'Napoleon was deposed by the French Senate on the ninth day of April, and surrendered on the fourteenth of the month! That frigate crossed the Atlantic in seventeen days! Just fancy that! Had excellent weather and steady winds all the way! Fine young captain!'

He was, thought Miranda, more excited about the performance of the frigate than about the defeat of Napoleon!

There was, of course, no news of peace with America. In fact, while the British community in Barbados celebrated the fall of Napoleon with balls, routs and soirées, the troops from the Peninsula were being shipped across the Atlantic to fight in Canada. Soon, the fleets which had been blockading the French ports crossed it too. Some of the men-of-war under Admiral Dawson's command were detached and ordered north.

'They are planning something,' the admiral growled, wishing he had been called upon to go too.

Eventually the news filtered through. An invasion of Chesapeake Bay had been attempted and repelled. Annapolis was in Chesapeake Bay. But Adam was probably on the other side of the world.

In fact Adam was not. The *Seafire*, up to full complement again with the return of the prize crew, which had successfully brought the *Othello* home, had been sent to join an American squadron serving in home waters. She was one of the scouting frigates which first sighted the approaching British expedition. Flags were hoisted reporting 'enemy in sight', the message passed from frigate to frigate until it reached the admiral, but the commodore in command of the frigates sent the *Seafire* flying back to the admiral's flagship carrying a more detailed report.

He was not in the thick of the action, since his next orders were to watch and warn, to be one of his admiral's eyes. As the British withdrew, however, the *Seafire* did enter into a fierce engagement with an enemy frigate, taking it at length by going alongside and boarding. Zachary West and Greg Merrick were both killed in the action, together with too many seamen. They towed the British frigate into port as a prize, but that could not relieve the sense of deep loss Adam felt.

Zack had returned home for a reunion with his wife and a first sight of his daughter after their return from Barbados. He had reported again for duty in the highest of spirits, proud and happy. Now he was dead, and Adam had the sickening task of writing to his wife. Of course he was used to writing such letters of condolence to the relatives of the Seafires killed in action or dead from other causes, but none of them could compare with the pain he felt as he penned his appreciation of a fine officer and attempted to convey his sympathy to Zack's wife.

He had treated Miranda badly, he knew. But Zack's death confirmed him in his opinion that a naval officer should remain a bachelor. He could not begin to contemplate Miranda's distress were she to receive a missive such as the one he was writing. Their parting had hit her hard, he knew, yet the pain of a clean break now, while she was young and had her life before her, must be preferable to the anxious wait which might end in news of his death.

Subsequent to the action at Chesapeake he was engaged in escorting convoys along the coast, chasing off any enemy attempt to attack the merchantmen. Slow, laborious and tedious work after the freedom he'd known on the other side of the Atlantic.

Miranda still engaged his thoughts far more often than she should. She had not written to him, so presumably their union had not borne fruit. Only at the last moment had he faced the possibility and sent her a note. He'd been unforgivably careless, he knew, careless of Miranda's feelings, of her welfare after they parted. But everything had worked out satisfactorily in the end.

Except that he could not forget her.

* * *

On her finger, Miranda wore an engraved signet ring. To anyone who exclaimed over her lack of a proper wedding band, she protested that there had been no opportunity to purchase one.

For several days after learning of Miranda's condition and supposed marriage, Chloe refused to speak to her sister.

'You deceived me!' she cried in outrage, and ran to her room to shed buckets of tears.

'She still cherishes a *tendre* for your supposed husband, Miranda,' explained their mother somewhat sharply. 'She is jealous of you at present, but she is very young and has a sweet temperament. She will soon recover. She will have plenty of other young men to take her fancy after her come-out.'

'I hope so, Mama. I did not realise how seriously she had become attached to Adam.'

'Her attachment is not serious, my love. She only thinks it is.'

The come-out reception was to be in a few days' time. On her mother's advice, Miranda had broken the news beforehand, slightly earlier than was absolutely necessary.

'We would not wish to distress Chloe during the excitement of her entry into society,' she had suggested. 'She will forget her disappointment all the sooner if she is engaged in a round of pleasure.'

The ball proved a great success and during the following days Chloe, still moping slightly, gathered about her a group of admirers, which lifted her spirits. The young gentlemen followed her from one function to another and, in her demure way, she flirted outrageously.

'Pooh,' she said at the end of the first week, gazing starry-eyed at a young lieutenant in a red coat with splendid gold frogging, white breeches and stockings. 'I cannot imagine what I saw in your Adam York, Mirrie. I do so much prefer an army uniform. His shako suits him wonderfully well, do you not think? Just see how the plume nods!'

Miranda smiled to herself. The peak of the shako shadowed the young man's features, but hadn't she been taken in by a fine uniform and a handsome face before she'd met Adam? And Chloe was far too young to appreciate Adam's less spectacular qualities.

In December, the supposed Mrs Adam York bore her absent husband a fine son, whom she named Adam Henry and called Hal. She nursed him herself and cared for him with the help of Lilah.

In the new year they heard that peace was being discussed between Britain and her former colony. By the end of February Miranda knew it was fact. The treaty had been signed in Ghent in January of 1815. Britain, for the first time in many years, was at peace with all the world.

Was Adam still alive? Would he come? When would he come? He might still be on a lengthy commission somewhere on the other side of America, in the Pacific. He would have to take leave or make an excuse to call in on his way to or from somewhere else, as he had done to bring her here. If he was still alive and wanted to see her.

The months passed. Her hope began to fade. And

yet, and yet... Something told her that Adam would come if he could. The exigencies of the service must be keeping him away. She had to believe that, or the mainspring of her life would be gone.

Hal grew into a sturdy baby, before long sitting up unaided. Soon he would be crawling. But even he could not take the place of his father.

All kinds of merchant ships, as well as warships, came into Carlisle Bay now. French, Dutch, American, even a few Spanish, though Spain still fought a losing battle to keep all the trade in the area to herself. Her pirate ships were the greatest threat Admiral Dawson and his squadron now had to face.

Miranda watched from her window, hoping to see the *Seafire* sail in. Although, of course, Adam might have been given command of a different ship.

When he did arrive, just ahead of the hurricane season, she was one of the last to know.

The tails of his blue coat flapping in the wind, Adam strode up the hill towards Admiral Dawson's residence with Daniel at his heels. Despite the heat, the sweat beginning to trickle down his neck, he did not slow down. Action was the only thing keeping him sane at the moment; he could not have borne to sit quietly in a gig while the horse clip-clopped along at a leisurely pace.

'Why, it's Captain York, isn't it?' the official who had greeted him at the jetty had exclaimed. 'Hardly recognised you in that garb, sir! Left the US navy, have you?'

As Daniel had leapt out to hold the boat while he stepped ashore, Adam had nodded.

'Your lady wife will be that glad to see you. Only saying to her the other day, I were, that the boy would be quite grown before his father set eyes on him.'

What he had said to the man Adam could never afterwards remember. He was too shocked.

His 'lady wife' could only be Miranda. And she had a child. That man believed the child to be his.

Why had she not written, as he'd told her to? He'd resigned his commission in the navy and, determined to overcome any obstacles raised by her family, had come to ask her to wed him. But now he felt uncertain of the wisdom of his decision.

She hadn't sent for him when she'd found herself pregnant. Did that mean she no longer wished to marry him? How could he know, until he saw her? Had her father intervened, forbidden her to write? If so he would not be welcome now. Yet Admiral Dawson had seemed to approve of him—but as a naval officer, not as a son-in-law!

Impatient for answers, he kept up the killing pace until the residence came into sight. He paused in a scrap of shade before entering the grounds. The walk had given him time to compose himself.

He took off his cap to wipe his streaming forehead, revealing his newly cropped hair. His stock was a dismal, damp rag about his neck, but that could not be helped. His plan to arrive looking smart and acceptable to a British admiral's daughter and her family had been doomed to failure from the start, given the heat. He eased his shoulders under the coat, trying to shift the damp shirt from his skin. It should be cooler inside.

'Wait outside the house,' he ordered Daniel briefly, and strode up to the open door.

From somewhere on the shady side of the house he heard the gurgle of baby laughter. With his hand on the bell, he stopped, turned, and set off towards the sound. It might be some other child, of course, a servant's offspring, or that of someone making a call. But he did not think so. Especially as, as he drew nearer, he heard Miranda's voice cooing at the baby.

He turned the corner and stood watching the scene. The baby, naked except for a napkin, had been set down on a rug in the shade of the veranda and sat with his mother kneeling in front of him, holding his hands while she talked to him. A native girl squatted on the ground nearby, holding his little dress.

Adam stared at his son with wonder and pride and the surge of emotion almost unmanned him before he turned his attention to the girl who was his son's mother.

More beautiful than ever, was his immediate thought, but her face and figure reflected a new maturity. Now the feelings which shook him were of another kind entirely. Had he lost her by his foolish refusal to keep her with him? Had she found another man to love? It had been more than a year since he had left her here. Plenty of time for her to forget him. . .except that she called herself Mrs York and had the baby to remind her.

Perhaps she held that against him. Was it resentment that had prevented her from writing to him?

He wanted to walk forward and greet her but he was overcome with fear and guilt. How was it that Miranda

Dawson so often reduced him to an awkward, faltering oaf?

The child's nurse—for that must be her function—saw him first. Her eyes opened wide, the whites rolled as she lifted her arm and pointed.

'Miz Mandy!' she cried.

Miranda looked up. For an instant she appeared turned to stone. Then such a smile lit her small face that Adam knew immediately that he had not come in vain.

She jumped to her feet, abandoning the baby, and as he took a step forward she ran into his arms.

'Adam! You came! I knew you would!'

'Yes,' he agreed gruffly, once he had thoroughly kissed her. 'I came. Why did you not send for me?'

'Later,' murmured Miranda, glancing at Lilah. 'Come and meet your son.'

She led him by the hand to the rug. Then she dropped it as she bent down and took the baby into her arms. Adam swallowed. He had missed so much over the last fifteen months—something he had vowed never to do. It would not happen again.

'I hope you will approve—I have named him Adam Henry,' she said softly, holding the child so that his father could see him properly. 'But I call him Hal. I thought it might be less confusing when you came for us.'

Such confidence! Adam felt ashamed all over again, for doubting her constancy.

Speechless, he held out a finger which Hal immediately clutched.

Adam cleared his throat. 'What a grip he has.'

'Do you want to hold him?'

The infant changed hands. As Adam tucked his son into the crook of his arm he thought he had never been happier.

Miranda watched Adam's reaction and rejoiced at what she saw. All her doubts had been groundless. He was already the proud father, chucking his son under the chin and saying all the foolish things one said to a baby.

And then she noticed his cropped hair, the change of uniform. For surely the dark blue coat with its brass buttons was some kind of uniform? She opened her mouth to ask but was interrupted by a little shriek of surprise from the house as a glowing, graceful Chloe came out onto the veranda on the arm of her lieutenant.

'Captain York!' she cried, to Miranda's great relief showing no consciousness, no evidence of tender feelings trampled underfoot. 'So, brother, you have come at last! My sister was quite beginning to despair! We had feared you lost at sea or something, and with your marriage being so secret—well, the authorities may not have known where to write!'

Adam did not let go of Hal. He used his free hand to bow over Chloe's and acknowledge the introduction to the lieutenant.

'My wife,' he said quietly, 'would have been informed had I been killed in action. Otherwise, our countries being at war, it was better that I did not write.' He looked straight into Miranda's eyes as he went on, 'But communications have been poor since the end of the war. Did you not receive the letter I sent in February, my love?'

They were playing a game; Adam had fielded Chloe's

ball and now she must pick up Adam's. Dear Adam, who had met the unexpected challenge of being supposed wed with such aplomb.

'No, my dear, I have received no letter from you at all. But I always imagined that you had written but the letter had gone astray. What must you have thought of me when I did not reply?'

'I feared you had forgotten me,' said Adam with perfect truth. 'Although I hoped it had been lost. So I came to claim you with all the dispatch at my disposal.'

'How romantic it was to be wed at sea aboard the *Virago*!' sighed Chloe, gazing up at her lieutenant, who, silent at the best of times, had now completely lost his voice. His lack of conversation did not appear to concern Chloe, who did the talking for both of them, content to bask in the adoration of her beau. 'And then Captain Judge was killed and your marriage certificate lost in the confusion which followed. You will have to wed her again, Captain, if you wish to convince the parson who baptised Hal.'

So that was the story Miranda had told. Plausible enough but not entirely convincing to all. 'I have every intention of doing so,' responded Adam seriously. 'I can allow no doubts as to the legality of our union to remain. Besides, we would both wish to receive the blessing of the Church.'

'When?' cried Chloe excitedly. 'And may I attend the bride?'

'Of course you may, sister, dear.' Miranda turned her radiant face to Adam. 'As to when, we must discuss that with others. With Mama, Papa and the parson. Mama is

resting and Papa is busy about his duties. You will see
them both at dinner.'

'Meanwhile,' said Adam softly, reluctantly handing
his son to Lilah, 'may we seek a little privacy? I have
much to tell you and much to explain, my love.'

Miranda nodded. 'Lilah will take care of Hal. Is
Daniel with you?'

Adam grinned. 'Of course. He is waiting at the front
of the house.'

'Then I must instruct one of the servants to look after
him.'

Saying which, Miranda led the way into the coolest
room in the house, speaking to a footman on the way.

With the door closed firmly behind them, Adam took
Miranda into his arms again. The kiss, a delightful
reminder of all they had been missing over the last
months, deepened from tender caress to almost desperate longing.

'Tonight,' murmured Miranda at last, 'you will be
staying here?'

He held her clasped firmly against his heart. 'If you
will welcome me into your bed.'

Miranda's laugh was shaky as her fingers tangled in
his short hair. The cropped style suited him splendidly,
she acknowledged, delighting in his distinctive looks all
over again. 'Oh, Adam, I have missed you so!'

'And I you, my love. When you did not write I tried
to forget you—especially after Zack was killed—but it
proved impossible.'

Miranda drew back a fraction to gaze into his face.
'Zack is dead? How? When?'

'During a duel with an enemy frigate at the close of the attempted British invasion of Chesapeake Bay. He was killed instantly by a cutlass blow as we boarded.'

'Oh, his poor wife!'

Adam nodded, his face sombre. 'I had to write to her, I did not have leave to visit. I swore then that I would never put you in a position to receive such a letter.'

'Adam,' she whispered, 'the war is over now; you are unlikely to be killed, though there is always the risk of being lost at sea. Is that why you have come?'

He led her to a rattan sofa before he answered. Once they were settled, entwined closely together, he explained, 'I'm here because I could not stay away, my dearest girl. The war ending made it possible, that I grant, for I could not have deserted while I was needed to serve my country. But they were putting me on the beach on half-pay, like so many others—'

'In the British navy too.'

Adam nodded. 'So rather than that I resigned my commission.'

'You've left the navy?'

Grinning, Adam pointed to the coat he had discarded on entering the room. 'There you see my new uniform, my love. I am now owner and master of the trading barque *Seafire*. She lies at anchor in the harbour.'

'The *Seafire*?' wondered Miranda. 'You named her for your frigate?'

'I could never forget my naval command. Neither did I wish to. I found my true happiness aboard her, Miranda.'

'So did I,' remembered Miranda wistfully.

'Why did you not write, my dear one?'

'I could not force you back to me, Adam. You had to come because you could not stay away. Otherwise you would have grown to resent your responsibilities, for you did not wish to be wed.'

'And you were prepared to be condemned by the world for bearing a bastard rather than hold me to my duty?'

'That was the point, Adam. I did not wish you to wed me from a sense of duty. I knew that for us to find true happiness together you must sincerely wish to marry me.'

'So you contrived that story about being married at sea—'

'For my parents' sake, really. I did not care for myself. And in the eyes of the world, if you did not come, I should simply be a wronged wife, you would not be hurt, while if you did come you would still have the choice. If you had not wished to wed me you had only to go away again. You still could.'

'Thank you, my dear, but I do not think I will, if you do not mind! I am hoping our happiness will continue aboard the new *Seafire*.'

'How? What do you mean?'

'Why, my love, I hope that you will sail with me. The accommodation is far superior to that of a warship, this *Seafire* will carry passengers as well as cargo and a necessary complement of crew and cannon designed to deter pirates. Abraham Windsor and Thomas Crocker are both with me as mates and I have no doubt you will be delighted to learn that William Williams and James Stirling are also in the crew, together with a number of the old Seafires.'

Miranda's eyes shone. 'You mean it, Adam? I may come with you? How wonderful to face the dangers of the sea together! No waiting at home for letters that do not come, no entertaining of desperate hopes that, somehow, even if the ship has foundered, you are safe.'

Then her face dropped. 'But what of Hal—and other children we may have?'

'He and his nurse, or they and their nurse, may accompany us, at least until such time as they either take to a life at sea or attend school on land. We will, of course, not be at sea all the time; we shall have a home somewhere—here if you prefer, or in the USA—and we can hire houses in London or anywhere else in the world we may find ourselves for any length of time.'

'London!' exclaimed Miranda. 'We may go to London one day? I have never been there!'

'It will be our first destination when we leave here, my love. The *Seafire* will make its way up the River Thames to dock below London Bridge, near the Tower. We may explore the city as much as you please.'

'Adam! I should enjoy that above everything! Though of course,' she added hurriedly, 'I long to see your home in Virginia and to meet your family.'

Adam smiled and squeezed her shoulders. 'We shall explore the USA, never fear. I believe your charm may even melt my father's irascible heart!'

'As you will my father's! You begin with an advantage, my love, for he dotes on Hal and found you congenial, a courageous and honourable officer until he discovered my condition! Then, of course, he fretted and fumed and took a deal of pacifying, but I do believe that beneath his outrage he still admires you. So he will accept our belated wedding with approval even if he does rant a little at first.'

Adam kissed her again. 'I am delighted to think so, although I should not allow him to deter me from making you my wife.'

'I am not yet of age, Adam. But I do not believe he will prevent our marriage.'

'If he tries, we will elope!'

'And sail the seas together for evermore!'

'We shall not be at sea all the time; we shall spend time at home; of that you may be certain. Abe and Tom between them are perfectly capable of making voyages without me. And if the venture is successful I shall purchase more vessels, train up more crews. We could own a fleet for our sons to command. What do you think?'

'I think it is wonderful, Adam!' She jumped to her feet. 'Let us go up to my room so that I may scan the harbour for sight of the *Seafire*!'

'Look,' said Adam a few moments later, pointing from her window, 'that three-masted ship there. She has a capacious hold for cargo and is a fine, seaworthy ship capable of making up to ten knots.'

'She's beautiful,' murmured Miranda, eyeing the barque's graceful lines. 'Oh, Adam, I am so happy!'

'So am I, my love. Who knows that we are not truly wed?'

'Only Mama and Papa. Forgive them if they are constrained with you at first, but I am persuaded that they will soon forgive you when they learn of our plans! Oh, Adam!'

Her arms crept round his neck. The bed stood invitingly behind them. Their full reunion could be denied them no longer.

The wedding became the social occasion of the year on Barbados. Even the governor and his lady attended, mostly on account of his having worked so closely with Admiral Dawson, though Miranda suspected his wife of sharing all the ladies' curiosity and speculation over the circumstances and legality of her first marriage. Let them wonder, she thought as, her face radiant, she walked from the church on the arm of her husband.

Despite the imminence of the hurricane season the *Seafire* sailed immediately after the ceremony and reception, bound for London by the northern route across the Atlantic. There were no passengers on this trip—Adam had turned down several requests for passage to England, for this was their honeymoon—but the holds were full of valuable sugar.

'The North Atlantic currents and winds are more helpful for a crossing from west to east,' Adam explained. 'It'll be icebergs we shall have to fear, not hurricanes.'

As the anchor was weighed and the ship sailed out of the bay he held her close.

Miranda watched until the island began to sink below the horizon, sad to leave her family again but so happy otherwise that the emotion soon passed. She left Adam on deck and went below to the sumptuous cabin they would share, all mahogany, satin and velvet, and looked in on Hal on her way, smiling contentedly to herself.

Lilah was busy settling him into his small swinging

cot. The girl had been reluctant to accompany them at first, but Daniel had persuaded her. Miranda doubted it would be long before Adam was asked to marry the pair. Daniel was clearly besotted with the lively young woman and she, despite the disparity in their ages, seemed taken with the big, genial sailor.

All the Seafires had welcomed her aboard with beaming smiles and exclaimed like old women over the baby. Tomorrow she would resume her boy's garb, take up her lessons in seamanship again.

But for now... When Adam descended the ladder to join her she once more gravitated straight into his arms. It seemed that, having been separated for so long, neither of them could bear to be far from the other for many months.

The ship was in good hands. The deck heaved easily beneath their feet, the water chuckled blithely along the sides of the vessel. To Miranda, being aboard a ship again was like coming home. The comfort of the wide swinging cot Adam had introduced awaited them. With a sigh of deepest contentment, she surrendered herself to the fire of her husband's embrace.

Historical Romance™

Coming next month

BETRAYED HEARTS
Elizabeth Henshall
CHESHIRE 1080

Lady Ghislaine de Launay had little choice where she
married, but she objected to being a pawn between the
Earl of Chester and Guy de Courcy…she would rather
enter the convent. As far as Guy was concerned the
convent was welcome to her—*after* he had cleared his
name of murder. A propitious start to their marriage!
However, despite all the uncertainty, their mutual
attraction was undeniable—but how could she love a
possible murderer with all the evidence seemingly against
him?

THE WOLF'S PROMISE
Alice Thornton
SUSSEX COAST 1809

Lady Angelica Lennard took matters into her own hands.
Her brother needed bringing out of France and Benoît
Faulkener owed a debt to her father. In view of her
father's blindness, she would go herself to persuade
Benoît to rescue Harry. Fully expecting a piratical
smuggler, Angelica was mortified to discover a
respectable shipowner—or was he? Some things didn't
add up, but somehow Benoît didn't seem a stranger. Was
she imagining the warmth and intimacy? When she fell
into danger and Benoît's steely will showed through, she
was sure of it!

MILLS & BOON®

Weddings ♣ Glamour ♣ Family ♣ Heartbreak

Since the turn of the century, the elegant and fashionable DeWilde stores have helped brides around the world realise the fantasy of their 'special day'.

Now the store and three generations of the DeWilde family are torn apart by the separation of Grace and Jeffrey DeWilde—and family members face new challenges and loves in this fast-paced, glamourous, internationally set series.

For weddings, romance and glamour, enter the world of

Weddings By DeWilde

—a fantastic line up of 12 new stories from popular Mills & Boon authors

OCTOBER 1996

Bk. 1 SHATTERED VOWS - Jasmine Cresswell
Bk. 2 THE RELUCTANT BRIDE - Janis Flores

Available from WH Smith, John Menzies, Volume One, Forbuoys, Martins, Woolworths, Tesco, Asda, Safeway and other paperback stockists.

GET 4 BOOKS AND A SILVER PLATED PHOTO FRAME

Return this coupon and we'll send you 4 Mills & Boon Historical Romance™ novels and a silver plated photo frame absolutely FREE! We'll even pay the postage and packing for you.

We're making you this offer to introduce you to the benefits of Reader Service: FREE home delivery of brand-new Mills & Boon Historical Romance novels, at least a month before they are available in the shops, FREE gifts and a monthly Newsletter packed with information.

Accepting these FREE books and gift places you under no obligation to buy, you may cancel at any time, even after receiving just your free shipment. Simply complete the coupon below and send it to:

MILLS & BOON® READER SERVICE, FREEPOST, CROYDON, SURREY, CR9 3WZ.

No stamp needed

Yes, please send me 4 free Mills & Boon Historical Romance novels and a silver plated photo frame. I understand that unless you hear from me, I will receive 4 superb new titles every month for just £2.10* each postage and packing free. I am under no obligation to purchase any books and I may cancel or suspend my subscription at any time, but the free books and gifts will be mine to keep in any case. (I am over 18 years of age)

H6IE

Ms/Mrs/Miss/Mr _____

Address _____

_____

_____ Postcode _____

Offer closes 31st March 1997. We reserve the right to refuse an application. *Prices and terms subject to change without notice. Offer only valid in UK and Ireland and is not available to current subscribers to this series. **Readers in Ireland please write to: P.O. Box 4546, Dublin 24.** Overseas readers please write for details.

You may be mailed with offers from other reputable companies as a result of this application. Please tick box if you would prefer not to receive such offers. ☐

MILLS & BOON®

Presents™

Can a picture from the past bring love to the present?

Don't miss Robyn Donald's intriguing new trilogy—
The Marriage Maker—coming up in the
Mills & Boon Presents line.

All three stories centre around an 18th century miniature
painting which brings luck in love to the present owner.

Look out for:

The Mirror Bride in October '96
Meant to Marry in November '96
The Final Proposal in December '96

Price: £2.10 each

*Available from WH Smith, John Menzies, Volume One, Forbuoys, Martins, Woolworths,
Tesco, Asda, Safeway and other paperback stockists.*